CHASING THE STAR GARDEN

Clockpunk Press, December 2013
Copyright 2013 Melanie Karsak

This is a work of fiction. References to historical people,
organizations, events, places, and establishments are the product
of the author's imagination or are used fictitiously.

Published by Clockpunk Press
PO Box 560367
Rockledge, FL 32956-0367
www.clockpunkpress.com
ISBN-13: 978-0615878775
ISBN-10: 0615878776
Edited by Cat Carlson Amick
Cover art and book design by Damonza.com

CHASING THE STAR GARDEN

THE AIRSHIP RACING CHRONICLES

MELANIE KARSAK

CLOCKPUNK PRESS

for Cat

CHAPTER 1

I was going to lose-again. I gripped the brass handles on the wheel and turned the airship sharply port. The tiller vibrated in protest making the wheel shake and my wrist bones ache. Bracing my knees against the spokes, I tore off my brown leather gloves to get a better feel. The metal handgrips were smooth and cold. My fingers tingled from the chill.

"Easy," I whispered to the *Stargazer*. I looked up from my position at the wheelstand, past the ropes, burner basket, and balloon, toward the clouds. They were drifting slowly left in a periwinkle blue sky. There'd be an updraft as we passed over the green-brown waters of the canal near Buckingham House. I locked the wheel and jumped from the wheelstand onto the deck of the gondola and looked over the rail. The canal waters were a hundred feet away. I ran back to the wheel and steadied the ship. If I caught the updraft, it would propel me up and forward and give me an edge.

"Cutter caught it, Lily," Jessup yelled down from

the burner basket below the balloon opening. "Up he goes," he added, looking out through his spyglass. The gold polish on the spyglass reflected the fire from the burner.

"Dammit!" I snapped down my binocular lense. I saw Hank Cutter's red-and-white striped balloon rise upward. At the top, he pitched forward with great momentum, catching a horizontal wind. I could just make out Cutter at the wheel. His blond hair blew wildly around him. He turned and waved to me. Wanker.

I was not as lucky. Just as the bow of the *Stargazer* reached the water, a stray wind came in and blew us leeward. The balloon jiggled violently in the turbulent air. I missed the air pocket altogether.

"No! No, no, no!" I cursed and steadied the ship. I had chased Cutter from Edinburgh across the Scottish and English countryside. He had been off his game all day. I'd had him by half a mile the entire race. With the bottom feeders lingering somewhere in the dis-tance behind us, I'd thought the London leg of the 1823 Airship Grand Prix would be mine. That was until St. Albans, where Cutter caught a random breeze that pushed him slightly in front of me. Cutter had a knack for catching favorable winds; it was not a talent I shared.

"We're coming up on Westminster," Jessup yelled down from the basket. "Lily, drop altitude. Cutter is too high. Come in low and fast, and you might overtake him."

The airship towers sat at the pier near the Palace of Westminster along the Thames. A carnival atmosphere had overtaken the city as it always does on race day. Colorful tents were set up everywhere. Vendors hawked their wares to excited Londoners and international visitors. I could hear the merchants barking from their tents even from this far above. I fancied I could smell roasted peanuts in the wind.

I jumped down from the wheelstand, ran across the deck, and pulled the valve cord, opening the flap at the top of the balloon. Hot air released with a hiss. I kept one eye on the balloon and another eye on Tinkers' Tower. At this time of day, the heat coming off of the Palace of Westminster and Tinkers' Tower would give us a bump. I looked up. Cutter had started preparing his descent. It would be close.

I ran back to the wheel.

"Angus, I need more speed," I yelled down to the gear galley, rapping on the wooden hatch that led to the rods, belts, and propeller parts below.

Angus slapped open the hatch and stuck out his bald head. His face was covered in grease, and his blue-lense monocle glimmered in the sunlight. He looked up at the clouds and back at me.

"Let's giddyup," I called to him.

"You trying the Tower sling?" he yelled back.

"You got it."

He laughed wildly. "That's my lassie," he yelled and dropped back down, pulling the wood hatch closed with a clap. I heard the gears grind, and the propeller, which had been turning nice and steady, began to hum loudly. The ship pitched forward. Within moments, we were coming up on Tinkers' Tower. The airship towers were just a stone's throw away.

I aimed the ship directly toward Tinkers' Tower. Just as the bowsprit neared the clock, I yanked the wheel. The warm air caught us.

"Whoa!" Jessup yelled as the balloon moved within arm's length of the tower.

The sound of "Ohhs!" echoed from the crowd below.

A mix of warm air and propulsion gave us some go, and seconds later we were slingshotting around Tinkers' Tower toward the airship platforms. Gliding in on warm air and momentum, we flew fast and low.

Cutter had kept it high, but now he was dropping like a stone toward his own tower. Damned American. I didn't blame him; I would have used the same move. His balloon was releasing so much air that I wondered if he would be able to slow down in time, not that I would have minded seeing him smash to the ground in a million pieces.

"It's going to be close," Jessup yelled as he adjusted the heat pan.

I guided the helm. The *Stargazer* was temperamental, but we understood one another. A shake of the wheel warned me I was pushing too hard. "Almost there," I whispered to the ship.

The Grand Prix Marshalls were standing on the platform. Cutter and I had the end towers. I was going to make it.

"Cut propulsion," I yelled toward the gear galley. On the floor near the wheelstand, a rope led to a bell in the galley. I rang it twice. The propeller switched off.

A soft, sweet wind blew in from the port side. It ruffled my hair around my shoulders. I closed my eyes and turned the wheel slightly starboard, guiding the ship in. Moments later, I heard a jubilant cheer erupt from the American side and an explosion from the firework cannon signaling the winner had been declared. My eyes popped open. I tore off my goggles and looked starboard. Cutter's balloon was docked. I threw the goggles onto the deck and set my forehead against the wheel.

The *Stargazer* settled into her dock. Jessup set the balloon on hover and, grabbing a rope, swung down to the deck. He then threw the lead lines and anchors onto the platform. The beautifully dressed crowd, gentlemen in suits and top hats and fancy ladies in a rainbow of satin gowns carrying parasols, rushed toward the American end of the platform to congratulate the winner.

I was, once again, a national disgrace. Lily the loser. Lily second place. Perhaps I would never be anything more than a ferrywoman, a cheap air jockey.

"Good job, Lily. Second place!" Jessup said joining me. He patted me on the shoulder.

I sighed deeply and unbuttoned my vest. The tension had me sweating; I could feel it dripping down from my neck, between my breasts, into my corset.

"You did great," I told Jessup. "Sorry I let you down."

"Ah, Lily," he sighed.

Angus emerged from below wiping sweat from his head with a greasy rag. He pulled off his monocle. He frowned toward the American side. "Well, we beat the French," he said with a shrug and kissed me on the cheek, smearing grease on me.

"Good job, Angus. Thank you," I said, taking him by the chin and giving him a little shake as I wrinkled my nose and smiled at him.

Angus laughed and dropped his arm around Jessup's shoulders. They grinned happily at one another.

"You stink, brother," Jessup told him.

"It's a wee bit toasty down there. Besides, I pedaled this ship across the entire fucking country while you were up here looking at the birds. That, my friend, is the smell of success."

I laughed.

"You pedaled the ship?" Jessup asked mockingly. "Like Lil and I were just up here playing cards? If I didn't keep the balloon aloft, your ass would be kissing the ground."

"Now wait a minute. Are you saying your job is more important that mine?" Angus retorted.

I could see where this was going. "Gents."

"More important? Now why would I say that? Just because I'm the one..." Jessup started and then his mouth ran.

"Gents."

"… and another thing…" Jessup went on.

"Gentlemen! Our audience awaits," I said cutting them both off, motioning to the well-shod crowd who waited for us on the loading platform outside the *Stargazer*.

I grinned at my crew. "Come on. Let's go."

I patted the rail of the *Stargazer*. "Thanks," I whispered to her, and we exited onto the platform.

A reporter from the *London Times* and several race officials stood waiting for me.

"Well done, Lily! Well done!" the British race official congratulated me with a pat on the back. "Second place! King George will be so proud. One of these days you'll have it, by God."

I was pretty sure that the last thing I needed was the attention of George IV, the extravagant, unpopular lush. But I bit my tongue and smiled politely.

"Lily, how did Cutter beat you? You led the entire race," the reporter asked. She was a round woman wearing a very thick black lace collar that looked like it was choking her. Her heavy purple walking dress looked hot under the late afternoon summer sun, and the brim of her black satin cap barely shaded her nose. I noticed, however, that she had a small clockwork fan pin attached to her chest. The fan wagged cool air toward her face.

I pulled off my cap, mopped my forehead, and thought about the question. "Luck," I replied.

"Lily, that was some move around Tinkers' Tower. How did you learn to do that?" another reporter asked.

"My father," I lied.

"Make way, make way," one of the race officials called, ushering a Marshall forward.

The Marshall looked like someone who lingered an hour too long at supper. The gold buttons on his satin, marigold colored vest would take an eye out if they popped. His overly tall top hat was adorned with a ring of flowers that matched his striking orange colored dress coat.

"Miss Stargazer, congratulations," he said, shaking my hand. "The Spanish airship is coming in now. Will you please join Mr. Cutter at the winners' podium?" he asked politely as he guided me forward by the hand.

From below there was a commotion. A man dressed in an unusual costume rushed up the stairs. The London constables, a full squadron of the Bow Street Runners, chased him. When he got to the loading platform, the man pushed through a crowd of well-dressed ladies and gentlemen, many of whom were gentry. It was then I could see he was dressed as a harlequin. He wore the traditional red and black checked outfit and a black mask. He scanned the towers until he caught sight of me. He jumped, landing on the tower railing, and ran toward me. A woman in the crowd screamed. Moments later the constables appeared on the platform. The race Marshalls pointed toward the harlequin who was making a beeline for me.

I let go of the Marshall's hand and stepped back toward the ship.

"Lily," Jessup warned, moving protectively toward me.

Angus reached over the deck of the *Stargazer* and grabbed a very large wrench.

Was it an assassin? Christ, would someone murder me for winning second place? I turned and ran toward the *Stargazer*. A moment later, the harlequin flipped from the rail, grabbed one of the *Stargazer*'s ropes, and swinging over the others, landed on the platform directly in front of me. Any second now, I would be dead.

He panted and muttered "Lily?" from behind the mask.

"Stop that man! Stop him!" a constable yelled.

"Get out of my way!" Angus roared at the crowd that had thronged in between us.

The masked man grabbed me, tugged on the front of my trousers, and leaned into my ear. The long nose of the mask tickled the side of my face. "Go to Venice," he whispered as he stuffed something down the front of my pants.

"We got you now," a constable said, grabbing him, raising his club.

The man shook him off, took two steps backward, and with a jump, leapt off the tower.

Several people in the crowd screamed.

I rushed to the side of the tower to see the harlequin lying at its base. His body was twisted, and his arms and legs bent oddly, contorted into three distinct points. Blood began pooling around him.

"Miss Stargazer, are you all right?" a constable asked.

"A man just killed himself in front of me. No, I am not all right."

"I mean, are you harmed? Did he hurt you?"

I shook my head and looked down at the mangled body which lay in the shape of a three-sided triskelion. It was the same symbol that was painted on the balloon of the *Stargazer*.

CHAPTER 2

"Absinthe," I told Rheneas, setting my trophy on the bar.

He laughed. "Of course, Lily. Hey, you did good today."

"Oh yeah, it was all great. Losing. Having a man kill himself in front of me. All good," I replied.

"You're getting to be a grouch in your old age, Lil," he replied with an injured laugh, his face crumpling.

"Sorry, Rhe," I said, feeling regretful for my sharp words.

"Well, nobody likes to lose to an American. Right, gents?" Rheneas called to the crowd who booed in reply. Rheneas set his hand on mine. He poured me a glass of the green fairy then slid me the iced water along with the plate of sugar cubes and a spoon. "That one is on me."

I leaned across the counter and kissed Rheneas on top of his bald head. I popped a sugar cube into my mouth and sipped the drink. The spirit dissolved the sugar on contact. My mouth filled with the exploding taste of sweet and the sharp taste of alcohol. I could smell the anise, fennel, and other herbs in the absinthe. I closed my eyes and let it slide down my throat. Heaven. After two more glasses, I was feeling remarkably better.

"I'm headed to the back," I told Rheneas.

"Why don't you leave that with me?" he replied, looking at the trophy.

I gazed at the cup. It was shaped like a hot air balloon. The stem of the trophy was the basket. The top of the balloon was open at the pinnacle and suitable for drinking. It was a heavy piece with inlaid silver filigree. The trophy, once I'd sold it, would probably keep the *Stargazer* outfitted until the next race.

With the death of the harlequin, the trophy ceremony had been suspended. The Marshalls had given Cutter, me, and the Spanish airship racer, Alejandro Fernando, our awards behind the scenes as the constables ushered everyone away from the airship platforms. Just like that, after two solid months of preparation, it was all over. Cutter had invited me for dinner at some fancy place in Kensington, but I passed. The boys headed to Scarlette's Hopper, a tavern near the towers, and I headed home to Covent Garden.

I looked at the cup and back at Rheneas. He was right.

"All right," I said, pushing it toward him. "I'll be back for it later. Either that, or I know where you live."

Rheneas laughed. "You should stop by. My wife has been asking for you."

Flying on absinthe, I wound my way back to the opium den. My head felt light and dizzy. The pent-up tension from the race finally started to leave my body. The green fairy had already led me to another plane. I was seeing stars by the time Miss O led me to my opium cot.

"Lily! You here to celebrate?" Miss O asked, her naked breasts hanging in my face as she set out the equipment for me, including my favorite pipe.

"Oh yes."

"You need anything else, baby? Want me to bring you someone? We got a new girl. How about a nice tickle?" she asked, rubbing her hands over my breasts.

I laughed. "Miss O. Go away," I replied, smacking her playfully on the ass as she headed out.

"Call if you need anything or if you change your mind," she said, wiggling her tongue at me, then closed the curtain.

I picked up the engraved brass and wood pipe and lit the opium. I inhaled deeply, the smoke filling my mouth. The sweet scent of the burning herb filled the air around me. I closed my eyes and let the opium do its work. After a few hits, I felt like the world around me had begun to slow. The voices outside my cot seemed drawn out, Miss O's laughter ringing like a slow gong. My head filled with a light haze. I felt deeply relaxed.

Finally alone, I decided to find out what, exactly, the harlequin had passed to me.

No one had seen him stick the package in my pants. When the constables questioned me, I declined to offer more information than they needed. I told them the clown had asked me to marry him, and I'd said no. Then, he jumped. They didn't need to know anything else.

The constables had bitched bitterly when they discovered the harlequin had nothing on him except his mask. Apparently he'd been making a ruckus across London all day. He had manhandled an undersecretary at a downtown office and made off with some papers, stolen something from a cathedral, beaten the priest who'd tried to stop him, and knocked out two of the Bow Street boys to get onto the tower.

They did, however, ask me to identify him.

When they removed his mask, we discovered he was young and very handsome. "I've never seen him before," I told them truthfully, a lump rising in my throat all the same.

"Well, that's it then. Just some loon. Probably was so depressed she rejected him that he killed himself. After all, no one goes around dressed like that," the Captain told his underlings.

"Unless they *are* a harlequin," I said.

"Well, yes, of course," the Captain replied, irritated. With that, they closed the case.

I pulled the package out of my pants and

unwrapped it. At first I thought it was a spyglass. It was long, gold polished, and had strange symbols engraved all over it. It looked very old. I lifted it, expecting to see magnification, but my eye was met instead by a waterfall of color. A kaleidoscope? Why had someone died to pass me a kaleidoscope?

I lay back, taking another hit of opium, and looked at the colors. They were exceptionally vivid. I had never seen a kaleidoscope so brightly hued. I turned the glass around and around. Inside the colors changed, at least in my imagination, from vistas of flower filled fields, to bouquets of lilies, to the floral pattern on my mother's everyday housedress. I stopped. That was an image I had completely forgotten until that moment. Sighing, I turned the kaleidoscope again while my eyes drooped.

I was sweating. I could not move. I stared down at my foster father's body lying on the cobblestone street, blood pouring from his mouth and ears. I wanted to scream, but I couldn't make a sound. I twisted and turned, unable to get away from the sight. It was so hot. I could not breathe.

"She's in here," Miss O's voice broke in. "You want me to bring a couple of girls again?"

"No. Not this time."

"Lily, visitor," Miss O called.

My eyes popped open. I gasped for breath.

"Bad dream?" he asked.

"Lord Byron?" I said, surprised, as I tried to pull myself together. I mopped the sweat from my brow.

As always, the fucking nightmares. Would it ever end? "Now, what brings you to this den of sin?"

"I looked for you after the race. I couldn't find you anywhere. Naturally, then, I knew you would be here," he said, sitting down on the cot beside me. He lifted the pipe and took a toke. How handsome he looked in the dim light, his chestnut colored hair curling around his ears, his skin, with its alabaster sheen, making him look otherworldly. His pouty red lips always seemed hungry. And then there were his eyes, as clear and blue as a spring sky.

"I've missed you, but why are you in London?" I asked him. He handed the pipe to me. I inhaled deeply. The opium made a haze of everything. I felt like I was experiencing the world from a forty foot distance.

"Some legal matters needed immediate and personal attention. And I came, of course, for the race. But I'm leaving for Athens at dawn," he said, stroking my leg. He toked again then poured himself a glass of absinthe from the small decanter beside the cot. He popped a sugar cube and drank the absinthe in one long swallow.

"So soon?" I said with a sly grin as I grabbed hold of his belt, my fingers inside his pants.

"That's time enough," he replied, "unless, of course, my absence has cured your love for me," Byron said with a smile.

"Love?"

"Of course. It is the duty of a lover to love. Ah, but I forget myself. I have a gift for you," Byron replied.

He reached into his pocket and pulled out a small wooden box. He handed it to me.

I took another toke then set the pipe down. "What is this for?"

"Your service to your country," he replied.

"Ah yes, how the British love a loser."

Byron leaned in and kissed my cheek and ear. "We are giants. That is the reason we cannot tolerate anything less than excellence. Open it," he whispered.

I opened the lid to discover a small metal pin tinkered into the shape of a lily. "It's beautiful."

"Ah, but that's not all. Watch," he said and tapped one of the intricately designed carpels extending from the center of the lily. With that, the flower came to life. The petals flexed up and down as if they were in the breeze, the carpels waving in coordination. "A lily that never loses its fragrance. A delicacy that never wilts. It is common metal, yes, but strikingly beautiful in its complexity."

I stared at it. It was amazing. I set the box down, and lying back, pulled Byron on top of me. I kissed him deeply, my tongue roving inside his mouth, my fingers twisting around his curly hair. I could taste the sugar and alcohol on his lips. His intoxicating scent of patchouli and orange blossom overwhelmed me.

He moved to unbuckle my corset. "No buttons?"

he asked. Puzzled, he eyed the corset with great interest.

Guiding his hand, I set it on the small metal rosette at the center of the corset between my breasts. "Press down."

When he did, the mechanism inside released and the corset fell open. At once, I was topless.

"Now, *that* is amazing," he said, spreading his hands wide.

"A friend designed it for me. I think it will become fashionable."

"If men have anything to say about it, indeed." He lifted a sugar cube off the tray and licked it once, rubbing it on my nipples. He then nuzzled my breasts as he pulled off my belt.

I slid out of my pants and pulled the corset aside. I helped Byron unbutton his vest and pulled off the blousy white shirt that lay beneath. Moments later his boots and pants were off too.

Byron was an infamous lover, and I think many wondered at the relationship between us. It was not that I was so beautiful, so smart, or so alluring that enchanted him. What Byron liked best about me was that I knew what he wanted-it was the same thing I wanted.

I grabbed my belt and pushed Byron down on the cot. He smiled at me. With a wink, I grabbed his hands and belted them together, cinching the belt tightly to the post. I straddled his waist. Then I leaned in and kissed him deeply. I sat back up. We were locked into a deep stare; then, I hit him hard. Blood leaked from the corner of his mouth. He stuck his tongue out and tasted it.

"Again," he whispered.

I did as he asked, again and again. When tears of pain finally came to his eyes, I stuck him inside me and rode him hard. After I untied him, he grabbed my breasts roughly, squeezing the nipples until I cried out. He was good, knowing just how and when to raise and lower his hips. The first moments were strikingly clear but then the rest became a blur of flesh and feeling. I remember untying him, being flipped on my stomach, and the sharp feel of a lash on my ass, but after that everything else was hazy.

I woke an hour or so later to find Byron lying beside me looking into the kaleidoscope. My post-opium head was already starting to ache.

"Where did you get this?" he asked, turning it.

"The harlequin passed it to me before he jumped."

"Why?"

"I don't know," I replied. I sat up and opened the curtain. "Miss O?" I called.

I could see from the open skylight that it was dark outside. An airship passed over; it was a passenger transport.

"Baby, your lip is bleeding," Miss O said when she came up to me. She handed me a handkerchief.

"Thanks. Can you bring some water?"

"Of course," she replied and walked away.

I leaned back in and blotted the blood from my lip. Byron smiled apologetically, but I shrugged. I noticed he had a dark ring under his eye. I said nothing.

"Did the harlequin say anything?" Byron asked, rolling over.

I looked at his naked body. I loved making love to him, but there was something so endearing about seeing Byron naked and unaroused that moved me. It almost made the great Lord Byron seem vulnerable.

"He asked if I was Lily, told me to go to Venice, and stuck this in my trousers."

Byron half laughed, half grunted. "When are you leaving?"

"I cannot afford a holiday to Venice, my Lord," I said jokingly, taking the kaleidoscope from his hands.

I put it to my eye again. Once more, I was treated to the beautiful colors.

"What about your prize money?"

"Used immediately to settle my debts. I still have to hawk the trophy; the money from that will cover most of the *Stargazer's* expenses with a few crowns left over to feed myself. But I need to take fares and get ready for the next race."

Byron looked at the kaleidoscope. "No. You should go. It is, after all, Venice," he said, looking wistful, "a place where dying glory smiles. It is the perfect place for an escape. I have people there who can help you. I will arrange a place for you."

I shook my head. "You already do too much for me. Besides, I have fares lined up starting tomorrow."

"My secretary will cancel them. Do this, Lily."

"Why?"

"Because this was given to you-specifically."

"By some crazed racing fan. It probably means nothing."

But both Byron and I knew it meant something, even if we were not sure what.

He took the kaleidoscope from my hands again and looked at the engraved symbols on the side. "Take it to Venice, to the clockworks in St. Mark's Square. Someone will know what it is."

I looked deeply at him, studying his handsome face as he examined the kaleidoscope. Every time I was with Byron, I felt a rush of excitement. While my stomach filled with girlish butterflies, my body ached for his rough embrace. I set my chin on his shoulder and inhaled deeply, breathing in his sweet scent.

He smiled wistfully at me then lifted the handkerchief and blotted my lip. "Lily," he whispered fondly.

I reached out and stroked his cheek.

"Water," Miss O called and handed in a serving platter.

Taking the tray, Byron uttered a distracted "Thank you."

Miss O nodded but said nothing. God knows what she had heard or what she was thinking. With a sigh, Byron started pulling on his clothes. I handed him a glass of water which he drank greedily. Then he pulled on his boots.

"Now," he said, and I could see that this was his goodbye, "I insist. Just go. Here," he said, handing me his coin pouch, "take this. My secretary will meet you in the morning with another sum and my contacts, and he'll settle with your customers."

"George…" I began, but I was not sure what to say. I wanted to go, but I did not want to take his money.

He rose then and came to stand outside of the cot. "Oh yes, this too," he said and handed me a bottle of amber colored laudanum. "For the trip. It takes the edge off. Trelawny found a great supplier. It's the best I've had," he said and leaned in. "Besides you," he added and kissed me. "Write and let me know what you discover. And Lily, have fun," he said with a sly grin then walked away.

"My lord… my lord," Byron was greeted by others in the den as he passed. Moments later, he was gone.

I lay back on the cot. Opening the bottle, I tasted just a small drop of the laudanum. It *was* good. I looked at the kaleidoscope again. When I looked inside this time, however, I thought I saw, for just a moment, a strikingly beautiful woman—all in gold gazing at me.

I lowered the kaleidoscope then looked again. This time, I saw only colored glass. It was probably just the laudanum playing tricks on me. I lay back. What the hell. I would go.

CHAPTER 3

I woke the next morning feeling like an elephant was thundering around in my head. I didn't remember how I got there, but I had made it home to my second floor flat on Hart Street. My mouth felt sticky and tasted like the bottom of my boots. I clanged around in my small kitchen and put on a pot of tea. When I pushed open the curtains I discovered it was already late morning. The sunlight made me wince. I put on my dark glasses and sat holding my aching head until the teapot whistled.

I stumbled back into the kitchen and poured myself a cup. The tart black tea washed away the gummy sourness in my mouth but did nothing to relieve the headache. From the pantry, I pulled out a tin of tobacco. Two months earlier I had raced in the New York City leg of the Grand Prix. I'd come in second, again, but Cutter was nice enough to give me a tin of his family's tobacco. It was good quality. I pushed a small pinch of the dried tobacco into a pipe. Despite my hopes, it did nothing to ease the headache.

I went back to the pantry to discover that, besides tea and sugar, I had nothing to eat in the flat. The days leading up to the race were always like that. I could only focus on one thing: winning.

I noticed then that the kaleidoscope was lying on the kitchen table wrapped in its cloth. I sat at the table considering it while I drank. After I finished the cup of tea, I looked down at the tea leaves. I was not a scryer, but I always impressed people with my ability to bullshit their fortune. I looked down at the pattern in the bottom of the cup. I saw, very clearly, the shape of a swan.

Forcing myself to get up, I washed my face and combed my hair. I took out the pin Byron had given me and fastened it on the side of my cap. It was already hot. I stripped off yesterday's clothes and redressed. I pulled on some belted stockings, leather shorts with suspenders, and a scoop necked white lace top. I slid on my black leather knee-high boots and a matching shoulder shrug with a large satin red rose. Securing the kaleidoscope in my satchel, I tossed on my cap and headed out.

The second I pushed open the door leading to narrow Hart Street, I regretted getting out of bed. The smell of the fruit and flowers being sold in the street coupled with the wafting smell of horse manure filled my nose. Unable to control myself, I leaned into the alley and vomited. That wasn't a good way to start the day.

I began the mile long trek back to the airship towers. My glasses on, I kept my head low. The sunlight burned my eyes and made my head throb. Hart Street was relatively quiet in the morning. The sound of the vendors and children and their mothers' scolding them filled the streets. It was quite different from the raucous sounds of the night when the theaters, taverns, brothels, and opium dens were in full swing. Traveling down the cobblestone, I was happy to notice the pillory stocks were empty; apparently the constables were leaving the man-loving dandies at rest today.

I had just turned toward King Street when I heard someone call my name.

"Miss Stargazer?" someone called from behind me.

Oh lord, the last thing I needed was an adoring fan or a problem. I kept walking, pretending I had not heard.

"Begging your pardon, are you Lily Stargazer?" someone called again, and I heard feet hurriedly crossing the street behind me. "Miss?" the someone asked as he came up alongside me.

I turned to find myself looking at a very young priest with a very bruised face. I knew at once who he must be.

"Good morning," I said.

I must not have smelled as good as I thought. I saw him take a sharp breath. I guess I'd grown used to the lingering smell of alcohol and opium. Regardless, he smiled tolerantly at me. He was quite young. His sandy brown hair was cut short, and he had alluringly blue eyes. He was not half bad. "Are you Miss Stargazer?"

"Obviously," I replied. Not many London women were in the habit of dressing like an air jockey.

"I'm sorry. I was just trying to be polite. I heard about the harlequin yesterday. He confronted me as well. I was hoping I could speak with you for a moment?" he said and looked suspiciously around him. Clearly, he was not comfortable being in an area of town with such ill repute. Even though I was in a hurry, I felt bad for him.

"Sure, why not," I said sympathetically. "There is a teahouse across the way." I turned and headed in the direction of Mrs. Mulligan's.

"Thank you," he said, relieved. "I am sure you are very busy. Thank you for your time," he said as he tried to keep pace with me. His long black skirts swished above the stone streets as he walked.

The bell on the door of Mrs. Mulligan's teahouse jingled when we entered. We took a seat close to the window. I pulled off my glasses and hat. I noticed that several of the patrons looked up to inspect us when we entered. An air jockey and a busted up priest, we must have made an odd pair. Someone said my name in a whisper.

The teahouse was quaint. The walls were papered with a blue and yellow floral pattern. Each table had a white lace tablecloth and a small bouquet of irises at the center.

"Mornin', Lily," Mrs. Mulligan said. She was a stout woman who wore a blue cotton gown and a stiff white apron. She set a chipped teapot on the table, clattered down two old cups and saucers, and poured the priest and me tea into mismatched cups: mine bore a yellow daffodil; the priest's had a dark blue stripe.

"Want anything?" she asked me.

My stomach still had not decided if I was hungry or sick. "Let's have two lemon scones," I told her. I could not remember the last time I'd actually eaten something.

I lifted two cubes of sugar and dropped them into the tea, splashing drops onto the white tablecloth. I stirred the tea and looked up at the priest.

He looked around, taking everything in, then slid a slice of lemon into his tea. "I'm Father Magill," he introduced. "I heard the harlequin attacked you at the race yesterday."

"Well, 'attacked' is a bit strong. You look attacked. I was just rattled," I paused. "You're a bit young to be a priest, aren't you?" I lifted the teacup and saucer. My hands were trembling terribly; the china clattered. I set the saucer down, took a quick sip of tea, and returned the cup.

The priest's watchful eyes took in my shaking hands.

"I haven't eaten," I explained in something of a lie.

He looked carefully at me. "You're a bit young to be an airship racer, aren't you?" he said with a grin. His face dimpled at the corners when he smiled. He was far too handsome to be a priest, black eye aside. Or, perhaps, included.

I decided then that I liked him. I smiled. "Yeah, I see what you did there. Now, what do you want from me?" I asked.

Mrs. Mulligan returned with the scones. They were baked to a golden yellow. I could smell the thin lemon glaze on the top and just a hint of the sweet scent of vanilla. My stomach growled.

Right away, Father Magill lifted his scone and took a bite. He sighed, savoring the flavors.

It was my turn to look carefully at him.

"The church pantries are somewhat limited," he said in what I suspected was something of a lie. "The harlequin stole an artifact from the church and left me with this little gift," he said pointing to his eye. "I'm trying to track down the item, and the constables have been no help. My superiors asked me to see if you knew anything. They are put out that it's missing, and ultimately, it is my fault it got away."

"Is it? What kind of artifact?" I asked and took a bite. The scone was good, and my stomach decided to cooperate.

"Well, I'm not really able to say," he replied, looking rather embarrassed.

I laughed. It figured. I then told Father Magill the same lie I had told the constables.

The priest looked disappointed. He took another bite of the scone and stared down at his plate. His forehead wrinkled with stressed distraction. I suspected that his superiors were more than a little put out.

"What's your name?" I asked, sipping my tea.

He raised his blue eyes and looked at me. "Arthur," he replied.

"Arthur. Savior from the Saxons. Wielder of Excalibur."

Arthur smiled. "And how did you end up with the name Lily?" he asked.

"When my mother dumped me at the orphanage before they hauled her off to debtors' prison, she left me with a bouquet of lilies. She hoped it would make the nuns like me. From then on, they called me Lily."

Arthur looked surprised. "How old were you?"

"About five."

"You said they called you Lily. Did you have another name?"

I grinned at him. "Guinevere," I lied.

"Really?" Arthur asked with a heavy laugh. He rubbed his knuckles across his lips while he looked me over. A moment later, he seemed to come to himself. He lowered his hand, and his eyes, and took a deep breath. "Your mother, what happened to her?" he asked, taking a sip of tea.

"Died in prison six months later."

"I'm so sorry."

"It happens," I said and suddenly felt a strong urge to get going. "Well, I need to get to the ship," I said. I polished off my tea as I rose. Fishing a couple of coins out of my pocket, I set them on the table. My eyes caught sight of the tea leaves in the bottom of my cup. Again, I spotted a swan. I pushed the plate with my unfinished scone across the table to Arthur. "Enjoy mine too. Sorry I can't help," I told him.

"Lily," he said, rising. It seemed he did not know what to say. "Thanks anyway. Congratulations, by the way, on second place yesterday."

"Thanks," I said, tossing on my cap. "Good luck, Arthur," I said and exited the teahouse.

CHAPTER 4

Rather than heading directly to the towers, I turned toward Hungerford Market. Walking briskly, I found myself in the middle of the busy market less than fifteen minutes later. I passed the fish mongers, fruit carts, and butcher stands on my way to the back.

Though my stomach felt better, my head still ached. Giving in at last, I stopped in a dark corner between two stalls and pulled out the small bottle of laudanum Byron had given me. I took one drop. I leaned against a beam, closed my eyes, and let it work. I took a couple of deep breaths, and soon my head began to clear.

I resumed my course to the back of the market. There, in the dim light, I found Tinkers' Hall. The tradesmen were hard at work. The fireworks vendors, clock makers, jewelers, and other gadgetry vendors were huddled into one end of the market. It was easy to find their section. A ten foot clock tower, an exact replica of Tinkers' Tower at the Palace of Westminster, which had been a gift from the London Tinkers' Society to Queen Anne, sat at the entryway of their stalls. A bell struck sharply at the top of every hour. The smell of sulfur from the fireworks makers burned your nose. A chorus of hammers struck metal, filling the place with a sound you could feel. Row after row of vendors displayed unique gadgetry, clothing, and mechanical parts.

I wove toward the back. Unlike the front stalls, here no one screamed out their wares. Old men with thick, white moustaches and bushy eyebrows looked up at me from behind monocles, their stalls filled with an assortment of gears and parts. I waved at Budgie, a vendor from whom I often bought spare parts. He had been working on a gun of some sort, adjusting the small gears with a very tiny tool. He had his jeweler's monocle wedged into his eye socket. He removed it when he spotted me.

"Lily? Didn't break a part yesterday, did you? I didn't see Angus-"

"No, we're good. I'm headed to see the Italian."

"Ah, good, good," he said with a wave then turned back to his work.

The Italian. It's how everyone referred to Salvatore. While Angus and Jessup called him that too, he was a good friend to me. His always had new, ingenious ways to improve the *Stargazer* or remarkable contraptions, like the clockwork bodice, for me to try. He was also incredibly attractive.

When I reached his stall, he was not in the front. He had his lanterns burning, but he was nowhere to be seen. I leaned across the counter to look at his workbench. He had several small gears and screws laid out as well as coils of copper wire and magnets. Sitting under a plate-sized magnifying glass was a small device with the tiniest clockwork gears I'd ever seen. The door to his workshop behind the stall was open. I hopped over the counter and headed back.

"Sal?" I called, knocking on the door. I looked inside. I didn't see him anywhere. "Sal?"

A hand dropped on my shoulder.

I jumped.

"Miss Stargazer, are you snooping?" he whispered in my ear as he gave my backside a soft squeeze.

I turned to face him. He had his long, silver-streaked black hair tied at the nape of his neck. His glasses had been pushed up onto his head. His steel gray eyes looked piercingly at me. "Hi Sal," I said, giving him a soft, sweet kiss.

"That's all?" he asked. "Well, I guess it must do for now. Please," he motioned me inside.

I went within and sat down.

"What can I do for you?"

"I want you to look at something. Something... secret," I said in a whisper. My eyes darted quickly back to the aisles outside.

Sal closed the workshop door. He went to the pantry and pulled out a bottle. He poured us two small glasses of grappa. He handed one to me. I could smell the sharp spirit. My mouth watered.

"Salute," he said.

Clinking glasses, we drank. He refilled mine; I drank again.

"Now, what does my Lily have that is secret?" he asked.

I pulled the kaleidoscope out of the bag and handed it to him. He unwrapped the device and looked closely at the markings on the outside. He lifted the kaleidoscope, aimed it at a nearby candle, and turned the dial.

"She's beautiful," he said, lowering the kaleidoscope again.

"What are these markings? Do they mean anything?" I asked, pointing to the images engraved on the sides.

Sal lowered his glasses. "Flora, fauna, some geographical markers. But there is something else here," he said. He took off his glasses then pulled on the thick pair of goggles he'd had hanging around his neck. He peered intently at the kaleidoscope. When he looked up at me, his eyes seemed ten times their size. "It's ancient Greek."

"Can you read it?"

"Of course. That is why you came to me, no?"

I grinned.

"It is like a poem: 'Celestial queen with the kaleidoscope mind, come to me once more,'" Sal recited as he read the words. He lifted the kaleidoscope again and looked within. "There is something special in the glass. I cannot tell what unless I take it apart."

"Oh no, please leave it as it is," I said quickly.

He lowered it again and looked at the symbols engraved on the outside. "Some of these seem random, almost decorative: flowers, doves, apples, shells, swans." He pulled off his goggles. "It is very beautiful. Where did you get it?"

"Someone died to get this to me."

Sal raised an eyebrow inquisitively then handed me the kaleidoscope. He then picked up the cloth covering to pass to me as well. When he did so, however, the wrapping caught the light. For a brief moment, I saw something on the fabric.

"Did you see that?" I asked, grabbing the cloth.

I held it back up to the light. There, just barely visible in the bright light, was the outline of a swimming swan holding a flower in its beak.

"Now, that is interesting," Sal said and took the cloth from me. He looked closely at it and then smelled it. "It is drawn with a very light water and oil mixture. If this cloth is washed, the image will fade. Clever."

I looked at the cloth. "What kind of flower is that?"

Sal looked closely. "It looks like an anemone."

I stared at the image then wrapped up the kaleidoscope and stuck it in my satchel.

"Do you like Venice?" I asked him.

"Ah, Venice. Oh yes. Very much."

"Good. Then you're coming. Be at the airship towers tomorrow at dawn."

"Coming? To Venice?" Sal asked hesitantly.

"Yes, to Venice," I said then stood.

Sal leaned back, put his hands behind his head, and exhaled deeply. He looked me over from head to toe. "You're looking so beautiful today. Why are you in such a rush?"

I grinned at him. "Well, I'm late to get to the *Stargazer*."

"If you are already late, what does another half an hour matter?"

"Only half an hour?" I smiled wryly at Sal and then, setting my bag down, slid onto his lap. Sal reached over and grabbed the bottle of grappa. He took a small sip and then pulled me into a deep kiss. The sharp spirit spilled between our lips, burning my mouth.

He gently pushed the shrug from my shoulders and slid the suspenders off. He then pulled my blouse up over my head and set it aside.

"My Lily, what is this?" He gently touched my breasts. I looked down to see that both breasts had dark fingerprint bruises.

"Byron," I replied.

"Ahh," Sal said, gently kissing the bruises, "someone must teach the great poet to be gentle with delicate things."

"He did like your corset."

"Well, he does have good taste."

I unbuttoned Sal's shirt and rubbed the thick hair on his chest. Pushing his shirt off, I kissed his neck and shoulders, my hands roving across his muscular frame. I could smell the light scent of sandalwood on his skin. Sal stroked his hands across my back as he gently kissed my breasts and neck. I rose and removed my shorts.

Sal stuck his hands between my legs and caressed me gently. "Tiger Lily," he whispered, leaning forward to kiss me through my lace underwear, feeling my breasts and backside. He leaned back and unlaced his pants. I slid my panties off, and he pulled me back onto him. Moments later we were flying.

Sal was not like Byron, but his moves were not tepid. He was fluid and skilled. He was precise in the way he touched me, knowing what would arouse me. Perhaps twenty years my senior, it was not surprising that Sal knew what to do. He loved women, but he rarely left Tinkers' Hall long enough to engage in any kind of real relationship. He was a perpetual bachelor, married to his craft before anything else. In this, and many other things, we were kindred spirits. And, I adored him. I enjoyed every sweet moment together. In fact, I was so lost in him that after both Sal and I reached release, I dozed off peacefully, nestled snugly against his chest.

Lost in the void of sleep, I jumped when the clock tower at the end of the hall chimed eleven o'clock.

"Oh, I'm so late. I need to go," I groaned. I grabbed the bottle of grappa and took a large swig.

"So soon?" Sal asked sleepily as he smoothed my hair.

"The boys are waiting," I replied. I could already hear the earful I was going to get from my crew. I took another drink.

"Ah, well, then you should go."

"You'll be there in the morning?"

"Of course."

I kissed Sal, who was looking very drowsy, then hurriedly got dressed and headed toward the airship towers. On the way there, I braced myself for a scolding I probably deserved. It would not be the first, and no doubt, it would not be the last.

CHAPTER 5

"Lily, where in the hell have you been?" Jessup demanded the moment I reached the *Stargazer*'s platform.

Angus was leaning against the hull of the *Stargazer* looking like he was trying to decide whether or not to be angry.

My head had already started to ache. Assembled outside the *Stargazer* were Angus, Jessup, Byron's secretary, who was holding a large package, and an impatient looking constable.

"I-"

"Lord Byron's secretary has been rerouting our fares all morning. What the hell is going on?" Jessup complained.

The constable opened his mouth and stepped forward, but Byron's secretary motioned for him to be silent.

"Miss Stargazer," Byron's secretary interrupted, "I did let your crew know I had rearranged your passengers' flight plans with your approval." He cast an exasperated glance at Jessup. "Now, I have a couple of items my Lord has asked me to pass to you, and I'll be on my way."

I felt sorry for the man, not because he had endured my caprice, as I am sure caprice was something he was used to, but because he'd had to hear Jessup and Angus bitch all morning.

The secretary removed a small metal bank box from a cloth bag and handed it to me. "My Lord said you would know the combination," he told me.

I nodded affirmatively. "Please send my gratitude."

"Ah, Miss Stargazer, nothing pleases my Lord more than being your sponsor," the secretary replied.

Jessup and Angus exchanged glances. Jessup's anger seemed to leave him at once, and his eyes shone excitedly. He grinned from ear to ear. Angus nodded knowingly and slid over the rail and onto the *Stargazer*.

"He also sent you this package," he added, handing a large box to me.

"What is it?"

"That, I don't know. Lord Byron passed me the package this morning. Can I be of any further service to you, Miss Stargazer?" Byron's secretary asked.

"No. Thank you. Please give Lord Byron my thanks."

The secretary nodded politely then made his way down the platform.

I felt the package with curiosity. I was about to

open it when the constable cleared his throat. I had forgotten he was there.

"Miss Stargazer, my Captain asked me to come see you regarding the harlequin."

"I already told your Captain I don't know anything," I replied, irritated.

The constable nodded. "Actually, he wanted to share some information with you. We learned something more about the man. After some research, they discovered that it was your adoption records that were stolen yesterday. The Captain thought you might wish to know; he was concerned for your safety. You're leaving town? Perhaps that is for the best until this matter clears up."

"My adoption papers?"

"Yes. Where are you headed so I can inform the Captain?"

"Italy."

"Very good. Have a safe trip. Congratulations, by the way, on second place yesterday. Cutter got lucky," the constable said and left.

I closed my eyes. Why would someone steal my adoption papers? And why was my head pounding again already?

I took a deep breath and boarded the *Stargazer*.

"All right, Lil, what's going on?" Jessup asked.

"We're off the transport circuit for a bit. We'll be taking a little trip," I replied.

"And where are we going?" Angus asked.

"Venice."

"Venice!" Angus and Jessup both declared at once.

I laughed. "So we need to get the ship ready. I want to leave by dawn tomorrow. Can we manage it?"

"Of course we can manage it. We can even leave tonight if you like," Angus said.

I shook my head. "That's okay. We'll go in the morning."

"Why Venice?" Jessup asked.

I pulled Angus and Jessup into a huddle and told them about the harlequin's kaleidoscope.

"Are you sure you want to get mixed up in this? There might be a mess waiting in Venice," Angus warned.

"I won't let it become a problem. And if it does, then to hell with it. Let's just consider this a little break. I think we all deserve one, don't you?"

Angus inhaled deeply and looked at his hands. His eyebrows arched as he mulled it over.

"I'm happy to oblige Byron and his coin, but Venice?" Jessup said. "You don't even speak Italian. How are you going to-"

"I have that covered."

"Covered?"

I nodded.

"Oh bloody hell. No," Angus said and looked at Jessup.

"She wouldn't."

Knowing what was coming, I looked away from them.

"No. No, Lily. You didn't," Jessup said.

I didn't look at him.

"Ahh, Christ, she did," Angus grumbled.

"Lily! The Italian? You know we *hate* that guy," Jessup said.

"He'll be giving us advice across the Channel and back," Angus said.

"My friend, why don't you use silk line rather than twine rope," Jessup said in a mock Italian accent.

"Grease it a bit more, Scotsman. If you set it counterclockwise it will get better pull," Angus jibbed.

"Come on, gents, he's not that bad," I told them with a grin. I had fully expected it. Not only was I late, but I knew they wouldn't be happy to hear Sal and his useful advice were coming. Angus and Jessup were masters at what they did; people came to them for advice, not the other way around. They just didn't understand Sal the way I did.

"Not only that, but we'll have to listen to Sal fucking you the whole way," Angus added.

"Lord Byron isn't bad, Lily, but Sal-" Jessup said.

"Mind your own business and get the ship ready," I said with a laugh and sent them on their way.

Once they had gone, I sat with my back along the bulwark of the *Stargazer* and opened the package Byron had sent. The brown paper wrapping on the package crinkled under my fingers. I pulled open the lid of the large box. Inside was a light yellow satin and chiffon gown. It had a scooped neckline with lace trim and puffy sleeves. A pair of dainty white leather shoes with rosettes had been stuffed into the bottom of the box. I also found a small ladies' top hat. Inside was a note: "No one doubted on the whole, that she was what her dress bespoke, a damsel fair, and fresh, and beautiful exceedingly. Wear a gown or the Venetian women will hate you. George." I stroked the soft chiffon and whispered a prayer of thanks. What fortune I'd won to have Byron in my life.

I leaned over the rail and looked down to where the harlequin had fallen. Why had he stolen my adoption records? And why had such a young man killed himself? And why had he passed the kaleidoscope to me? Moreover, what was its significance? I could only hope my trip to Venice would bring some answers.

CHAPTER 6

When I returned to my flat to prepare for the trip, I found the place in shambles. Everything had been tossed around; my clothing had been heaved out of drawers, the kitchen cupboards, still embarrassingly bare, were flung open, and my tool box had been torn apart, the tools strewn everywhere. They had even cut open my mattress. They had not taken anything, not even the trophy. They were looking for the kaleidoscope. Clearly, someone had not believed the lies I had told. For a moment, I envisioned Father "Arthur" Magill ripping my flat apart, a desperate expression on his face.

As I stood in the middle of the mess, I felt violated. Someone had made themselves privy to my private world. One of my opium pipes lay on the floor, the small supply of dried opium sprinkled on the old carpet. I tried to tidy up. I picked up my clothing to put it back in the wardrobe, but the thought of unknown hands on my clothes made me feel sick to my stomach. Maybe Angus was right. Maybe I had no business in this mess, but a man had died to pass the kaleidoscope to me. People only sacrifice their lives for a few reasons: love, religion, or money. Unless I went to Venice, I would never know why he had died. I threw the clothes into a heap in the corner, collected just a few of my belongings, and headed out. I bolted the flat shut and went to spend the night on the *Stargazer*. There, with the tower guards on patrol, I would be safe.

—•—

Sal joined us the following morning, and the four of us headed out at dawn. The weather patterns over the English Channel could be unpredictable. The higher we went, the more likely we'd get trapped in a rapid east-west air current. If we stayed closer to the water, we'd be hit with marine conditions. And I hated the water. I always got nervous flying over it, and I liked flying over the Channel, renowned as it was for air pirates, even less. The *Stargazer* was fast, so I had no doubt we could outrun anyone, but I'd rather not find myself in the position of trying. Angus and Jessup were not as uptight. After getting over the initial surprise, they were both happy to be on holiday, even if Sal was along for the ride.

As we passed over the white cliffs of Dover, I stood at the wheel of the ship and looked out at the waters of the Channel. A strong wind blew, but it was warm and sweet. It was the beginning of July, and while the hot summer air lingered in the streets of London, in the air I felt free. I could breathe there. I held the wheel steady as the ship glided from over the land to above the water. The balloon joggled with the change in air pressure then steadied.

"Let's have ten percent more lift," I called up to Jessup who immediately adjusted the heat pan. Moments later the balloon pulled the gondola upward. The propeller worked steadily, easing us out over the water.

The waters just offshore were a soft greenish blue. Once Dover was a speck behind us, the water grew deep. Its color faded to dark navy. It was not a far trip to Calais, a mere 48 kilometers, but I would be nervous the entire time. I held the wheel tightly; I did not want the others to see my hands were shaking.

I gazed out at the waves. The sight of the water took me back in time. Once again I was a little girl sitting beside my mother on the bank of the Thames in Southwark. It was early morning, and the Thames was covered with thick mist. There was a heavy, fishy smell in the air. The Thames' waters rippled, curling and breaking against the bankside. I wasn't sure why we were there. My mother had woken me before dawn, and we had left the small London apartment we'd been sharing with three other families.

My mother was crying hysterically, her face buried in her hands.

"What's wrong, mama?" I'd asked.

My mother lowered her hands and looked at me.

Her eyes were red and swollen. Wild wisps of dark brown hair had pulled from her bun and framed her face. "I just don't know what to do with you!" she moaned hysterically.

I remembered being scared, and it was not the first time. We'd left our farm in far-flung Cornwall after my father had disappeared. My mother never told me what had happened to him. He'd simply stopped coming home. When I asked her where he had gone, she would not answer me. I remembered that men came and took all of the furniture from our house. My mother made me pack a small bag and told me that we had to go to London or we would starve. My mother cried a lot and spoke little. I don't know how long we lived in the cramped London apartment, but I remember my mother leaving before dawn and returning at dusk looking exhausted and smelling like body odor and raw meat. But no matter how much she worked, men still came and demanded money from her.

That morning, beside the Thames, I was terrified. I didn't know why. But I did know my mother was sad, maybe sadder than she'd ever been. I put my small hand into my mother's and smiled at her, trying to comfort her.

My mother looked down at me, pulled me into a tight embrace, and kissed me on the cheek. She then whispered in my ear. "It's for the best. Mama loves you," she said, and picking me up, threw me into the briny Thames.

I hit the cold water with a startle. The fast waves began to pull me under at once. I was so young, I didn't know how to swim. The Thames pulled me downstream.

"Mama!" I screamed. "Mama!"

I saw my mother standing on the bank, her arms folded across her chest. She stood completely still, as if she was either shocked by or was making peace with what she had just done. As the water of the Thames carried me away, I fought. I kicked my legs hard and screamed for my mother.

"Mama! Help me, please!"

"Oh my god," I heard a man yell and moments later saw someone jump into the water.

The waves had begun to fill my skirts, and they grew heavy. I could feel them pulling me down. I fought against the current as the deep reached for me, my head bobbing under again and again. My arms and legs were numb from the cold, and I could barely move them. As I was about to lose to the river, someone grabbed me.

"Hold on," a young man said. "Hold on."

He held me by the waist and pulled me, swimming against the current, toward the shoreline. The Thames fought him, as if the river sought to keep the prize it had won.

With a heave, he pulled me out of the water. I lay in the grass on the bank. A young man, perhaps no more than fifteen years of age, looked down at me. He was dressed in a dark blue velvet suit.

"Can you breathe? Are you all right?" he asked.

My mother ran up to us. "Is she all right? Baby, are you okay?" She sounded hysterical.

"What happened?" the boy asked.

"She was dawdling and fell in," my mother lied.

The mist had been thick. He had not seen.

I sat up, coughing out water.

"Are you all right?" he asked me again, patting my back.

I nodded mutely and turned to face my mother.

She would not meet my eyes.

My mother then pulled the young gentleman aside and thanked him and God for being there in her most desperate moment. After that, her words grew quiet, and she talked with great intensity to this young gentleman who only nodded solemnly. Wordlessly, the boy carried me back to the road. He loaded my mother and me into his vehicle. Lifting the hood covering the boiler, he checked some instruments. I heard the hiss of steam. He hopped in and pulled a chain attached to the throttle. Steam puffed from three brassy pipes on both sides of the transport. The air around us grew dense; it was like we were driving in a cloud. We set off with a jerk. I shivered in my wet clothes.

As we entered Southwark, my mother spotted a cluster of lilies growing at the side of the road. She asked the young man to stop, and she picked a large bundle. When she got back in, she whispered to the boy to carry on and shortly thereafter we were at the door of the St. Helena's Orphanage and Charity School.

The young man stopped the vehicle, and pulling a lever, let it sit in idle. I could hear the hot water rolling in the boiler. My mother lifted me out. She tried to take my hand, but I pulled it from her. I was wet, freezing cold, and frightened out of my mind. I followed ruefully behind her.

My mother knocked loudly on the door. We waited for several minutes, but no one came. She knocked again; still there was no answer.

My mother sighed heavily and looked back at the waiting gentleman. She knelt and looked at me.

"Give these to the nuns," she said, passing me the large bouquet of lilies.

I stared at her.

"I have made so many mistakes," she said miserably then looked at me, large tears falling from her eyes. "I will go to debtor's prison, and I don't know how long I'll be there. I will try to work off the debt then come back for you. Be a good girl," she said then kissed my forehead. "I'm so sorry," she added, her voice cracking as she held back a sob. She turned and went back to the vehicle. Moments later the young gentleman and my mother pulled away.

The boy looked back, a worried and despairing

look on his face. My mother never looked behind her. It was the last time I saw her.

"Lily, problem," Jessup yelled, shaking me—thankfully-from my memories. He was looking out his long spyglass. I followed the direction of his gaze and adjusted my goggles: indeed, a problem. Behind us, a large but tattered pirate ship had dropped out of the thick bank of clouds. Oh yes, this was a problem.

❦

CHAPTER 7

"What kinds of weapons do you carry?" Sal asked as he stared through the spyglass at the ship coming in behind us. The ship had double propulsion—a modification illegal for a racing ship—and was moving in fast.

"Side arms only. We run light and lean. Right now, an emphasis on run." I looked up at the clouds. On the horizon, a tower cumulus cloud was forming. Having spent the last three years ferrying around a renowned cloud scientist, Luke Howard, and exchanging everything we knew about clouds and airships, I knew the tower would propel us up-fast. With a punch of propulsion, hopefully we would outmaneuver and outrun them.

"There," I said to Jessup, pointing to the tower cloud.

"Oh Lily, you sure?" he asked.

Sal had opened the hatch to the gear galley; Angus was looking out.

"Better belt in," I told Jessup then turned to Angus.

"Ready?" I asked him. "When the time comes, I'm going to need some punch or we're all going to see stars."

"Just say the word," he said then dropped below. Sal crawled into the galley to help.

I kept one eye on the ship behind me and another on the cloudbank ahead. The pirate ship would break starboard to avoid the cloud tower—any ship would and should break starboard. It would be a game of nerves.

The propeller on the *Stargazer* kicked up a notch, the gears turning quickly, and soon we were rocketing across the sky. Regardless, the pirate ship dropped in close behind us. I looked back and adjusted the lenses on my goggles, trying to make out the symbol on the side of their balloon. As the ship edged starboard, I saw it. The balloon bore a burning castle tower painted in red with a black bird perched on its top: *Burning Rook*. Dammit.

"*Burning Rook*," I yelled up to Jessup.

"Bloody hell," Jessup grumbled, his hand holding the heat valve tightly.

The *Burning Rook* was one of the most notorious ships to troll the Channel. Captain Sionnaigh piloted the vessel and was well-known for dumping riders into the water while sorting out their goods. While the *Stargazer* carried no cargo or treasure, the famous ship was worth a nice ransom. Suddenly I wished I had painted over the triskelion before we'd left.

"Miss Stargazer, please cut propulsion and allow us to board for a little chat," a voice boomed across the sky.

I looked back. Toward the prow of the *Burning Rook* they had rolled forward an enormous horned speaker. I could see the sun glinting off the brass. The captain, wearing his red tricorn hat, stood behind the horn.

"Lily, there's lightning in those clouds," Jessup called as he looked at the tower cloud.

Dammit again. A forming storm cloud was one thing. A formed storm cloud was something different. I heard the rumble of thunder.

I looked back at the *Burning Rook*. The captain was pacing at the front, waiting for me, expecting me to slow, to bear starboard. I could see the pilot shouting at him. His crew knew it was time to break starboard. Any minute now the air current would pull us in and up.

I held the wheel steady. A strong wind came in, shifting the *Stargazer* slightly port. I turned the wheel and headed directly toward the cloud. Behind me, the *Burning Rook* started to slow and turn. I caught sight of the captain once more; his spyglass was centered on me. I blew him a kiss, turned my back to him, and held tight as the *Stargazer* rolled into the cloudbank.

The bow of the ship lifted slightly. We were there. Angus, feeling the movement, punched propulsion, and we cut a hole into the updraft.

"Whoa!" Jessup yelled as a moment later we were being thrust upward in a draft with enormous speed.

It was like we were being sprayed out of a water fountain. My heart dropped into my boots. I braced myself against the wheel, holding on for dear life. Wind gushed around us. The Channel and the *Burning Rook* sank into the distance below us. The air was dewy wet. I heard the low rumble of thunder. I knew that if we shot too far up the air would get thin, and we might black out. I had an altimeter, but I kept my eyes on the *Stargazer's* balloon. It would soften as air pressure decreased. She would tell me when it was time. A moment later, I saw the balloon deflate. I reached down and pulled the rope connected to the galley bell. We needed to cut out of the upstream. The propeller groaned. I was thankful that Sal was there. Alone, Angus would not have been able to give enough speed to catch the out draft in time. The gears kicked hard, and I felt the gondola thrust horizontally against the vertical lift. The balloon ropes strained, tipping the gondola slightly backward from the bow as the ship protested. One tether at the very front snapped.

"Jessup, release air," I yelled.

Holding on tight, Jessup opened the flap and let the hot air release from the top. The balloon softened further. The gondola dragged the balloon with it as we searched for the out draft.

"Be ready," I called to Jessup. We both knew that moments after we came out of the cloud tower, the balloon would need lift or we would fall like a stone toward the water.

With one last hard push, the *Stargazer* broke free of the upward draft. Lightning rocked the clouds behind us. We were flying fast through the air, tossed by the cloud and running on propulsion. The *Burning Rook* was nowhere to be seen, but in the far off distance, I spotted the air towers of Calais.

"Now, Jessup! Now!" I yelled. He set the burners on high; an inferno of gold and yellow leapt into the balloon.

The *Stargazer* shot forward, and despite the propeller kicking hard, it suddenly slowed to a stop. There was simply not enough lift. Then, she dropped. For a single, terrifying second, we were free-falling toward the water. Suddenly, the lift caught us. The heat in the balloon made up the gap, and we were coasting.

After several minutes of fast and very, very high flying, Angus opened the gear hatch, and he and Sal came onto the deck.

"I don't think we've ever flown so high," Angus said, looking over the side of the ship.

A strange silence overcame us. We were all filled with a mixture of relief and awe. Perhaps we'd risen too high; I felt lightheaded. Below the ship, the sea birds flew toward the shoreline. Angus was right. We had never been at this high of an altitude before. Far below, the waters of the Channel were glossy in the early morning light.

Sal took my hands, kissing each one. "So young but so talented."

"I'd like to see Cutter try that," Jessup called down.

Everyone laughed, and we cruised toward Calais.

CHAPTER 8

As we came in over Calais, we lowered altitude to catch the main ferry routes across Europe. The total trip from London to Venice would take about twenty-four hours at the *Stargazer's* normal cruising speed. We'd planned to put in near Zurich before we crossed the Alps. It would be dangerous to cross the mountains at night, and we would need an update on the range's weather conditions. After outrunning the *Burning Rook*, I figured a little 4,000 meter mountain range would be no problem.

It was near midnight when the red lanterns of Zurich's airship towers appeared on the horizon. We were grateful. It had been a long day. The laudanum was keeping my headaches at bay and my mood light, but I looked forward to sneaking off for a few hits on a pipe. In Zurich, it would be easy to find somewhere to smoke. It was always easy to find opium; you just had to know where to look. What I wasn't looking forward to was "the look" Jessup would give when he knew my habit was getting the better of me. Angus never said much. Our history was longer, and he understood me better. I also understood him. I'd fished him out of the bottom of a bottle of Scotch more than once.

There were a dozen ships docked at the Zurich towers, a popular stop for any traveler before and after the Alps. There were transport ships, personal yachts, and some single-person aircrafts, one of which even had an apparatus that looked like wings. Armed watchmen patrolled the platforms. Jessup settled with the stationmaster, and we tethered in for the night.

"Let's go have a drink," Sal called encouragingly.

We took the lift down to the wharf at the base of the towers which were situated near Lake Zurich. There were a dozen or so buildings situated there. The wharf was an outpost for travelers: air, land, or sea. The merchant shops, many of which were still open, showcased all manner of supplies. A stone gateway with a clockwork mermaid sitting on top stood over a road that led away from the lake toward the city.

There were a couple of taverns open; we chose the busiest. We could hear the raucous noise within as we drew close. Outside the tavern were parked a dozen or so steam or pedal vehicles, their brass and copper gears glimmering. The tavern lights were powered by a small windmill on the roof that caught the air coming off the lake. The lights flickered from bright to dim, illuminating the sign over the tavern door.

"The Crow's Nest," Sal said, reading the German name over the door.

"German too?" I asked.

"It is a dialect of German, but yes, of course," he said with a smile as he held open the door for me.

Jessup rolled his eyes.

When we entered the tavern, the smell of roasting meat and freshly baked bread nearly overwhelmed me. There was a large stone fireplace at one end of the tavern; a whole lamb turned on the spit. My stomach growled hungrily. I was intrigued, however, by a small clockwork figure at the wheel of the spit. The small machine had arm-like appendages that kept the spit rotating. Behind the bar was a similar contraption pouring ale at what appeared to be the perfect pace.

"Let's grab a table," I called.

The place was filled with travelers: air jockeys and their crew, grease stained pedal riders, and steamboat sailors. There were also the usual carnal delights. The barmaids wore black lace or red satin corsets decorated with metal trim, short black skirts or shorts, and lacey stockings. Breasts were more than half heaved out; the customers pawed at the fleshy displays. To add to the bawdy atmosphere, a mostly naked woman sat on a pedestal in a stone alcove near the fireplace playing a callioflute. The instrument, powered by steam and water, created sharp, alluring sounds. Water sprayed onto the woman's body as she worked the mouths of the flute. The steam made her hair curly and skin dewy.

A tavern girl came to our table. The girl wore heavy

black eyeliner and had thick, black hair that fell to her waist. She wore a metal choker with a large glass evil eye pendant. She looked decidedly exasperated.

Sal took her gently by the hand and whispered to her in low tones. He worked his magic on her. She left with a smile. After a few minutes she returned with two large trays: four heaping plates of food, two ales, and two decanters of wine. She set every item down with the ease of someone who knows her trade. Sal slid her some coin, whispered something in her ear, and she left smirking.

"Are you always so successful with women?" I asked him as I eyed my plate.

"When I choose. My only thought was to make sure my Lily had the best cut of meat and the finest wine. And, I have been successful," he said as he poured me a glass from the decanter. He set it down and kissed me on the earlobe.

It was my turn to smile.

"Aye, well, I don't know what you said, but this is fucking delicious," Angus said, his mouth already full, as he shoved in a second bite.

We all laughed.

I downed the glass of wine and poured another. While my eyes took in the spectacle, I also noticed traffic moving in and out of a room in the back of the tavern where, no doubt, opium could be found. I felt relieved. I picked up a slice of bread. It was still warm from the oven. The tang of the sourdough filled my mouth. The bread was golden and crunchy on the outside, but the soft bread tucked within melted in my mouth.

We finished our meal, rehashing again the incident with the *Burning Rook*, and soon we were all drunk and feeling very sated. Like two mother hens, Jessup and Angus chided me for not eating enough. They then headed back to the *Stargazer* to keep watch. In London, we knew and trusted the airship security. Zurich, however, was another matter.

Sal and I sat at the table relaxing, but curiosity got the better of Sal and soon we were standing at the bar. I ordered an absinthe while Sal asked the bartender about the clockwork contraptions at the spit and the tap.

"You have come on the right night," the bartender told Sal in English with a heavy German accent. "Master Vogt is the tinker. That's him," he said, pointing to a very old man sitting by the tavern window.

Sal smiled at me. "I'll only be a moment," he said. And while I am sure that's what he intended, I knew better.

I tipped my cap at him then watched as he approached the old man. After a few pleasantries, Sal joined the tinker at his table. I eyed the patrons coming in and out of the back. There was an old woman sitting just by the door. One would barely notice her. She was dressed in all black, her hair covered, her face deeply wrinkled. Each patron spoke to her as they entered, passing her some coins. I popped one more sugar cube, finished off the sharp spirit, and went to the old woman.

"May I?" I asked, gesturing toward the back.

She nodded and held out her hand. I pressed two coins therein. She looked them over then motioned for me to enter. Once I was in the room, the smell of opium filled the space. Others with the opium habit were sprawled on cots. A naked girl who looked like the tavern maid led me to the back where there were a few private, curtained cots. As we passed, I saw all manner of people enjoying the pleasure of opium; some sat in silent stupor, others lay back toking sweetly, one man was being serviced by two beautiful young women, and a man and woman were in the heat of full-on fucking as I passed by. No one paid me any mind. Wordlessly, the girl brought me a pipe and an enormous supply of opium. She smiled at me, motioning to a small bell at the bedside, then closed the curtain and left. I filled the pipe, a dark wood and bronze piece, and lay back. Moments later, I was drifting.

My head felt hazy, and the passage of time seemed to slow. My body had been aching since we left London. Now, I felt fine. In fact, I felt great. I was giddy, and the colors of the kaleidoscope, which safely stowed in my bag, spun in my imagination. I tapped my foot to the callioflute music coming from the tavern and drifted away.

In my mind, a vision of a woman all in gold

appeared: her hair, her clothes, her jewels, and even her skin were golden hued. I'd seen her once before, in the kaleidoscope. She danced now to the callioflute music. She spun quickly, trailing colorful veils around her. She spun and spun, her beautiful body bending erotically with the music. Then, at once, she stopped. With a sly grin, she lowered herself to the ground and crept toward me, her back arching catlike. When she neared me, she stroked my cheek and peered deeply at me with her striking multicolored eyes. "Lily," she whispered. "Wake up!"

Startled, I awoke from my opium stupor. When I opened my eyes, I was shocked to see a man leaning across my body. Was he trying to rape me? A second later, however, I realized he had his hand on my bag: the kaleidoscope.

"Well, mother fucker," I exclaimed, surprising him.

The man, who had thus far been sneaking, made a grab for the bag. I pulled one leg free and kicked him toward the end of the cot. He tumbled then righted himself, pulled a knife from his belt, and lunged toward me. His greedy hand aimed for my satchel. I slid sideways and with a fist, hammered him hard in the side of the head. His knife hit the pillow. He rolled, grabbing at the bag once more. I jumped backward out of the cot, knocking over the bell the attendant had left.

I stood in the hallway. I was trying to pull my sidearm out of my satchel, but my head was spinning; everything was a muddy haze. The man burst forward. The cot curtains twisted serpentine around him, snagging his arms and legs. He fought them off as he grabbed for me.

Finally pulling my gun from my bag, I was just taking aim as a figure appeared behind the man and dropped a very large mallet on the thief's head. The man wilted under the blow. Clutching his bleeding head, he turned and fled out the back door.

I ran to the doorway and raised my gun. Though injured, the thief disappeared into the darkness before I got off a shot. I lowered the weapon.

"Are you hurt?" someone with a very thick French accent asked.

Shaking with rage, I could not answer.

"Mon dieu, Lily. Are you all right?" the person asked again, setting their hands on my shoulders.

I turned to find myself face to face with Etienne Souvenir, the French airship racer. "Etienne?" I asked. I thought I might be seeing things. The opium did that to me at times. I stuffed my gun in my bag, put both hands on Etienne's cheeks, and eyed the Frenchman over. Etienne had long, soft looking strawberry blond hair which was pushed back by his goggles. He was fair; his features were petite and sophisticated. His frame was lean and muscular. He wore tan leather travel breeches and a navy colored jacket, its buttons undone, with a blousy white shirt underneath.

Etienne laughed. "Oui, c'est moi. I think I just

saved your life... or at least your satchel. You owe me a drink."

"I'm not sure what the hell just happened."

"I was in the cot next to you. I heard a noise, looked out, and found Lily Stargazer in a knife fight in an opium den in Zurich. But I was not surprised," he shrugged and laughed.

I chuckled, but my stomach had pulled into a knot. I felt angry. Was the man just a thief or was he after me in particular? Did he know what I carried? Would someone kill me for the kaleidoscope? I didn't even know what the bloody thing was! The sooner I got to Venice the better.

I pulled myself together and followed Etienne back into the tavern. It seemed that no one else was alarmed by the commotion in the back. Such disturbances must have been commonplace. We joined Etienne's crew at the bar. I smiled nicely and tipped my cap at them. The French team was not a bad racing crew. They usually placed fifth or sixth. Their problem was they were too hesitant, playing the race too safe.

The tavern was still very busy, but Sal was nowhere to be seen. Though I was pretty sure I knew where he'd gone, I was worried.

"Where did the man I was with go?" I asked the bartender.

"With the tinker," he replied, sliding a glass of water toward me.

"Thank you. By the by, I was just in the back and someone tried to kill me."

The man nodded nonchalantly but said nothing.

I laughed at the absurdity and ordered Etienne a drink. The tavern keeper set a glass of chartreuse down in front of him.

"I did not see you when I came in," Etienne said, lifting the drink.

"You rarely see me, Etienne. I am always too far in front of you," I said with a sly smile as I took his drink from his hand and sipped.

"Ah, she plays with me, no? And after I just saved her life," he said to his crew with a laugh, taking back his drink. "So why is someone trying to kill Lily Stargazer?"

"That was just an act to see if you would save me," I said playfully. "I wanted to see if the French are still chivalrous." I grabbed at his glass for another drink.

Etienne laughed and swiped the glass away from my grasp. "As you can see… to a fault. Why are you in Zurich?"

"I am headed to Italy. Why are you in Zurich?"

"I am here for work on my ship. Eh, you know how it is, constant improvement. I was supposed to meet a tinker here, but I find no one." While his green eyes sparkled, I noticed he had dark rings underneath.

"Was it Master Vogt?" I asked.

"Quelle surprise," Etienne said. "How did you know?"

"I think my companion ran off with him," I replied then turned to the bartender. "Where can we find the workshop of Master Vogt?" I asked.

"Turn left out of the tavern. The building with a clock."

"Shall we?" I asked Etienne, motioning to the door.

Etienne exchanged a few words with his crew. I exchanged a few words with the old woman and nabbed a supply of opium for the road.

The air outside was cool for a summer night. Etienne and I walked through the fog toward the workshop. The opium made me feel equally foggy. While I relished the giddy and blissful relief of opium, the drug also made my mind dull and muddy. My eyelids felt heavy, and I strained to focus. When I did, I noticed that Etienne's mood had shifted. He was sulking. It was not like him. Witty and sardonic, he was one of the few other racers I honestly liked. At every race we managed to find a way to exchange a few jabs. The fact that I was one of the few other racers fluent in French helped. We always made fun of the others, especially Cutter.

"It is not like you to eat opium," I said. "What's wrong? Love sick?"

"Eh, your jest, unfortunately, is correct. Do you remember Benoit? He broke off with me before I left Paris."

"Oh Etienne, I'm so sorry." It was just like me to say exactly the wrong thing.

"Perhaps I should try to win him back... I don't know."

"I'm not the best person to give advice on love."

"You? The whole world knows you are the lover of Lord Byron."

"It is one thing to be a lover and another thing to be loved."

"That is my problem. I always want to be loved. It never works for me."

"That's why I gave it up."

"I thought you were a romantic. No husband in your future? No children? No domestic life for Mademoiselle Stargazer?" he jested.

His comments silenced me. If I continued like I did, what *would* be my end destination? The answer to that question was not pretty. I'd stopped asking it long ago.

Etienne noticed my silence. "Now *I* have made *you* sad. Pardon, Lily. You must not worry. A woman like you will burn for a time and then cool. No doubt someone is already waiting for that to happen."

Was he right? "Well, it's not happening tonight," I replied with a grin and elbowed him in the ribs.

Etienne chuckled. "Ah, here it is," he said, looking up at a building with a clock tower.

The clock face was flanked by clockwork figures holding mallets, ready to chime the hour. I knocked on the door. After a few minutes, the old man appeared.

"Ah, Etienne... Fräulein Stargazer," the old man said and motioned for us to come inside.

The front of the workshop was dark, but I could make out a myriad of shapes. There were huge piles of metal, gears, wheels, and various clockwork figures in heaps everywhere. Etienne and I followed the tinker through a path in the clockwork labyrinth. I tried not to knock over anything. Light poured in from an open doorway in the back. Once there, I found Sal gazing at the gears of a machine lying on a workbench.

"Lily, you should see this. It is amazing," Sal told me, distracted. I wasn't sure if he realized I hadn't been with him the entire time.

I snickered. "Sal, you should meet Etienne Souvenir," I told him, "the French racer."

Sal looked up. He had a faraway look in his eyes, his brilliant mind distracted by the machine in front of him.

"Monsieur, my pleasure. Salvatore Colonna," he said, shaking Etienne's hand before turning back to the clockwork on the bench.

"Tinkers," I whispered to Etienne who chuckled.

"Eh, what is this, Master Vogt?" Etienne asked.

"A metal man," the tinker replied, "designed to replace your galleymen," he added, looking from Etienne to me.

At that moment, I was very glad Angus was not there. Etienne and I came closer to the workbench as the tinker explained how the clockwork man would have the strength of three men. Such new and illegal modifications were rampant amongst pirates. The racing league kept tight restrictions on the design of airships and the composition of their crew, but there was a strong call for the allowance of double propulsion such as the *Burning Rook* used.

"And look at this," Sal said, pointing to a model balloon hanging from the ceiling.

"The balloon has a semi-rigid structure," Master Vogt told us. "It will keep buoyancy better and be easier to navigate. It is a prototype."

I gazed upward but said nothing. I suspected I was seeing the future.

"But, I do have business with Monsieur Souvenir for which I am late. It has been a pleasure to meet you, Mr. Colonna," Master Vogt said.

I could see the crushing disappointment on Sal's face.

"My thanks, Master Vogt, for showing me your creations. They are genius."

The old man smiled. "Please, stop again on your way back to England. There is more!" the old man said happily.

I looked up at Etienne. "See you in Valencia," I told him and pulled him into a hug. "Don't despair. As they say, the course of true love never did run smooth," I whispered into his ear.

He kissed me on the cheek. "Thank you, mon amie."

With that, Sal and I left the workshop and headed back to the *Stargazer*. Sal was lost in thoughts of the clockwork man, but he had wrapped his arm around my waist and kept me close. Coming down from my opium high, I was left with mixed emotions. I was confused, afraid, and angry. Was someone really following us or was the thief just looking for easy pickings in the opium den? It wouldn't be the first time someone had lifted my belongings while I was out cold, but it angered me all the same. I'd accepted that the trip to Venice might entail unpleasant interruptions, but I wasn't expecting someone to try to stab me. I needed to be more careful and to keep my sidearm a bit handier.

I also thought about Etienne's words. They left me feeling confused. Would my life only consist of an endless string of lovers? Why was I so unable to allow myself to really connect with anyone? Even I knew I was a ridiculous mess. At least I was having fun, wasn't I?

I sighed heavily. It shook Sal from his thoughts.

"Are you all right?" he asked.

I smiled at him. "Thank you for coming."

"Who can say no to an adventure with Lily Stargazer?"

We stopped. The moonlight shone down on us. Sal put his hand on the back of my neck, stroking the nape. I gazed up at him. His steel colored eyes glimmered. He pulled me into a kiss. It was a soft, warm, but passionate kiss, the kind of kiss that left you feeling dizzy and seeing stars. I didn't remember him kissing me like that before.

"Italians… you are so passionate," I said with a grin.

"Indeed, you give me much to be passionate about. Come," he said, and we headed back to the *Stargazer*.

CHAPTER 9

Jessup and Angus were already sleeping in their hammocks. They had even been nice enough to string up mine. I led Sal to my hammock, and we lay down for the night. I snuggled into Sal's arms and no sooner had we lain down then Sal was asleep. At first I was surprised, but then I remembered that Sal was much older than me, and it really had been a long day. Perhaps I had tired him out.

From below, the sounds of a fight drifted upward. I listened as the two men swore at one another in German. Their argument was heated; both men shouted loudly. Soon I heard the grunting sounds of physical fighting. The sound took me back to my days at St. Helena's.

"You say that again, and I'll do you like they did Mary Queen of Scots," I threatened Maggie, another girl at St. Helena's, sliding my finger across my throat as I stared the doe-eyed girl down. We were about six years old, and she had just told me for what seemed like the hundredth time that day that I was a piece of rubbish.

Maggie gritted her teeth and lunged at me.

I picked up a handful of dirt and threw it in her face. She screamed, the dust burning her eyes. I took the opportunity to punch her in the gut. Crying, she fell to the ground. After she was down, I gave her a solid kick in the side of the head, the other girls cheering me on. Suddenly Sister Margaret was standing over us. Her towering shadow cast a gloomy pall.

"What is going on here?" she asked aghast. Sister Margaret yanked me away from Maggie, her fingernails digging into my skin. She squeezed my wrist until it ached.

I pulled my arm free. Knowing I would be punished either way, I decided it was best not to lie. "Maggie was calling me names so I beat her a good one," I told Sister Margaret.

She looked down at me, her face furrowing deeply. She had an odd look on her face like she was suffocating rage. "This is the last time-" she began to say but stopped short when she heard Sister Sarah approach.

"Are you sure, Mr. Fletcher? You did say you wanted a lad. The boys will be out any moment," Sister Sarah said as she came up behind us. She sounded nervous.

I turned to look. Sister Sarah escorted two gentlemen onto the yard. The man she referred to as Mr. Fletcher had long, curly gray hair. He wore small, round glasses, a tight blue shirt buttoned to the neck, breeches, stripped stockings, and a top hat. The other man, also gray haired but balding, looked like he'd just rolled out from under a greasy transport. He wore a checked top with tan trousers, both of which were stained with grease. His two front teeth were missing.

"No need. This one fights like an alley cat. She'll do," the man she referred to as Mr. Fletcher said, looking down at me. "What do you say, Mr. Oleander?" he asked his companion.

"Let me see your hands, girl," the other man, Mr. Oleander, said to me.

I stuck out my hands and let them inspect me.

"Dirty under the nails. Scratches on the knuckles," Mr. Oleander observed. Both men seemed impressed.

"But gentlemen, a young lady will need some refining, a womanly influence," Sister Sarah said.

"We've got a woman, don't we, brother?" Mr. Oleander answered chuckling as he elbowed the other man in the ribs. They both laughed.

"What is your name, young lady?" Mr. Fletcher asked.

I looked up at Sister Margaret. Only once had I ever been asked my real name and that was on my first day there. A very old nun had written it and my parents' names on a paper. She died a few days later. Otherwise, everyone called me Lily on account of my mother's bouquet. Both Sister Margaret and Sister Sarah had come to St. Helena's later, and that's all they and all the others knew of my name. And in my mind, that other girl, the one my mother—who had never come back-had thrown into the Thames, *was* dead.

"Lily."

"Lily what?" Mr. Fletcher asked.

"Just Lily," I replied.

Both of the men laughed.

"Yes, she'll do. Where do we sign?" Mr. Oleander asked Sister Margaret.

Sister Margaret and Sister Sarah looked at one another in shocked silence. After a moment, Sister Margaret looked down at me, her face still wearing the shadow of rage. I realized then I had chosen the wrong day to infuriate her. Indeed, it would be the last time. "This way to my office, gentlemen," she said, directing them back to the orphanage. "Sister Sarah, please get Lily ready to go."

Lost in my memories, I was about to doze off when I heard a gunshot. Sal snored in his sleep and turned but did not wake. I rose and looked over the side of the *Stargazer*. In the dim light of the gaslamps, I saw a man run off. The shot man lay still in the street. Clearly, he was dead. The tower guards were soon on the scene. I sighed and crawled back into the hammock. I pulled out the laudanum and took double my usual dose. I snuggled close to Sal, reminding myself that the days with Mr. Fletcher and Mr. Oleander were long behind me. They were now ghosts who could only harm me in my memories. And then, just as I had wanted, every-thing went black.

CHAPTER 10

Early the next morning we bundled up and set sail. Despite my best efforts, I could not shake Mr. Fletcher and Mr. Oleander. The memories added to feeling tense about the altercation in the opium den. I was unnerved. I woke at dawn feeling groggy, nauseated, and irritable. In fact, no one was feeling very happy once I shared how someone had tried to manhandle me in the opium den.

"You think it was just a thief or did it seem like he was after you specifically?" Jessup asked.

"I'm not sure," I replied, hoping not to alarm them.

Angus sighed. "I warned you. That kaleidoscope came with blood on it."

"Then the sooner we know what it is, and we get rid of it, the better," Sal said encouragingly.

Angus, however, went below and returned with loaded sidearms which he passed to Jessup and Sal. Both men took a gun without speaking a word about it.

Angus handed me an extra box of ammo. "Keep

your weapon loaded, your head clear, and watch your ass."

◆—⋯—◆

The snow covered Alps, streaked with block rocks, went on as far as the eye could see. Even in July, the air was cold. It was, however, very fresh, so pristine I could nearly sense the divine. Navigating this beauty would be tricky all the same. I had done it before, but I was not in a mood for a challenge that morning. Low level clouds or stay winds would be certain, but I knew it would be manageable.

"It's like a fucking painting," Angus said as we all stood at the bow of the *Stargazer* and looked out at the mountain range.

"There are, in fact, several famous paintings of the Alps. There has been much consideration of the painting *Napoleon Crossing the Alps* by Jacques-Louis David who painted it for the King of Spain," Sal offered.

I pretended not to see the gestures Angus and Jessup exchanged.

"Let's just hope we meet with a better end than Bonaparte," I replied.

We did. After several crisp, beautiful hours of smooth flying, we cruised toward Venice. We passed over the forests, mountains, and farmland in Switzerland, and we were over Italy shortly after the lunch hour. By late afternoon, we approached the Vento area, and air traffic became much busier. At first we saw mainly European transport ships rigged for long haul travel. A steam yacht passed us; it was an unusual contraption held aloft by a cluster of balloons rather than a single balloon. Steam poured from the back of the ship. Since it carried water, it was heavy and low to the ground. As we neared Venice, however, we noticed more brightly colored personal yachts and transport air gondolas. The Venetian air gondolas shone with thick black lacquer, their balloons dyed scarlet red. The air gondoliers wore the same black and white striped shirts as their lagoon counterparts, but the straw hats were replaced with tan leather skullcaps. The colorful ships sailed toward the Venetian air towers on the Lido; it was like a slowly moving painting. I could feel I was in Venice. As I navigated the ship over the city toward the Lido towers, Sal narrated the sites.

"We're over the Grand Canal, Lily. There is the Rialto. Ah, there is Saint Mark's… the Doge's palace," Sal listed.

I took a peek below; the dark teal colored waters of the canals glimmered in the late afternoon light. From above, the orange-red tiled roofs of the palazzi reminded me of a jigsaw of bread loaves. Excited, I smiled. I had been around the world racing, but I had never truly been anywhere on holiday. It was an excitement I knew Jessup and Angus—both of whom had always worked for every crumb in their mouths—shared.

"Go in port, Lily. There are international transport docks open on the upper platform," Jessup called from above, his spyglass on the towers.

The breeze off the Adriatic Sea made for a bumpy ride into the towers. There were more air towers located in Venice than I had seen anywhere else. Big ships like the *Stargazer* were anchored on the upper levels. There were at least a dozen large ships tethered there. I eyed the symbols on the balloons but didn't recognize any of them. I did notice a British diplomatic vessel parked in one of the private bays. About twenty feet below the international transports were ports for the local gondoliers, yachts, and personal crafts.

A Venetian ground crew, all dressed in scarlet, guided the *Stargazer* into her dock. Soon, Jessup and Angus were hard at work getting the ship tethered in. Once we were anchored, Sal spoke with the stationmaster.

"My Lily, it seems Lord Byron has cleared the path for you. The *Stargazer* was expected, and your docking account has been settled. The stationmaster saw the *Stargazer* come in. As Lord Byron requested, ground transport has been arranged to take us to our lodgings," Sal informed me as the Venetian stationmaster smiled appreciatively at the *Stargazer*. "And he is a fan of yours," Sal added with a lowered voice.

Angus and Jessup leaned on the deck rail, listening to the exchange.

"Ask him if he'd like to take a look," I replied motioning to the *Stargazer*.

Sal spoke to the man. The stationmaster smiled excitedly at me, and with a nod, Sal led him aboard.

"Well, Miss Important Friends, our lodgings, eh?" Jessup said with a laugh. "Where you suppose Byron set us up, Lily?"

"Us? Well, I am sure a palace awaits me. I think I saw some stables on the Lido for you lot," I replied with a laugh.

Angus chuckled.

The look on Jessup's face told me he had not considered that Byron had only arranged for me, not all of us. But, I knew Byron. He took care of those he loved and trusted. Despite his reputation as being mad, bad, and dangerous to know, Byron had a good soul and treated well those who did not abuse him—unless, of course, he had asked for it.

After Sal's tour was over, the stationmaster—who kissed me on each cheek and spoke excitedly to me in Italian, thanking me and blessing my next race, or so Sal told me-led us to the lift. I was glad a race fan was keeping watch on the *Stargazer*; I knew she would be safe.

The clockwork gears ground as the stationmaster operated the lift levers. The massive gears turned, and the lift lowered us slowly toward the sandy beach below. A warm wind blew in from the sea. As much as I disliked the water, Venice was truly beautiful.

Sal and the stationmaster exchanged a few words, and when we reached the Lido, we headed off in the direction of the vaporetti, the steamboat taxis. Sal was wearing a knowing smile.

"What is it?" I asked.

"Ah, my Lily, how Lord Byron must love you."

"Why do you say that?"

Sal only smiled.

"Sal," I warned playfully, sliding my hand under his shirt to tickle his ribs.

"You'll see," he replied, grinning as he grabbed and kissed my fingers.

Sal spoke a few words to the vaporetto taximan who transported travelers by water from the Lido to the city. The vaporetto itself was a sleek, dark wood boat with a thick coat of polish. A blue and white striped awning covered the taxi seats. The taximan guided us aboard. As we settled in, I followed Sal's gaze to the copper piping that created the steam propulsion. Angus, too, was straining his neck to get a look.

As we set off, the taximan eyed me over. My belongings were stuffed into a sack hanging over my shoulder, but under my arm I carried the box containing the gown Byron had sent. The sailor's gaze had made me feel self-conscious, and though I was not inclined to wear the dress, I was suddenly glad I had it. As we approached the city, passing more Venetians, I better understood the look. The Venetian women looked like china dolls. Their hair was done perfectly. Their ornate dresses looked like bouquets of wildflowers strewn in the wind. While they had their intricately designed jewels and tinkered trinkets, overall their look was soft. English women had their own style. Air jockeys more so. In Venice, however, things were different. I now understood Byron's gift.

The vaporetto slipped into the Grand Canal. Moments later we were gliding past the pastel colored palazzi: pink, peach, white, and tan façades faced the water. Most buildings, though somewhat decayed, were decorated with white marble or stone trim. Arching windows with ornate trefoil, carved cherubs, theater masks, regal animals, and other designs trimmed the elegant palazzi. Much like the Venetian women, the buildings were refined in their beauty.

"Palazzo Mocenigo," the taximan called as we approached a Venetian palace. The tan façade of the palazzo was trimmed with both wroughtiron and stone balconies that hung over the water. The palazzo looked to be four stories in height. In all, the palazzo had four buildings. The gondolier guided us toward one of the middle buildings.

"Holy Christ," Jessup whispered. He had grown up on a farm in Norwich and was, no doubt, as impressed as I.

Indeed, the palazzo was striking. I looked up at the building to see the various carvings of lions' heads looking down at me.

Sal smiled at me. "You see," he whispered.

The taximan docked and extended a hand to help me debark. A Venetian butler who was fluent in English came to meet us.

"Signorina Stargazer, welcome to Ca' Mocenigo. I am Vittorio and am at your service," he introduced, kissing the back of my hand.

I introduced the others. Vittorio led us down a marble hallway, the floors polished to a mirror shine, to a stairwell with an ornately carved banister. Golden sconces and magnificent oil paintings lined the walls.

"You will have two floors, Signorina Stargazer," Vittorio explained as we went upstairs. "On the second floor you will find the piano nobile where you may entertain guests. Please let me know if you would like to arrange any dinners, and we shall be at your service. Are you expecting Lord Byron?"

I could hear the excitement in the man's voice. Byron was famed for his poetry but was infamous for his behavior. He'd been in Venice the few years prior. I'd heard a story about how he'd swum naked in the Grand Canal, holding a torch aloft so he would not be hit by a gondola. I'd laughed until I cried when I heard it. Given Byron's ways, I had no idea if I was expecting him or not. That was partially why our relationship worked so well.

"We'll see. We are not expecting visitors at this time," I told the man politely.

He smiled, but his disappointment was evident.

"Now, this is the sitting room," Vittorio said. He pushed open heavy double doors at the top of the stairs to reveal a Renaissance style parlor. The wear on the ornate plaster was evident, and discoloration marred the pale blue walls, but the beauty of the place could not be denied. The grey-flecked marble floors gleamed. The walls were trimmed with gold leaf. Tapestries, oil paintings, and statuary filled the place. An elaborate bird cage contained two doves who cooed nicely when we entered. The place was filled with vases of cut flowers—all lilies—and sumptuous furniture.

"Follow me," he called, leading us through the room to a second set of doors. He pushed these open to reveal a dining room with soft yellow paint and glimmering white marble floors. A gold and crystal chandelier hung from the roof where plaster was chipped away. Filigreed mirrors and oil paintings of Dionysian delights lined the walls.

"This is your formal dining room," Vittorio said then led us through one final set of doors to reveal a sunny room in the front of the palazzo. "And finally we come to the drawing room," he said. The room, painted pale peach, looked out on the Grand Canal. It was comfortably arranged with small groupings of chairs for private conversation, and again, the room was filled with lilies.

"If you need a private work space, Miss Stargazer, there is also a small office through here," Vittorio added, opening a door just off the drawing room to reveal an office in which a large desk, and only a large desk, sat in the very middle of the space. "Lord Byron worked here when he was in residence," he added proudly.

I nodded, and for a brief moment, envisioned Byron laboring over the desk, his dark curls falling into his eyes as they were sometimes apt to do. I smiled.

"This way." Vittorio led us upstairs and showed us each to a bedroom. We arranged to have dinner in a couple of hours, and Vittorio left. Angus and Jessup, examining their lodgings, grinned like school children. My room, which was the same Byron stayed in when he was in Venice, as Vittorio had informed me, looked out onto the canal. Double glass doors opened to a magnificent vista. The heavenly smell of lilies filled the room. The bedroom was papered with red brocade that was torn in the corners. Gauzy white fabric draped the tall, four-poster bed.

Since the men were settling in, I was alone. I took a drop of laudanum and stood in the opened doorway overlooking the canal. Gondoliers poled passengers and crates up and down the green-blue canal waters. As one singing gondolier passed, he tipped his hat at me and called out what sounded like a compliment. I blew him a kiss, and he smiled. Moments later, Jessup and Angus burst into the room behind me.

"Can you believe this, Lil?" Jessup said excitedly.

"My màthair would not believe her eyes," Angus

added, pulling Jessup and me both into a hug as we stood looking out at the Canal.

"Gents, just think. If we can start pulling first place wins, we could really live like this from time to time," I said.

Angus and Jessup both turned serious. "If we place first in Valencia and then in Paris, and if Cutter drops to third at least once, we can pull it off," Jessup said.

"Cutter doesn't race well in Valencia. This year we might take him," Angus added.

"We need modifications," I said. "I saw Souvenir in Zurich. He was getting work done to his ship. We need to consider what we can do to reconfigure the *Stargazer*. Truth is, we need more speed."

Sal, who had been leaning against the door frame and listening to the conversation, spoke up. "In Master Vogt's workshop he showed me a reconfiguration of one of the propulsion gears which requires less muscle to give speed, using centrifugal force over raw power. May I draw it and show you, Angus?"

Angus looked at Sal, and the look on Angus' face told me that in that moment he'd finally figured out what Sal was all about. Sal *was* arrogant. And Sal *did* offer more suggestions than were needed, but Sal was also a genius.

"Let's have it. In fact, why don't we adjourn to the drawing room and further consider the matter," Angus said, putting on a mock sophisticated accent that made us all laugh.

With that, the four of us spent the next two hours huddled over a table as Sal and Angus considered what could be done to reconfigure the *Stargazer*. The smell of food wafting in from the kitchens on the first floor had my stomach aching. When Vittorio returned to tell us it was time to eat, I was grateful.

Vittorio opened the doors to the dining room to reveal a table heaped with a sprawling array of Venetian cuisine. Footmen dressed in grey uniforms with silver buckles seated each of us. Vittorio presented our meal. As he went over each dish, a footman poured us all bowls of brodo di pesce, a fish soup with saffron, and glasses of white wine. At the very center of the table was what he called an antipasto de frutti de mare, a massive plate of seafood from the lagoon dressed with lemon and Italian olive oil.

"A favorite of Lord Byron," he told us.

Also on the table were Venetian style sardines, carpacci, muscles cooked in wine, heaps of fresh fruit, bread, and a dish called baccalà manteceta. "You might like this one, Scotsman," Vittorio told Angus. "It is salted cod minced with oil, garlic, and herbs."

Angus looked hungrily at the food, eyeing the salted fish dish in particular.

"Let us toast," Sal said. We all raised our glasses. "To the lady with a kaleidoscope mind," Sal said, referencing the line written on the kaleidoscope.

I smiled knowingly at Sal.

Angus looked at Jessup who shrugged, and they called "Cheers."

Jessup and Angus ate excitedly, commenting on everything. I noticed that Angus asked the footman again and again to put more of the baccalà manteceta on his plate. I sipped my wine and took in the scene. I felt happy to see them happy. Whatever the harlequin had died for, it had led to this pleasure: good people enjoying a rare treat, something they surely worked hard enough to deserve. I *would* find the meaning of the kaleidoscope and discover the lady of the kaleido-scope mind—but not just now.

CHAPTER 11

That evening, Angus and Jessup, exhausted, overfull, and excited to try their rooms, headed to bed. Promising Sal I would be by later, I went to the small garden terrace on the roof. Once there, I found a comfortable wicker chaise and laid back. I pulled out my pipe and opium supply and lit up. I lay smoking as I looked at the stars. Air transport ships and gondolas, their lanterns blinking, passed overhead. The sounds of the canal gondoliers singing as they rowed past filled the night air. It was warm with a soft breeze coming in from the sea. The air smelled sweet and salty with a hint of a fresh seaweed scent. I gazed up at the early evening sky and noticed an extremely bright star located just beside the moon. In fact, it seemed almost brighter than the moon. I had not noticed it the night before.

I pulled out my spyglass to look at it more closely. It was exceedingly bright. Digging in my bag again, I pulled out the kaleidoscope. I hoped the starlight would illuminate the colors. When I centered the kaleidoscope onto the star, I was surprised. In fact, I was so surprised I jumped up, knocking over the glass of wine I'd brought with me. It shattered on the floor. Very clearly reflected in the kaleidoscope were a series of numbers. The colors of the kaleidoscope had rotated so the purples and blues fell together and clearly wrote out numbers: 36.6858. I dug around in my bag for one of Sal's beautifully tinkered fountain pens. Unable to find paper, I wrote the numbers on the hem of my shorts. I looked again to be sure I had noted the digits correctly. I panned the kaleidoscope to another part of the sky only to see the numbers disappear. They only appeared when pointed to that bright star. Kaleidoscope in hand, I ran back downstairs.

I ran to Sal's room, flung open the door, and rushed to his bedside. "Sal," I whispered, shaking his shoulder. "Sal, wake up," I said again, jostling him.

"Ahh, my Lily, here you are," he said sleepily, raising his hand to stroke my hair.

"No, no, no. Not that. Sal, come on, I've seen something in the kaleidoscope! Please, get up! Come on," I said, pulling him out of bed.

Sal rose sleepily.

"Sal, you're naked," I said with a laugh.

"Ah yes, I thought to save time," he said smiling as he pulled on a robe. Sleepily, he followed me upstairs. "Ah, what a sight," he said when we entered the terrace.

"Careful," I said, guiding him around the broken

glass. I thrust the kaleidoscope at him. "There," I said pointing. "Aim it toward the bright star beside the moon. Tell me if you see it."

Sal yawned then lifted the kaleidoscope toward the sky. After adjusting it a bit and moving it toward the bright star, Sal sighed an excited "ahh," his eyebrows rising.

"You see it? The numbers?"

"Oh yes. 36. Is that a dot? 36.6858. Lily, did you write it down?"

"Of course. What is it? What does it mean?"

Sal was still gazing upward. After a moment, he lowered the kaleidoscope. "That is Venus as the evening star. She'll sink from the sky in an hour or so," Sal said.

I pulled Sal down onto a chaise beside me. Once we settled in, I lit the opium pipe again and took a toke. I handed the pipe to Sal and then drank a slug from the bottle of wine I'd brought with me earlier.

"What are the numbers? A combination?" I looked back up at the sky with a naked eye. Venus' bright light held steady.

Sal coughed heavily as he smoked then set the pipe down. "I'm not sure," he replied. I noticed then his eyes had taken on a glossy sheen. He examined the numbers I had written on my hem. "I'll need to consider it a bit."

I lifted the kaleidoscope again and shone it at the night's sky. I centered on the moon and a few other stars; there was nothing. Only with the backdrop of Venus, the evening star, did the numbers appear.

Sal watched me move the kaleidoscope across the sky. "We must seek Venus. She holds the answer," he said.

"Seek Venus? Like the Goddess Aphrodite?"

"As the Greeks called her, yes."

"We all seek Venus, don't we?" I joked.

Sal kissed me sweetly on the cheek. "Yes, we do," he whispered in my ear.

I curled up into his arms and lay looking at the stars, the kaleidoscope hugged tightly to my chest.

We both must have slept then because I woke up on the chaise the next morning still lying against Sal. We were covered in morning dew. At a nearby palazzo, I heard the voices of workers and the sound of boxes being unloaded. It was just past sunup. Lingering pink light was fading from the sky.

I woke Sal who was still groggy and led him downstairs and back to his bed. Settling him in, I pulled his covers to his chin and kissed him on the forehead. I stroked his silver-streaked hair away from his face. How sweet he looked.

I then wandered back to my room where I startled a maid who looked like she'd been looking for me. She spoke some English so I tried to explain I had slept on the terrace. She seemed puzzled but told me to come with her. She was waiting to help me with my bath.

She led me to the small bathing room where an

arsenal of oils, astringents, perfumes, combs, and two more handmaids waited. At once, I felt ill at ease. My mind, startled by the smells of the bathing oils, went back in time to my first day at Mr. Oleander's and Mr. Fletcher's alley flat on Neal's Yard just off Covent Garden.

"Now Lily, this is Nicolette," Mr. Fletcher had said. "She will get you cleaned up. We thought we were getting a boy so the only clothes we bought are men's fashions, but you'll be more comfortable on the *Iphigenia* dressed like that anyway," he continued. "Oh yes, and Nicolette is French. She doesn't speak English very well." With that, he left me in a small room in their flat with a blue eyed girl who was about fifteen years in age. The girl looked at me like I was a rodent.

"What is the *Iphigenia*?" I asked her.

"Take off your dress," she said in a heavy French accent as she began to pour water from a pan over the fireplace into a washing tub. "It is their air transport."

"Like a balloon?" I asked.

Nicolette nodded then helped me pull off my shift. She then lowered me into the hot water. "I thought they were getting a boy," she said.

I didn't know why Nicolette seemed so annoyed. I was so happy to be out of the orphanage that I decided I didn't care if two old men had been my saviors. I was going to make the best of it. "I'm sorry," was all I could think to say.

"Non," she said, "it's only... well, we'll see. Come,

let me clean your hair," she said then poured warm water onto my tangled and dirt-covered tresses. She worked soap into the hair then rubbed in sharp smelling oils, lemon and lavender, trying to break the tangles free. "I will need to cut some," she said, taking the scissors from the fireplace mantel. With a snip, she rid my hair of about six inches of length. I fingered my hair which now sat on my shoulders. "I'm sorry," she said then threw the hair into the fire. The smell of burning hair filled the room.

"You speak English just fine," I told her.

"Don't tell them," she said with a smile as she combed what was left of my tresses.

I was confused. After she got done scrubbing a year's worth of dirt from me, Nicolette plaited my hair into a braid and helped me redress in the clothes the brothers had purchased: tan trousers, black suspenders, a mandarin colored shirt, and black socks and boots. She looked at me and frowned. "You are looking too pretty even dressed like this," she said and then sighed. "Come. They will want to see." Taking my hand, she led me back to the sparse sitting room where the brothers sat at worn wooden table looking over some papers. Light shone in from two dirt-stained windows at the front of the flat.

"Monsieurs," Nicolette said with a curtsey, her eyes downcast.

I looked at the two men. Mr. Oleander rose to take a better look at me. "Well, look at the alley cat now," he told Mr. Fletcher who laughed. "She looks like a girl again, don't you, pretty kitty," he said, tickling my chin.

Nicolette stiffened.

I tried to turn my face but his sharp fingers followed, poking at me.

"Now, now," Mr. Fletcher chided Mr. Oleander, who sat back down.

"Can you read, Lily?" Mr. Fletcher asked me.

"Yes, Sir."

"You see, even British orphans can read. French girls only look pretty," Mr. Fletcher told Mr. Oleander.

"Well, Nicolette earns her keep on her back, not at the books," Mr. Oleander replied as he poured himself a drink.

Both men laughed.

Nicolette's face had gone pale. She looked at the floor and said nothing.

"You're excused, Nicolette. Please go get Lily's trundle ready. Come here, Lily," Mr. Fletcher called and then motioned for me to come beside him. "What does this line say," he asked, pointing to a sentence written in a book which otherwise contained lists of numbers.

"Fares for the month of May," I read.

"Ah, very good. You know your numbers?"

"Yes, Sir."

"Then read these lines," he said pointing to a row of figures which I read off.

"Can you do mathematics?"

"Only a little."

"I'll teach you."

"We didn't go to get a bookkeeper. I need a galley monkey," Mr. Oleander said and grabbed a few tools from his toolbox. He was about to set them on the table when Mr. Fletcher stopped him.

"Not where we eat, brother," he said.

Mr. Oleander nodded and motioned for me to come to his tool chest. "Which ones do you know, pretty kitty," he asked.

I recognized most of the instruments but only knew the names of the wrench and mallet. "It's a good start," he told me, then schooled me on the names of the remaining tools. I paid close attention, wanting to impress my new caregivers. When he was done, he quizzed me, asking me to name the tools again. Thankfully, I was able to remember them all. "She's a good choice," Mr. Oleander finally determined.

"Indeed," Mr. Fletcher said then leaned back in his chair and took a long, hard look at me. "Run off now, Lily. We've work to do," he said and leaned back to look at his papers once again, pushing his small glasses up his nose. "Tomorrow we'll take you out to the *Iphigenia*," he added as I scampered back to the room where Nicolette had gone.

I found her sitting in my cold bath water. She looked like she had been crying.

"What's wrong?" I asked. The room still smelled

strongly of lemon and lavender. She shook her head but said nothing. The answer would become all too evident soon enough.

"All done, Signorina Stargazer," the maid told me, interrupting my thoughts. She handed me a mirror. She had bathed me thoroughly and rubbed my skin with sweet smelling basil and rose oils. My hair was dressed in the same fashion I had seen the Venetian women wearing; it was woven into a bun at the back of my head and wisps of loose ringlets fell around my face. I gazed into the mirror. I felt like I was looking at a stranger.

"Beautiful. Thank you," I said. I suddenly felt sick to my stomach. She offered to dress me, but I declined and hurried back to my room. I closed and locked the door then sat down on the bed. My damp skin prickled with cold. Tossing the lid aside, I looked at the contents of Byron's dressbox. I pulled the lily pin from my pilot's cap and affixed it to the satin top hat. I then took a drop of laudanum to build up my courage.

After I dressed, I went downstairs. I could hear the others in the dining room. The door to the room was shut. I took a deep breath and opened the door a crack. The men went silent.

"Lily?" Sal called.

"Promise not to laugh," I said.

"At what?" Angus asked.

I stepped into the dining room. "At this," I replied, entering in Byron's chiffon gown.

Jessup set down his bread. Angus stared. Sal rose and took my hand. "Truly, a lily," he said, kissing my hand. He guided me to my seat.

"Where the hell did you get that?" Angus asked.

"Byron. It was a gift."

"You look like a dessert," Jessup told me.

"Doesn't she always," Sal said with a wink, making me grin.

"I don't like it," Angus said.

"Well, we need to go into the city today, and I can't wear my normal clothes," I replied.

"Why the hell not?" Angus asked with a frown.

Vittorio entered before I could answer. "Ah, Signorina Stargazer, out of your traveling clothes I see. I have arranged for a gondolier. Signor Colonna suggested you might be going out?"

"Yes. Thank you, Vittorio."

He nodded then exited.

I sighed. "Well, gents, ready to see Venice?"

CHAPTER 12

The Piazza San Marco was bustling with people and pigeons. The square, framed on its sides by shops and market stalls and capped by the Basilica, was an image of Venice I'd known only through paintings. Now I stood in the shadow of the Basilica watching the Venetians stroll past. The place was a feast for the senses. Warm wind blew in from the canal. The small cafes and bakeries surrounding the square offered up sweet aromas. Textile vendors sold brightly colored silks at outdoor market stalls. Glassmakers showcased a rainbow of delicately blown plates and goblets, trimmed with golden filigree, which caught the morning sunlight. Prisms cast rainbows all around. And then there was the sound of the thronging market crowd and clink of hammers from the tinker stalls. I watched, intrigued, as one vendor displayed his small clockwork pets to two delicately dressed women and their very clean looking children. The little girl squealed with terror and delight as a clockwork spider crawled from the tinker's hand onto hers. Opposite the clockwork creatures, a vendor displayed wrist-holstered guns to two men wearing matching blue silk suits and top hats.

Angus and Jessup, armed with Sal's drawing of propulsion modifications, headed into the market in search of parts. Byron had suggested I consult the clockworks about the kaleidoscope, but I wondered who I could trust. Sal, however, knew a man from Rome with whom he'd grown up. The man kept a small workshop at Torre Dell'Orologio, St. Mark's Clock Tower.

"He's on the second floor," Sal said as we stared up at the building. The signs of the zodiac on a starry background spun around the Roman numerals on the dial. Above the clock face, the winged lion of Venice, also with stars at his back, stared down at us.

We headed into the building and followed a twisting staircase to a small room at the front of the tower on the second floor. The sound of the massive clock gears clicked loudly through the walls.

Sal knocked on the door.

From within, we heard a rustle and the sound of metal clanging to the floor. Moments later the door opened and a man wearing a leather apron appeared. He was about Sal's age. He had cropped silver hair and twinkling blue eyes. He was a tinker, of that there was no doubt. Everywhere I looked in the room behind him I saw clocks: wrist watches, pocket watches, cuff watches, necklace clocks, wall clocks, zodiac clocks, replicas of the clock tower, and more. The tick, tick, tick sound of the room was nearly deafening.

"Salvatore?" he said, seemingly shocked.

"Anthony," Sal said with familiarity in his voice.

"Salvatore!" the man yelled and pulled Sal into a hug, kissing him on both cheeks. The man turned and looked at me. "Chi è questo?"

"This is Beatrice. My wife," Sal said.

Beatrice? Both Anthony and I were stunned to silence. I raised an eyebrow at Sal who simply smiled lovingly at me.

"English, eh? Well, she is still beautiful! Oh, Salvatore, you old devil. Someone finally captured you! And I thought you would never find a girl good enough for you. Too bad your mama is not alive to see it. She would be so proud of you," Anthony said with a laugh then turned to me. "Mrs. Colonna," the man said happily, kissing me on both cheeks.

"Beatrice, this is Anthony Arcumenna," Sal introduced. "We grew up together in Rome."

"Pleasure to meet you, Signor Arcumenna," I replied.

"Come in, come in. My goodness, I cannot believe I am seeing Salvatore in Venice. And I thought you swore you'd never return to Italy."

"Yes, well, under the right conditions, we all outgrow our past," Sal said simply.

I looked deeply at Sal. I had never questioned him about his former life, his youth in Rome. It suddenly seemed odd to me to think he had a mother, a mother who would have been proud of him for marrying me... well, at least Beatrice. And I hadn't known he'd forsaken Italy.

"Let's have a drink. It is early, but I like this news," Anthony said with a laugh and poured us all a small glass of sambuca. I tried not to drink mine the way I knew how.

The two old friends made conversation; I paid attention. They exchanged news on common friends and people from home. They reminisced a bit. Their youth was typical of most boys, except they were both geniuses. Then Anthony turned serious, asking Sal about the matter with his brother. "He is what he is," Sal said dismissively, but I saw a line of worry furrow on Sal's forehead that I'd never seen before. "I do have a favor I need help with, old friend," Sal added.

"Of course. Anything," Anthony answered.

Sal motioned to me to give Anthony the kaleidoscope. I unwrapped it, leaving the wrapper safely stowed in my bag, and handed it to him.

"Ah, now, this is something," Anthony said, pulling a jeweler's monocle from his pocket and pressing it into his eye.

"We've come by it with a bit of trouble attached, I must warn you," Sal said. "I can see there is some tampering in the colored glass display, but I cannot make out what is there without taking it apart, which we do not wish to do. What do you see?"

As Anthony looked over the kaleidoscope, he too translated the Ancient Greek lines. "The symbols on the side, Salvatore, are not just decorative. These are all symbols of the Goddess Venus: the doves, swans, apples, shells. I use these in my jewelcraft. Ah, and here I see the anemone flower. Do you know the story of Venus and Adonis, Mrs. Colonna?"

I shook my head.

"It is a very romantic tale fit for a young bride. The Goddess Venus once loved a mortal man, Adonis, with a depth of passion she had never felt for another. Adonis, a rough young youth who liked the hunt, flirted with danger in an effort to impress his Goddess lover. Though Venus told him she did not need his bravado and advised him to be cautious, Adonis insisted on showing his strength. He hunted a wild boar, piercing it with a spear. But the boar would not be defeated. It snapped the spear from its side and ran Adonis through with its tusks, mortally wounding him. As Adonis lay dying, Venus came to his side and wept bitterly. Adonis died in her arms. In her grief, Venus transformed his spilled blood into the anemone flower. The red blossom, which can bloom and die in the same strong wind, is a memorial to the fragility of love. That is why the anemone is called the wind flower. A tragic story, is it not, Mrs. Colonna?"

"Truly," I replied. I suddenly felt like I needed another drink.

"Without dismantling it, I can only tell you it is

very old," Anthony said, handing it back. "And by that, I would guess it is from the ancient world. It is quite a find. I've never seen its like. You say it came along with some trouble?"

"Indeed, so I would appreciate it if you did not mention having seen it—if anyone asks. Now... let's have a gift for my bride. Let me see your cases, Anthony."

Anthony rose. "Oh, indeed! Yes, yes, let me see. Let's have a nice ladies' cuff," the man muttered distractedly as he began pulling cases from the shelves. He set several in front of me. Inside were beautifully crafted cuff watches. I looked them over. I could not help but notice a petite watch decorated with freshwater pearls crafted to look like cattails. They surrounded a watch face adorned with a swan. Gold and brass colored gears gleamed in the background of the watch face. Dragonflies with topaz wings and abalone shell lily-pad charms decorated the cuff.

"That one," I said, pointing to it.

"Ah, of course, Mrs. Colonna. After such an excellent story, that is the right choice. After all, swans are the very symbol of love."

Anthony looked at Sal who nodded permissively then boxed up the watch. Sal thanked Anthony heartily, passing him an uncomfortable amount of money, and promised to stop by to see him again before we returned to London. Sal asked again for Anthony's discretion, and we left. By the time we were out of the room, the ticking of the clocks had given me a headache.

"Your friend is very sweet, dear husband, but his head must pound all day long," I said as I leaned against the wall at the bottom of the stairs. I rooted around my bag for the laudanum. I pulled out the bottle and turned from the crowd to take a drop. I offered the bottle to Sal who imbibed as well.

Sal handed me the box containing the watch. "For my Lily," he said with a smile.

"Oh Sal, it was too expensive. Please, let me pay you back."

Sal shook his head, and as he put the box into my satchel, he leaned close to me and kissed my neck. "I liked you as Mrs. Colonna," he whispered, wrapping his arm around my waist.

I grinned. "Beatrice?"

"Well, who else could lead me to heaven but Beatrice?" Sal leaned back and looked deeply at me. He had a sentimental look on his face. Perhaps taking him out of his workshop had been a bad idea.

"Sal... I didn't know you had forsaken Italy. Why did you agree to come with me?"

"Did you give me a choice?" Sal replied. He stroked my cheek. "I would not miss out on a chance to be with you."

I laughed nervously. "Let's find Angus and Jessup," I said, giving him a quick kiss, then led us back toward the crowd.

The piazza thronged with people. The smells that had formerly delighted me now made me feel nauseous. My head was aching, the bright sunlight hurting my eyes. I put on my dark glasses and followed behind Sal. It was reaching tea time and the market was packed. The crowd of people bumped and pushed us. I don't know how, but soon Sal and I got separated. I don't even know how long I stumbled along before I realized Sal was gone.

"Sal!" I yelled into the crowd of ladies and gentlemen who glared at me. "Sal!" I turned around in the rushing crowd, but Sal was nowhere to be seen. I walked deeper into the market, thinking I would find Angus or Jessup amongst the tinkers, but I couldn't find them anywhere.

I was just about to head back to the gondolas when I realized I was being followed. Behind me, a man in a dark suit tried to look nonchalant as he perused a stall displaying carnival masks. The random nature of my searching made his presence obvious, but in true Lily fashion, I didn't know I was in trouble until I was already in the middle of it.

I slipped my hand into my bag and grabbed my sidearm. I turned then and advanced on the man. Startled, he turned and began walking in the other direction. He passed between two tents; I followed him. When I made the turn, he grabbed me.

"What are you doing in Venice, Lily?" he asked,

knocking my gun from my hand then twisting my arm behind my back as he tried to reach into my satchel.

With my free arm, I elbowed him hard in the side. He let go. I turned and kneed him in the crotch. When he fell to the ground, I grabbed my gun and fled.

Thankful I had forsaken Byron's dainty heels for my boots, I hiked up my skirts and took off through the crowd. I turned back to see the man picking himself up off the ground. I ran. I rushed through the crowds, dodging between the tents, then under the arched walkways of the piazza to an alleyway behind the square. I ran into the belly of Venice, my assailant pursuing me. I dodged between buildings then paused, peering out of an alley to see the man talking to two other gentlemen also dressed in dark suits. While I could not make out their words, they were speaking English. All three men had sidearms drawn. Taking a deep breath, I slid down the alleyway. At its end, I found myself stuck between a four-foot wide trench and the alley leading back to the street and the men who pursued me. I pulled my dress up to my knees and taking a running jump, I leapt across the water.

"There she goes," I heard one of the men yell. He spotted me just as I landed on the other side. I ran between the buildings, dodging children and workers on velocipedes. I turned and looked back to see one of the men emerging from the buildings behind me. I ran over a footbridge, down another street, then found myself cornered between three palazzi. There was no way out. I looked around for a means of escape. To my surprise, I noticed that above the door directly across from me was a façade carving of a swan with an anemone flower in its beak.

"You've got to be kidding me."

"Go that way," I heard a man yell from the alley.

I ran to the door and knocked hard. A confused looking maid answered. "Please, let me in," I told her.

She shook her head.

"Please," I said, gesturing toward the swan, but the woman did not budge.

Just then a startlingly beautiful woman with raven black hair and round, gold colored eyes appeared behind the woman. "What's the matter?" she asked.

The men's rough voices floated toward the alley. "Please, let me in," I said, trying to push my way inside.

The woman started to push the door closed. "I don't invite trouble."

Desperate, I grabbed her hand. "I have the kaleidoscope."

Her big eyes grew even larger. She peered closely at me then pulled me inside. She clapped the door shut behind her.

"She's not here," one of the men called from the alley outside just moments later.

The woman peered out the window. The mid-morning sun shone in on her causing flecks of blue to sparkle in her black hair. After a moment, she leveled her golden eyes on me.

"Hello, Lily," she said in a rich voice that poured out of her like liquid velvet, "I didn't recognize you dressed like that. Please, come with me," she said, offering her hand. "I'm Celeste. Welcome to Palazzo del Cigno, the House of the Swan."

CHAPTER 13

Celeste led me through the kitchens to a sitting room in the front of the house. She asked me to take a seat while she exchanged whispered words in Italian with someone unseen. Moments later the back door of the palazzo opened and shut. Pensive about Sal and the others, I paced the room.

"Please, Lily, you're safe here," Celeste said. Taking a seat opposite me, she gestured for me to sit.

"I was with my crew, a friend… they will be looking for me."

"I've sent a messenger to Ca' Mocenigo," Celeste said.

"Wait, how did you kno-"

"Gossip flows like the water in Venice. When Lord Byron moves, people talk."

"All right. Then how about you tell me what the hell is going on?"

Celeste smiled at me as she leaned forward to pour us both a cup of tea. Her hands were long and elegant. Her light blue chiffon dress was cut so low that it revealed the very tops of her nipples. While the back of the gown was floor length, the front was cut into a very short skirt. Her long legs were covered with garters and white silk stockings; she wore painful looking high heels with metal rosettes and spiked bronze heels. I looked around the room. Nude statuary and painted images of lovers decorated the place.

"Sugar or lemon?" she asked with a smile.

"Who are you?"

Celeste raised an eyebrow at me in assessment. "Sugar," she decided and stirred two cubes into a cup and slid it toward me. "It depends on who you ask. I am known as a courtesan. The House of the Swan is a house of love."

"A brothel?"

"Not quite. I am a courtesan… the lovers I take are of a certain level, a certain repute."

"I see, a high class brothel," I said and paused. "You said, 'it depends on who you ask.' What does that mean?" I forced myself to sit and drink tea in hope it would calm my nerves.

Celeste frowned at my bluntness. "My associates and I are practitioners of Venus. We are, in fact, priestesses of her cult, her ancient and secret worship. That truth would have us all in the stocks, but since you've made it here with the kaleidoscope, it seems you are trusted."

"By whom?"

"Venus."

"Okay then," I said, having heard enough. I set the cup down. Again, the tea leaves had fallen into the shape of a swan. "I really don't know why someone passed me the kaleidoscope or what I am supposed to do with it, so why don't I just give it to you and be on my way."

"Lily," Celeste said, looking at me very seriously, "we need you. That is why the kaleidoscope came to you."

"Need me for what?"

Celeste sighed. "A very ancient treasure is about to fall into the wrong hands. We need to recover it and secret it away before that happens. But we needed the kaleidoscope to find it, and we need you to make the kaleidoscope work."

"I don't understand."

"More than a thousand years ago, a treasure was stolen from the cult of Aphrodite. Our early efforts to recover the artifact were in vain; we never found it. The passage of time has kept this treasure hidden, despite of our best efforts to locate it. Now your countrymen are roaming around the ancient world raping it of all its goods. Your new British Museum is slowly filling with more Ionian artifacts than there are in Greece. My order is on a quest to recover our lost item before your countrymen find it first. What we seek to recover is something very special, not something to display in a museum. It is something your countrymen are desperate to find. We must find her before they do."

"Her?"

"The Aphrodite of Knidos. The famed sculpture by Praxiteles." Celeste rose and crossed the room. She took a small statuette from a pedestal and set it before me. "A replica," she said. I looked at the statuette and realized I had seen the sculpture of naked Aphrodite, her hand in front of her pubis, before. My parents had one in our garden in Cornwall.

"The real statue is no ordinary thing," Celeste continued. "She is something special. For many years we have promoted a lie, saying she was destroyed in a fire in Constantinople. We thought our lie would help us hide the truth until we could recover her ourselves, but the British are good at examining details. We must recover her before the Dilettanti learn her location."

I had heard of the Dilettanti before. They were a group of Englishmen, mainly drunken gentry, who had a passion for antiquities. They were, in fact, building up the artifacts in the British Museum.

"The Dilettanti see the Aphrodite of Knidos as a key artifact for their erotic collection, a crowning jewel," Celeste continued. "She is, after all, the first nude ever sculpted, but she is so much more than that. They are desperate to find her, so desperate they stole the kaleidoscope, our only key to her true whereabouts, from our people in Paphos. They are so desperate, in fact, that you were just on the run from them. Yet, Venus saw you safely here."

"Why do you need me?" I asked.

"Do you know the Greek dialogue called the *Erōtes*?"

I shook my head.

"In the dialogue it relates the tale of how three friends visited the Aphrodite of Knidos and contemplated the nature of love. The story is a bit absurd, but buried within the tale is the allusion to a second story told by a temple priestess. The priestess tells a story from the time of Praxiteles, nearly 1500 years ago, about a man who so loved Aphrodite that he spent night and day in worship before Praxiteles' statue. So in love, he hid in the temple one night and made love to her. He was discovered, his lusty guilt left on the statue's thigh. The man, a citizen of Knidos of high repute, was banished from the city. His name was Dorian Temenos."

I froze. It was like a ghost had walked into the room. Temenos. My family name. My real family name. That dead girl who had been thrown into the Thames awoke when she heard the name Dorian Temenos spoken aloud; it was her father's name.

"Yes, the name Dorian is repeatedly used down your family line. It was your ancient ancestor, Dorian Temenos, from Praxiteles time, who stole and hid the Aphrodite of Knidos. Upon his banishment, he secreted away the sculpture. The oracle at Delphi foretold that when the time came to protect her, only a true lover, a Temenos, would be able to recover the Aphrodite. Now you understand why we sought you.

With your father dead, you are now the only remaining descendant of the ancient Dorian Temenos. It took us some work to find you. Who would have guessed that the world-famous airship racer Lily Stargazer was actually Penelope Temenos."

I rose then, took the kaleidoscope from my bag, and set it on the table. Without saying another word, I walked back to the door that led to the alley.

"Lily? Lily, please wait," Celeste called behind me.

I did not turn around.

I pushed open the back door and entered the alley where I had, not an hour before, scratched like a stray dog. I put on my dark glasses and walked away.

Celeste ran after me. She grabbed my arm.

"Lily, please, we need you."

"When I knocked on your door you told me 'I don't invite trouble.' Let me tell you the same. I'm really sorry that a bunch of old men are after your statue. And I'm really sorry that you are still running around after ancient prophecies and dead gods, but it's none of my business. Please don't bother me again," I said, shrugging her hand off.

"But Lily, don't you understand? The statue is not just a statue. She is more; she is the embodiment of love. Will you forsake her? "

"I'll forsake her only as much as she has forsaken me," I replied and walked away.

CHAPTER 14

I flagged down a gondolier and returned to Ca'
Mocenigo rattled and confused. When I arrived,
I found Vittorio in a worried huff. Moments before
Celeste's messenger had gotten there, Jessup and
Angus had gone to the *Stargazer* to look for me, and Sal
had gone back to the Piazza.

"Lord Byron would never forgive me if something
happened to you," Vittorio said.

I asked Vittorio to send someone to the *Stargazer*
to retrieve the crew then turned to head upstairs. But
Vittorio stopped me.

"Oh, Signorina, I nearly forgot," Vittorio said, looking pale and shaken himself, "there is a British gentleman, a former Parliament member, or so he introduced
himself, waiting to speak to you. I did try to get rid of
him, but he was insistent. Will you see him?"

"A former member of Parliament?"

"Yes, um, Richard Payne Knight. He is an older
gentleman. I believe he is in the antiquity trade."

Good lord, the day was getting better and better. "I need a minute to get out of this dress," I said.

"Of course," Vittorio replied and motioned for a maid to take me upstairs through the servant stairwell.

As I slipped into my regular clothes, I tried to remember anything I knew about Richard Payne Knight. He was, as Vittorio suggested, an antiquarian. Knight's exploits into Athens were well known; he had spent the last decade cataloging and collecting the ancient world on behalf of the British Museum. It did not take a genius to figure out what he wanted from me.

When I entered the drawing room, he was standing at the window looking down toward the canal. In his youth he had no doubt been impressively tall. He was still more than six feet in height but stood slumped, supported by a cane. His gray hair curled around his shoulders. He wore all black save an expensive looking white silk shirt with a ruffled collar.

"Sir," I said generously, considering he was likely behind the little jog I had taken across Venice earlier that day.

"Ah, Miss Stargazer at last," he said, crossing the room to take my hand.

Reluctantly, I extended it. His hand was extremely white, wet, and luke-warm to the touch. When he kissed my fingers, a feeling of revulsion rocked my stomach. "Richard Payne Knight," he introduced.

"Seems you already know who I am. Would you

like to take a seat?" I offered, wiping my hand on my trousers.

"Yes, thank you. Sorry to surprise you, Miss Stargazer. I had actually heard Lord Byron was in residence and had come by to see him. When I learned that it was, in fact, Lily Stargazer at Ca' Mocenigo, I thought to make your acquaintance. Old as I am, I love the races. We're rather proud to have a lioness battling it out in the air on behalf of the crown. Do you know some have nicknamed you the valkyrie?"

I did not like his face. His long nose was situated over too wet looking lips. Fat hung two-fold under his chin. While he spoke, his pale colored eyes roved around my body like snakes. "Do they? Can I offer you something to drink?"

"Ah, no, Venetian hospitality has been hard at work in your absence. I am already full on the house wine."

Terrific, he was drunk. "What can I do for you, Mr. Knight?"

"Ah, straight to the point, are you, Miss Stargazer? Perhaps that is why Lord Byron likes you, aside from your obvious qualities and talents. I'm looking for something, actually," he said with a tap of his cane. I noticed then that the handle on his cane was shaped like a phallus.

"Aren't we all?"

He laughed. "Well, what I am looking for is rather special," he said and looked piercingly at me, "something that was recently stolen from my associates and me."

"I'm sorry to hear it."

"Yes, well, it was a rather unique ancient artifact. We suspect it was the work of the ancient astronomer Eudoxus. We are a bit desperate to recover it."

My patience had worn out. "Mr. Knight, I beg your pardon, British as I am I do appreciate tact, but I am not patient with intrigue. I already told Father Magill that I don't have what you're looking for... and in truth, I don't have anything."

"Yes, yes, Arthur told us. Miss Stargazer, the Dilettanti are very fond of Lord Byron. He defines a level of eloquence we most admire. As well, from time to time, Lord Byron has been generous to us. We seek only to return his generosity and to support icons of our realm such as yourself," he said very carefully, measuring his words as one might measure salt. "Our main interest lies in recovering what has been lost—on many levels—and that is all."

Celeste was right; this was a man on a crusade. I leaned forward and looked closely at him. "I don't have anything, and I am not interested in being involved in finding anything. I am a simple air jockey."

The old man eyed me over and considered my words. "I understand," he said finally. "Well, thank you for your time. We do wish you luck in Valencia," he said, rising to leave.

I followed him to the door, motioning for an

attendant to show him out. He was about to leave when he paused and tried once more. "Lily, did you sell it? You've, I'm sorry for saying, a reputation as a bit of an opium eater. Perhaps-"

"Good day, Mr. Knight," I said, cutting him off. I closed the door on him and listened to the tap, tap, tap of his cane as he was led out of the palazzo. I leaned against the window and watched a gondolier load the old man into one of the sleek vessels. I was about to turn from the window when I heard an odd trumpeting sound. I looked out in time to see a pair of swans fly overhead.

I rolled my eyes. I was beginning to feel like the Goddess of Love was stalking me. I took a deep breath and headed upstairs.

CHAPTER 15

"What a crock of shite," Angus exclaimed after I told him and Jessup about my meetings with both Celeste and Richard Payne Knight. While I had given them most of the details, I had left out the Temenos prophecy. I was still reeling from having heard the name spoken aloud. "You did the right thing, lassie. Best not to get mixed up in matters that aren't your concern."

Jessup sat looking at his hands. It was not like him to mull over his thoughts.

"What?" I asked him.

He shrugged, spreading his hands, but didn't answer.

"Out with it."

"Well, this Celeste, she's right, isn't she? Doesn't it seem wrong for a bunch of crusty old buggers to go ripping about the Mediterranean taking everything they want and hauling it back to London?"

"The rebellious tribe of Boudicca speaks," I said.

"You have a point, but should I be risking my neck over it?"

Before either of them had the chance to answer, the door to my bedroom burst open, and a wild-looking Sal came in. He said nothing but scooped me into his arms and crushed me against his chest. Taking their cue, Jessup and Angus made silent departures.

"I can't breathe," I told Sal after a moment.

"Are you all right?" he said, stepping back, smoothing my hair around my face.

I relayed to him the sequence of events that had unfolded.

"I went back to Anthony's workshop. They tore the place apart and bloodied his nose. They were looking for the kaleidoscope. My Lily, I am so sorry. You were right behind me. I stopped for just a moment, and when I turned around, you were gone!"

"Sal, I'm fine. How about Anthony? Is he all right?"

"Surprised. Angry. But fine."

"I left the kaleidoscope with that woman. We came here to find out what it was and now we know. I've got too many of my own worries to get involved in this sort of mess."

Sal looked distressed. He held my hand, stroking my fingers. "The statue they seek is a rare treasure. Praxiteles is the most renowned sculptor of the ancient world. Thousands of people sailed to the ancient city of Knidos to view the Aphrodite. I thought the statue was lost in a fire in Constantinople."

"Celeste said it was a false lead, that the real statue was hidden by one of its admirers."

"The ancient cults, Lily, are very serious. To them, the Gods of the ancient world are as real as they were in the time of Troy. Praxiteles' statute was created for the cult of Aphrodite Euploia, the goddess of fair voyages. A voyager yourself, you must see there seems to be some connection between you and this goddess. After all, only a stargazer would notice coordinates in a kaleidoscope," Sal said.

"Coordinates?"

"I have been thinking about the kaleidoscope, the numbers, and why the object came to you specifically—your knowledge, your skills. The numbers seem to be a line of latitude. Venus is a morning and evening star. You saw the numbers in the evening star. What would we see if we viewed the numbers at the morning star?"

"Another set of numbers. The exact coordinates?"

"Perhaps."

"But surely someone else would have noticed after all these years. Knight said the kaleidoscope was ancient, the work of someone names Eudoxus."

"Eudoxus was an astronomer. He studied under Plato and was contemporary to Praxiteles. He may have also belonged to the cult of Aphrodite. It is certainly possible he tinkered the kaleidoscope. If the kaleidoscope was only meant to be used in a time of need, then no one may have ever known it was anything other than a colorful looking glass."

"Celeste said the Dilettanti stole it from Paphos."

"The Dilettanti have two sides. They are lovers of art and culture. On one hand they preserve history that would otherwise sit buried under rubble and grass, but on the other hand, they are dangerous connoisseurs of sexuality. They hold a secret museum of erotic art, so naturally all of London knows about it. They have shaken Pompeii loose of her riches and collected art from every ancient city they have unearthed in search of the divine physical form. No doubt, the Aphrodite of Knidos is a coveted prize, the most dazzling game piece of the ancient world. The courtesan likely did not exaggerate the dire nature of the situation. If the Dilettanti think they have a lead on the Aphrodite, they will not stop until they recover it."

"And if they do, then what? It will sit in the British Museum. Is that so bad?"

"We will all go and marvel at Praxiteles' creation whereas the cult of Venus, when they see her, will marvel at divine love."

I looked at Sal who was staring at me with great intensity. I giggled. "What, are you marveling at divine love?"

Sal gently took me by both arms and pulled me into a deep kiss. Something felt different. There was a shift, a minor change in pressure, intensity, chemistry, between us. I felt the sweet softness of his lips and breathed in his comforting scent of sandalwood. For just a moment, my heart fluttered open.

Sal laid me down and whispered in my ear. "When I thought something had happened to you, that I might have lost you…" he kissed me gently, and our eyes locked on one another.

This was not Sal, the Italian, of Tinkers' Hall talking to me. This was Salvatore Colonna of Rome, Sal who had old friends, a bad relationship with his brother, and a dead mother who would have liked me. This Sal was not distracted by inventions and devices. A different man, or, perhaps, the real Salvatore was looking down at me. I kissed this man back as Beatrice—or maybe Penelope-might have kissed him. Outside my open bedroom window, the swans sounded again, their calls reverberating deep in my soul.

❧

CHAPTER 16

E ven though I was young when I was adopted, it didn't take me long to figure out that my new situation was far worse than anything I could have ever imagined. Mr. Oleander made no effort to hide his repugnant behavior.

My first night there, Mr. Oleander came into my and Nicolette's room after Mr. Fletcher had gone to sleep. I could hear Mr. Fletcher snoring loudly in his room on the other side of the flat.

The door creaked when Mr. Oleander entered.

"Sir?" I said. I had been lying on a trundle rolled out from under Nicolette's bed. Still worried about making a good impression, and desperate not to go back to the charity school, I sat up.

"Go to sleep, Lily," he said as he neared Nicolette's bed. He bore a candle before him; his bent shadow moved along the wall. Nicolette never stirred. I guess, after all those years, she had grown to expect him.

Puzzled, I stared at Mr. Oleander.

"Mind your own business, pretty kitty, or I'll make *you* my business. Lie down and close your eyes."

I was confused, but I did as I was told.

"Don't pretend you're sleeping," Mr. Oleander whispered to Nicolette.

"Non. I am only tired," I head Nicolette whisper.

"Well, I won't be long. Come on now. Let's get acquainted," he whispered.

I heard Nicolette sit up, followed by a lot of wet sounds and Mr. Oleander moaning. I didn't dare to look. After a few moments, I head Mr. Oleander direct Nicolette to lie down. The bed creaked. My trundle shifted when he crawled onto the bed with her.

Then the bed started shaking. Mr. Oleander was groaning. Curiosity got the better of me. I peeked out from under the blankets to look. Mr. Oleander had pushed Nicolette's skirts up to her neck and had poised himself between her open legs. He was pumping hard, his face contorted into a weird grimace. Nicolette, her body rocking, stared at the skylight overhead. Her expression was as empty as the full moon.

Feeling sick, I pulled the blanket back over my head. My trundle rocked as Mr. Oleander relieved his lust on Nicolette. My bed shaking, I began to feel like it was happening to me too.

"Ahh, by God, there we go," Mr. Oleander said finally. Moments later he belted up and left, taking his candle with him.

I crawled out from under my covers and looked at

Nicolette. She lay motionless, staring up at the starry sky. Her dress was still pushed up around her neck, her body exposed. Not sure what to do, I gently pulled her skirts back down and covered her. She didn't resist. In fact, she barely seemed to notice. I took her cold hand and sat beside her.

"For some reason, I thought he was your father," I whispered.

She turned and looked at me. One tear slid from the corner of her eye. "He might be."

I was shocked by her answer. "Where is your mother?"

"Dead. Oleander was one of my mother's clients. He took me in when she died, brought me here."

"From France?"

"Oui," Nicolette said in an exhale.

"How long ago?"

She sighed. "I don't remember anymore."

I lay my cheek on her hand and said nothing else. I was frightened to my core that I would share Nicolette's fate. Maybe it would have been better if I had drowned in the Thames. What a choice: be left for dead or be abused until you were dead inside. All I knew was that I did not want that man's hands on me. I swore that no one would ever touch me without my permission. But I never could have anticipated what was to come.

◆—◆

Standing on a pedestal above an adoring crowd, I felt eyes roving over my naked body. I tried to cover myself, but my arms, stiff as stone, were frozen in place. Inside, I burned. All eyes devoured me: my lips, my thighs, my bare breasts, my secret female parts. Men and women gazed on me with desire and envy. I could read their lusty thoughts in their eyes. At night, as they made love to their paramours, they would imagine the upturn of my nipples, the roundness of my bottom. And I could not prevent them. Their thoughts raped me. They circled around me, gazing, absorbing my every curve. They would comment on my buttocks, my breasts, on which view was more preferable, back or front. The Phoenicians, the Koans, the Knidians, and the Greeks would all come and see what Praxiteles had made. With eyes of stone, I stared out at the blue-green waters of the Aegean and pretended they did not molest me. I thought of what I would say if I could speak, but my stony lips never uttered even a murmur.

"Be silent. Be still," Mr. Oleander whispered as he crawled into Nicolette's bed.

Moonlight poured in through the skylight, illuminating the room. Nicolette's face was white, almost translucent. Her glazed over eyes were staring at some far-off point no one could see but her. Her body rocked back and forth. Mr. Oleander's shadow rolled over her like a storm cloud.

Nicolette turned her head. She wore the face of the

Aphrodite. Her glossy eyes met mine. Her hand slid from the bed. I took it. It was cold as stone.

"Lily," she rasped. "Save me!"

I sat bolt upright. Outside, a gondolier was singing as he poled past the palazzo. I was shaking and drenched in sweat: fucking dreams, as always, the fucking nightmares. I tried to catch my breath. Undisturbed, Sal lay sleeping in the bed beside me. I poured a glass of water and rose. Still naked, the rub of lovemaking fresh on my skin, I leaned against the frame of the balcony window. A wind blew across the Adriatic. It cooled my sticky flesh. Moonlight shone down on me. Its luminescence made the canal waters sparkle with silver light.

I tried so hard to forget everything, to forget the years with Mr. Fletcher and Mr. Oleander, to forget what had happened to Nicolette and me, but the dreams wouldn't let it go. Now my dreams were a confused mess, a mix of the mystery of the statue and the pain of the past. And every time I saw Nicolette, even if it was just in a dream, my heart broke again.

As I gazed out at the canal waters, I thought I saw Nicolette's porcelain face appear amongst the waves. The image disappeared under the water. And again, I could not save her. But I could save the Aphrodite. Celeste was desperate. Sal was willing. Byron was encouraging. And an ancient prophecy said someone from my family line-my real family line-would protect the Goddess of Love. I didn't set much stock in such intangible things as prophecies or the familial duty of a family with which I had no connection. But Nicolette had been tangible, someone who had been family. She too had been the victim of hungry eyes. Would I let the sculpture fall to the same fate?

I closed my eyes and calculated. It had been about nine years since she died-no, no more of this. I wouldn't think of it anymore. I calculated again. I had not smoked opium for hours. The laudanum was supposed to have the same effect, but it didn't. Nothing made me feel better than smoking opium. Nothing made me forget better than smoking opium.

As silently as possible, I pulled a chair to the open balcony doorway. I dug in my satchel and pulled out my pipe. It had gotten tangled up in the kaleidoscope's cloth wrapping which lay forgotten in my bag. After a couple of hits, my hands started to steady. The images from the dream started to melt. I was able, once again, to push Nicolette's memory back into the dark place inside me where I kept her. Where I kept her safe. My eyes floated, my head humming. I looked at the cloth; the image of the swan was hidden in the darkness. As a gondolier passed, he looked up to find me sitting naked in the starlight.

"Bellisimo!" he called excitedly, extending both arms to the night's sky.

Feeling momentarily modest, I dropped the kaleidoscope's wrapping over my cunny.

"Venere pudica," the gondolier called with a laugh then poled way.

"Modest Venus," Sal said from the bed behind me.

I looked back at him. The moonlight fell on his naked body. He looked beautiful, his silver-streaked hair shining. "What did you say?"

"Venere pudica means 'Modest Venus.' That is the Aphrodite of Knidos' common title."

"Just how do you know so much about this statue?"

Sal shrugged. "My brother donated a copy to the Pope a few years ago."

I considered for a moment then laughed out loud.

Sal smiled wryly. "What is it, my Lily?"

"Well, I guess we have to find her."

Sal rose and came to stand behind me. He kissed my earlobe. "I know," he whispered.

CHAPTER 17

It was sometime after midnight when there was a knock on the door. Sal and I had been lying in bed entwined in one another's arms. Sighing heavily, I reluctantly got up and pulled on a robe while Sal, a sheet wrapped around his waist, answered the door.

"Ah, Signor Colonna..." Vittorio said, looking a little embarrassed, "pardon the intrusion. Signorina Stargazer, I am so sorry to bother you, but someone, a woman, has come through one of the secret passages between the buildings of Ca' Mocenigo. She wants to speak with you. Her name is-"

"Celeste."

Vittorio nodded.

"Can you escort her to the dining room? I'll be down in a minute."

Vittorio nodded and headed back down the hall.

"Shall I come?" Sal asked.

"Give me a minute with her first?"

Sal's expression was gentle. "As you wish."

I slipped on a pair of slippers and headed

downstairs. When Celeste entered I was a bit startled; she was wearing a hooded cape and a carnival mask. The porcelain mask was intricately decorated around the eyes and cheeks with inlaid filigree metalwork. Copper and brass rosettes trimmed the brow line.

"One of the benefits of living in Venice," she said, removing the mask, "is that we are deft at subterfuge. Of course, in my trade, I also know everyone's secret stairwells," she said with a smile.

I wondered then if we shared something-someone-else in common but decided not to ask.

"Thank you for agreeing to see me," she said and took a seat beside me.

I nodded. At once, my senses were overcome by the smell of her perfume; the rich scent of gardenia emanated from her. Thanks to the opium, everything in the room seemed amplified yet slightly out of joint.

"Lily," she said then, leveling those huge golden eyes on me, "I need to apologize to you. Have you ever been so passionate about something that you just assume everyone else around you cares as much as you do?"

"I'm a professional airship racer," I replied with a grin.

Her serious demeanor cracked. She laughed but then smiled sympathetically and took my hand. "I never thought about why you changed your name. To be honest, I never even cared. It was not until I spoke of your father, of your past, and I saw the look on your face... I'm sorry I have pried into something very private." With the accuracy I would expect from an expert on matters of the heart, she had hit her mark.

"My father... you said he's dead. That is certain?"

Celeste looked sympathetically at me. "As far as we were able to ascertain, yes."

I had always considered myself an orphan, but something about knowing for sure saddened me. I thrust the feeling away as soon as it arose, holding back tears that welled, choking them down.

"Who was the harlequin? The man who died to give the kaleidoscope to me?" I asked.

Celeste's forehead furrowed, and her lips pulled back tightly. "His name was Demetris. He was someone very special to me. He was one of us... a priest, really, from Paphos."

The look on her face explained it all. Her love had died to save the Aphrodite.

"I want you to meet someone," I told her. "We made a discovery, but you must promise not to discuss prophecies, or ancient ancestors, or... my father. If you can promise that, I'll help you."

The lines around her mouth softened. "Of course."

I rose and asked Sal to join us. Now dressed, he'd been waiting in the drawing room. He entered carrying a rolled map. He smiled at Celeste and introduced himself. After simple pleasantries, we got down to business. I relayed to Celeste what I had seen in the kaleidoscope.

"I believe the numbers represent a line of latitude. It is virtually useless without the line of longitude. But I do have a theory," Sal explained.

"Sal believes that when Venus is a morning star it may reveal the longitude coordinates," I said.

Celeste opened a small leather journal and set it on the table. "Venus is about to fall into a period when she is not visible from Earth. But Demetris, the other person searching for the Aphrodite, also saw numbers in the kaleidoscope. And he saw them on the morning star. We didn't know what they were. Here," she said pointing to a page where copious notes had been jotted in Greek and a series of numbers.

Sal picked up the journal and read over the notes. He handed me the map then opened a wooden chest he'd carried with him from London. I spread out the map. From inside the chest, Sal took out a number of small measures, a modified sextant, and a very old looking astrolabe connected to a series of dials. Sal went to the front of the palazzo with the sextant and journal, returning several minutes later with numbers scratched down the margin. He then worked the measures and finally set the dial. We sat back and watched; the astrolabe turned, the gears on the dial rotated, clicking into place. Sal took out a pen and drew two lines on the map. Where they crossed, he drew a circle.

Celeste leaned over the map. "That's not Knidos," she said.

"No, that is the isle of Kos," Sal replied.

"The Aphrodite statue was originally created for Kos, but the citizens were shocked by her nudity. They purchased a second Aphrodite by Praxiteles instead, a draped figure. The nude stayed in Knidos," Celeste told us.

"Maybe Kos ended up with the nude after all," I suggested.

"But why would Temenos take the Aphrodite to Kos?" Celeste mused.

Sal looked confused.

"A man named Temenos hid the Aphrodite," I explained away.

"We must go to Kos," Celeste said.

"Lily, you can't take the *Stargazer*. The Dilettanti will follow," Sal warned.

"I have an associate with a ship. Veronica will let you take the *Bacchus*," Celeste offered.

"The *Bacchus*?" I asked.

"It is a pleasure craft."

I frowned.

"I'll arrange it. Can you be ready by dawn?" Celeste asked.

Sal and I looked at one another. Dawn was only four hours away.

"I will need some things. If you can arrange for them, we'll be ready," Sal said then began jotting a list on one of the blank pages of Demetris' journal. He handed the book to Celeste. She read over the list, looked at Sal inquisitively, then nodded.

"I'll make the arrangements," she said and rose to go. Celeste smiled at me with gratitude before she donned her mask and left.

Sal and I stood staring down at the map.

"The Greeks and Ottomans are at war," I commented absently.

"Yes," Sal replied with a sigh. He wrapped his arm around my shoulder, pulled me close, and kissed the nape of my neck.

We were going. Now I just needed to figure out how to tell Angus and Jessup.

CHAPTER 18

"You're just looking for trouble, lassie. Don't you have enough problems of your own? And what the fuck are we supposed to do if you get yourself killed?" Angus grumbled.

He had a point. "Look, I'm just trying to help. Once it's done then it's done. Besides, Sal will be there. You and Jessup can stay in Venice and work on the modifications to the *Stargazer*. I promise I won't be longer than a week."

"We've heard that before," Jessup said with a sour face.

"I mean it. If this turns into a rabbit hole, I'll come back to Venice."

Angus sighed heavily and shook his head. "One day, you need to quit running," he said, his dark blue eyes meeting and holding mine.

I sighed.

Sal looked from Angus to me but asked nothing.

"No more than a week. You promise," Jessup said,

pointing his finger at me. "We need to get ready for Valencia."

"I'll be back," I promised.

◆–▪–◆

By dawn, Sal and I were standing on the roof of Palazzo del Cigno staring up at the airship I would pilot on loan.

"Flying the *Bacchus* is a lot like navigating a bathtub in a squall, but the old float chugs along," Veronica said with a laugh. Veronica, or Roni as she told us to call her, had wild brown hair that looped out of control. A lock of pure white hair jutted out from her temple and trailed away from her face, getting lost in a forest of curls. Not even her goggles could keep the wild locks at bay. Her husky voice told me she smoked and drank strong liquor. She wore black boots reaching up to her thighs, short black leather shorts, and a chainmail and leather bodice. Standing side by side with Celeste, Roni made the courtesan look as rigid as the statue she sought.

But Roni was right. The *Bacchus* was a heavy old airship. Its gold and purple striped balloon, decorated with the image of the Dionysian god, shifted in the morning air. Its deck was covered by a gold tarp. At the front of the ship was a massive figurehead of *Bacchus*. Roni's gear galleyman and balloonman, both trained not to ask questions, were along for the ride.

I felt uneasy helming someone else's ship, but neither Roni nor her crew seemed to mind.

"I'd give you a few pointers, Stargazer, but there's nothing here you won't be able to manage. Just don't get too fast or too fancy, and he'll cooperate," she told me. She then turned her attention to Sal. "And who are you?" she asked abruptly, looking him over from head to toe with a sparkle in her eye that evoked a twinge of jealousy. My reaction surprised me.

"Salvatore Colonna," he said graciously, bending to kiss her gloved hand.

"Nice to meet you," she said prettily. "Colonna? Gee, Stargazer, you have a thing for important men," she said with a laugh.

I didn't understand the joke. Puzzled, I looked at Sal who simply shrugged.

Roni and Celeste then exchanged a few words. Roni checked in with her crew one more time, and then with a wave, she headed toward the door that led to the palazzo below.

"Have fun," she called to me then passed Sal a naughty wink that made him chuckle. The door to the palazzo closed behind her with a bang. I got the impression that wherever Roni went, noise followed.

Celeste, Sal, and I stood looking up at the *Bacchus*. The rope ladder leading upward wagged in the breeze.

"You going to be all right?" I asked Celeste as I eyed the ladder. While she had changed into more reasonable tan colored travel trousers, laced suede boots, and linen top, something told me that most of her physical exertion usually happened between the sheets.

Celeste followed my gaze up the ladder. It was about fifteen feet to the ship. "I'll manage," she replied. And with courage that impressed me, she headed up. Sal and I followed behind.

Once aboard, Sal pulled up the ladder and set the astrolabe. With a few words to Roni's crew, we set sail. Once we'd risen over Venice, I turned the ship, and we headed south-east. The good thing about the *Bacchus* was that it was rigged for overnight passengers and long trips. The bad thing was that the trip to Kos was nearly 2200 kilometers. It would take almost two days to get there. Because Greece was, in fact, in a war for independence, we would need a route that avoided the conflict. After considering options, we decided we would fly first to British-held Malta. From Malta we would cross the Mediterranean Sea to Kos. It was a roundabout path, but it kept us out of the war. Malta was a sailors' port. Supplies, news, and other luxuries would be in abundance. And if anyone did spot me there, well, no one could guess where I was headed.

Sal stood at the wheel beside me as we slipped out of the lagoon and began following the Italian shoreline south. The sun was just rising on the horizon. It illuminated the receding night's sky with a yellow sheen.

"Well, Mr. Colonna, seems like you are keeping secrets. What did Roni mean?" I didn't like the idea that Roni knew more about the man at my side than I did.

Sal wrapped his arms around my waist and leaned his head against mine. "Ah, yes, important Colonna men. There are many Colonnas in Italy who are important, but I am not one of them. The Colonna family is very rich and very powerful. My father was a Colonna; my mother was a serving woman. I am just a tinker with an important name and a father who never thought I was good enough to worry about," he said and paused, "and a famous brother not interested in his father's bastards."

There was an odd tremor in Sal's voice I had never heard before. I was suddenly very sorry I had pried. "Well, they don't know what they are missing," I said and turned to kiss Sal sweetly on the lips.

"My Lily," he whispered, kissing me again. And then, with a playful pat on my ass, he went below to the gear galley.

As I watched him go, I wondered about my own secrets. Like Sal, another life lived locked inside of me. Long ago I had a mother and father. Long ago they called me Penelope. Then the woman who'd given me life tried to take my life. When she didn't succeed, she'd left me like a piece of rubbish at a stranger's door. Was this division of self what caused me, and

Sal, from really connecting? Was that why now, with our secret selves circling around the edges, we were starting to feel something more than lust? The thought both enthralled and terrified me.

Before teatime we neared Pescara, and I navigated the *Bacchus* westward over the Italian countryside toward Naples. Roni's crew had made the trip to Malta at least a hundred times. Malta had a reputation as a good place to stop if you were in the exotic commodities trade. Given Roni's and Celeste's professions, exotic commodities were all they traded.

In the late afternoon, after passing Naples, I turned the *Bacchus* south for a ride over the Mediterranean Sea. We would pass over the southern tip of Italy, east of Palermo, and break again across the sea to Malta. We should put in by sunset.

The *Bacchus*, while bulky, turned out to be a very sturdy old vessel. Its hearty endurance, rather than the charismatic finesse of the *Stargazer*, reminded me a lot of the *Iphigenia*. Like it or not, it was on Mr. Fletcher's and Mr. Oleander's *Iphigenia* that I had learned to fly. That behemoth was just as cumbersome as the ship whose wheel I now held.

As we came to the shore of the Mediterranean, Celeste and Sal stood at the side of the ship and gazed out at the water. The Mediterranean's gleaming waves made my eyes crinkle. I pulled down my dark goggles and tried to fight the memories that seemed to insist themselves upon me, but the feel of the *Bacchus*, so like the *Iphigenia*, and the image of the pair at the rail took me back.

I was almost thirteen when the seams of my adopted family life started to unravel. The balance between Mr. Fletcher, Mr. Oleander, Nicolette, and I could easily be likened to a broken vase that had been poorly mended; with the slightest bit of pressure, it would collapse. And that is exactly what had happened.

Despite Mr. Oleander's initial insisting that my soul purpose in life would be to slip between the gears in the galley and help mend, grease, and run the airship propellers, Mr. Fletcher saw something else in me. Over the years, Mr. Fletcher had taken an interest in my education and taught me everything he knew, which was a considerable amount. I learned how to keep books, bargain for parts, charm clients, and navigate an airship through the worst weather conditions. There were times when no airship was in the sky save the *Iphigenia*; Mr. Fletcher did not fear the wind.

Mr. Fletcher was like a father to me. When he would catch Mr. Oleander looking sideways at me, or calling me to sit on his lap, Mr. Fletcher always gave him a look.

"Yes, brother, yes, yes," Mr. Oleander would reply then shoo me away. But I could always feel Mr. Oleander's eyes on me, watching, waiting. I never dared get far from Mr. Fletcher for fear of Mr. Oleander. But then, as time would tell, Mr. Fletcher was no saint either. While I had become apprentice to Mr. Fletcher, Nicolette bore the largest burden on our ship. We were not dubbed a pleasure craft the way the *Bacchus* was, but everyone knew about the French girl on the *Iphigenia*. Nicolette's body was often the reason why we had so many fares. When I was about ten, a well-dressed man had inquired on so-using me. When Mr. Fletcher said no, Mr. Oleander cursed him.

"If I didn't know better, brother, I'd say you'd be willing to sink us all on account of that alley cat," Mr. Oleander had said.

Mr. Fletcher, who was drunk at the time, had hit Mr. Oleander so hard that his mouth had bled. After that, I think Mr. Oleander hated me. It was, in my rec-ollection, the only instance when the two brothers had quarreled. Of course, they were not really related.

"Mr. Oleander used to be married to Mr. Fletcher's sister. I overhead someone say she died in an acci-dent, fell from the *Iphigenia*, before I was brought to England," Nicolette explained.

This seemed odd to me. No one ever mentioned the woman. And given the mood of our house, neither Nicolette nor I would dare ask. Despite having had previous romantic attachments, Mr. Oleander never remarried. Why would he? He had made Nicolette his in-house concubine. It was this miserable attachment Mr. Oleander had to Nicolette that led to the ungluing.

Nicolette was about twenty-two the year it happened. For the last year, she had grown increasingly distant and secretive. Every night, after Mr. Oleander used her as was his custom, she'd slip out of our room only to return before sunup. Despite my quizzing, she would never tell me where she was going. All she would say is, "Don't tell. Promise me, Lil. Promise you won't tell." Then, to my terror, she would climb out of the skylight and make her way across the roof. I could hear the timbers overhead creaking as she walked.

It went on like this for months. I never knew where she went, and she would never tell me. When pressed, she'd say: "it's for your own good. The less you know, the better." One day, however, I was sent on an errand with Nicolette to the Hungerford Market. Nicolette had tried to shake me in the crowd, but I was not easily dissuaded. I knew something was going on. I followed Nicolette and found her locked in the arms of Abbot, the son of our parts vendor.

"Mon dieu, Lily!" Nicolette exclaimed when she spotted me staring at her.

Angry she had not trusted me with her secret, I ran away from her. When Nicolette finally found me in the crowd, she had tears streaming from her eyes. "Please, please don't tell them! You don't understand! Please,

Lily. Not now. Not now that I'm-" she fell sobbing into a heap.

"I would never tell them!" I stammered out angrily. How could she think I would betray her?

"Lily," she said then, smoothing the hair away from my face. "Don't be angry. I just don't want them to know because Abbot and I are going to run away. You know they would never let me go, but I am going to have a baby. I have to go!"

She was right. Mr. Oleander might just as well kill her before he let her go, and I told her so.

"That's why it must be secret. I am going to leave this Friday before Mr. Oleander takes the ship to Dublin. I can't bear the thought of a bunch of old fuckers riding me while I'm pregnant with Abbot's child. I love him, Lily. He is going to marry me. Please, please promise me you will keep it secret," she said in desperation.

"Don't you know how much *I* love you!" I retorted hotly. "I would never betray you."

"Of course... it's just... I just can't think straight. I didn't want you to know. I didn't want them to suspect you knew anything. I am afraid for you. What if Mr. Oleander-"

"Mr. Fletcher won't allow it."

"You mustn't trust him so much. He has used me from time to time as well. They are both wicked men.

You should come away with Abbot and me. Come with us and be a big sister to our baby."

Could I really just run off? Wouldn't they come after us? And didn't I owe Mr. Fletcher better than that? I thought about Nicolette's words. I knew Mr. Fletcher had been with Nicolette but always in the privacy of his room. And she was always given something new, a dress, a scarf, something, the next day. He wasn't like Mr. Oleander.

Despite her best intentions, things had not gone as Nicolette had planned.

"Get up, girls! You lazy lot. Up! Good for nothin' pack of women," Mr. Oleander had screamed at Nicolette and me. We'd been sleeping in our small room in the Nell's Yard flat. "Why Fletcher ever loaded us up with a house full of no good whores..." Mr. Oleander muttered to himself as he slammed the door behind him. In the main room of the flat, I could hear him slamming his tools around.

I opened my eyes sleepily and gazed up at the skylight. It was still dark outside. The smell of alcohol emanating from Mr. Oleander lingered in his wake.

"Oh non," Nicolette whispered. "Why is he up so early?"

The terror in her voice snapped me out of my sleepy state. Nicolette had planned to slip away in the morning after Mr. Oleander left to prep the ship. Our usual routine was for Mr. Fletcher, Nicolette, and me to go to the ship about an hour after Mr. Oleander had departed. With Mr. Fletcher in Paris for the weekend to look over a new ship, Mr. Oleander had changed his schedule.

"Lily! Nicolette! Move it!" Mr. Oleander screamed from the other room.

"What do I do? What should I do?" Nicolette asked breathlessly. I could see she was starting to panic.

"Wait. Just wait. Just hold on. Tomorrow. Go tomorrow."

The door burst back open. "Lazy whore! Get up!" Mr. Oleander stormed across the room, grabbed Nicolette by the hair, and tossed her out of the bed and onto the floor. "Now move! Our well-to-do clients are already in Dublin and are waiting on a ferry back. We need to be there first thing."

I was already pulling on my boots when Mr. Oleander turned in wrath toward me. Seeing I was almost ready, he grunted at me and left.

Hurriedly, Nicolette dressed and tried to fight back her tears. Her face had gone deathly pale. While her misery was readily apparent, Mr. Oleander had not even noticed. He herded Nicolette and me out onto the foggy London streets all the while cursing about his capricious clients.

"Come to Dublin. Can't they just take a fucking Irish ship back? Come to Dublin. Of all the weekends for Fletcher to go to Paris," Mr. Oleander muttered angrily. I noticed that Mr. Oleander staggered as he walked. He was either still drunk or drunk already. I wasn't sure which.

Nicolette and I followed Mr. Oleander through the fog toward the airship towers. The flickering lights of the gaslamps cast long shadows on the nearly empty streets. Besides the other servants and tradesmen already at work, the rest of London was still in bed.

I tried to choke back the terror that had my heart slamming in my chest. I hated being alone with Mr. Oleander in the first place, but now I could feel a storm brewing. With Mr. Fletcher gone, it was up to me to pilot the ship across the Irish Sea. It was not a difficult trip, but my hands shook. I cast a glance at Nicolette. All the blood had drained from her face. I feared she would faint. I feared even more that Mr. Oleander would finally realize that something was wrong. Though I was filled with dread, I went through the motions regardless.

Once we were aboard the *Iphigenia*, I set about prepping the ship and tried not to draw attention to the fact that Nicolette was curled up against the bulwark crying. We debarked, and soon were flying over the summer country. After we passed over the coast of Wales, Mr. Oleander came out of the galley to check the balloon.

"Get changed," he barked at Nicolette.

Nicolette was standing at the rail looking out at the

water. I'd feared she was going to throw herself over-board. When she did not move, Mr. Oleander crossed the deck toward her. They stood side by side, just like Sal and Celeste stood before me, when it all happened.

"I told you to get changed," Mr. Oleander bel-lowed at Nicolette.

"Non," she finally replied.

My whole body froze. It was as if we, aloft and gliding over the Irish Sea, were the only people in the world. It was early morning. The sun had barely risen. Only the first of the sea birds had taken flight. The world was quiet. With only the wind and balloon burner making sound, Nicolette's "non" carried on the breeze.

"What did you say?" I could hear the anger in Mr. Oleander's voice.

I wanted to call out to Nicolette, to encourage her. She just had to wait a little while longer. But I knew I should stay silent: hold the wheel, keep the ship steady, try not to draw attention to myself.

"I told you no, you creepy old bugger," she replied.

He hit her so hard I heard her nose snap when it broke.

Nicolette suppressed a yelp as blood came spray-ing out. He grabbed her by the throat and pushed her against the rail, leaning her over the water. When he did, her obviously pregnant stomach protruded pronouncedly. I saw him take in the sight. He pulled her back.

"So you went and got my baby in your belly after all," he said, his hand reaching toward her stomach.

She slapped his hand away. "What makes you think you have life in that old, dead stump of yours? You've been pounding me for years with no results. You're just a dried up old tool."

A lump rose in my throat, and I wanted to scream out to her to be quiet, but I could not speak.

"One of our clients? No, not that. Got yourself a young man, did you?" Mr. Oleander asked. His words were low and calm, making the danger all too apparent.

"I'm done with you. When we get back to London, this is over," she said.

"And what makes you think I'll let you go?" Mr. Oleander replied.

"You can't stop me. I'm not a slave."

"You're no slave, you are right about that, by God. But I can stop you," he said, and with a hard shove, he pushed Nicolette into the sea.

I suppressed a scream and ran to the side of the *Iphigenia* in time to see Nicolette hit the water below. She smashed into the waves with such impact that it no doubt knocked her unconscious. She floated for a moment on the waves but then her clothes, made heavy by the water, began to pull her under. Her blonde hair fanned out like a halo around her as the waves pulled her down. I saw her face, clear and pale as the moon, slip from the light and fall under the dark waves. Moments later, she was gone.

Mr. Oleander and I stood alone on the deck of the *Iphigenia*, both of us watching the murdered girl simply disappear.

I looked away from the water. Gazing upward, I noticed there was a star in the morning sky. I took a deep breath, knowing Mr. Oleander had turned his eyes to me, and went back to the wheel of the ship. I checked the coordinates then turned the wheel, piloting the ship northward toward Dublin. I said nothing, only held the wheel, because I knew my life depended on it.

CHAPTER 19

"Lily?" I heard Sal's voice break in. From his tone, I could tell it was not the first time he'd said my name.

"I'm sorry. What is it, love?"

"Wine," he said with a laugh, pushing a glass toward me.

I pulled off my goggles. The sun was already setting. I looked across the deck of the *Bacchus*. Celeste raised her glass to me in toast then took a drink. I took the cup from Sal.

"The crew says we will near Malta within the hour," he said, taking a drink from his goblet. "Ah, as I suspected. On the *Bacchus*, they have good wine. Drink, my Lily, it will clear your head," he said then, eyeing me with perception that made me uncomfortable.

I locked the wheel and took a deep drink, swishing the dark red wine in my mouth. The dry flavor of the grapes, with undertones of cedar and lavender, crept up my nose.

"Are you all right?" Sal asked me.

"Do you remember a boy named Abbot? A parts vendor? Bradley's son."

"I think so."

"Whatever happened to him?"

"Hmm, yes, I remember," Sal said taking a sip of his wine. "He died. Bradley closed his stall for a week. The boy became a sailor and was drowned at sea. Why?"

"I just remembered him… from before." It grieved me to know his fate. It was like the ocean had taken their little family. Having barely escaped the water myself, I shuddered. I tried to shift my attention away. "Have you ever been to Malta?" I asked Sal.

"Oh yes, many times," he said as he swirled the wine around in his cup. "Interesting place," he added with a grin then drained the glass.

"Very interesting," I said with a smirk as I took a long drink. Indeed, how many times had I woken up in Malta not knowing how I'd gotten there? One of my best memories was of waking up on board a yacht docked in Malta with Byron at my side. We played near the tranquil and startlingly azure waters of the Blue Lagoon until Byron's fans became too overwhelming. Byron did like attention, but only when he wanted.

The airship towers came into view just as the sun was beginning to set. They were situated around St. Mary's Tower, a stone fortress turned sailors' port on the small Maltese isle of Comino. The scene below the towers was raucous. Loud, cheerful voices rose upward into the night's sky. From the fireworks exploding in the air to the tall bonfires burning along the beach, it seemed that nothing about Malta had changed.

I piloted the *Bacchus* into port on the most distant tower. Most of the air docks were already occupied, and in the water below, boats of every fashion were anchored all around the island. Roni's crew checked in with the stationmaster. We would spend the night in Malta and leave for Kos in the morning.

"Let's get into trouble," I told Sal after the *Bacchus* had been anchored.

"While I couldn't agree more, we must be careful in case someone recognizes you," Sal said.

I looked below. The platform around the tower, the stairs leading to it, and the tower rooftop was bustling with people and excitement. I was itching for a drink, a smoke, and a nice dark corner for Sal and I to play in. "Fuck it," I said. "By the time news travels anywhere, we'll be gone." I tossed on my cap.

Sal smiled. "Lead the way."

Celeste, however, was apprehensive. "I'll stay aboard," she said. "I'd rather not show my face here just now," she added, looking up from a book she'd been reading. "Are you certain you should go?"

I shrugged. It was only one night, and nothing in life was certain. And it was Malta.

As Sal and I debarked, Celeste followed us to the side of the ship. "Please be careful, Lily. And do come back," she added with a knowing smile.

"I'll do my best," I replied, and we headed down to St. Mary's Tower.

Malta was just as I'd left it. The stairs leading to the tower were packed with people. Common whores were displaying their tits and almost everything else, a group of Persian men with billowing pants were smoking hookah, and spice vendors, gun traders, and even pirates—of both the air and sea—were everywhere we looked. Sal and I went into the massive stone tower.

Constructed by the Knights of St. John, St. Mary's was originally a military watchtower. It was the only structure on the isle of Comino, a small archipelago between the two larger islands of Malta. It had four proper tower spires on the cardinal corners, and its roof was still mounted with canons. While Malta was now under British rule, the military had little use for the traders' port of Comino and kept instead to the main isle of Malta. Something told me that I was not likely to see any aged antiquities collectors.

Sal and I went in search of the Arabian opium vendors. The arched hallways of the massive stone building were congested. We could buy almost anything, from elaborate wood carvings to delicacies from every corner of the world, from colorful silk scarves from the east to tobacco from the west. The sharp smell of animal urine burned my nose as we passed cages full of monkeys. They shrieked at us. In one dimly lit alcove, I spot a group of air pirates standing around a comrade being tattooed by a Moorish ink artist. Women with alluring eyes outlined with charcoal peered at us from above their veils as their hands worked busily shifting Maltese cumin and other rare spices into bags and vials. As expected, tinkers hawked their wares; a myriad of vibration and crystal powered instruments were on display. To my surprise, Sal only eyed the items and kept moving.

The opium vendors kept a room in the corner of the tower. The smell of burning opium made them easy to find. When we entered, we were immediately seated under a private, draped canopy. There were at least a dozen such satin tents in the room, the drapes for which were suspended from the ceiling. All the tents opened toward the center of the room. We sat on satin pillows and watched a topless woman do a belly dance while she held a snake around her shoulders and balanced a sword on her head.

"Dance like that for me. Please," Sal said jokingly.

"I don't have a snake," I replied with a laugh.

"I'll buy one for you. I saw a basket of them in the hallway."

We both laughed.

In another corner, two old men played enchanting rhythmic music on long-necked stringed instruments. In the hallway just outside the room, I spotted a man moving slowly along, his metal leg, a tinkered contraption attached where his knee should have been, clacked as he stepped. Sal eyed him with curiosity.

Soon they brought us a decanter of vinum opii, a

wine made of distilled opium syrup, sugar, cloves, and other herbs. For me, it was like an appetizer. We drank the wine and let its effects sink in. Shortly after, a man wearing a white satin turban brought a tray on which he had a syringe and vile of refined and extracted opium: morphine. Sal, whose use was not as frequent as mine-in fact, I think I brought out the worst of in him-passed. I, on the other hand, motioned for the man to proceed. After wiping my skin with alcohol, he stuck me with the syringe. At first the morphine burned, but then a warm sensation took over, and I smiled from ear to ear. At once, Nicolette and every-thing else was forgotten. This was what I had wanted.

I leaned back against Sal, who, on second thought, asked the man to bring him an opium pipe. Sal's hand slid down the front of my shirt, and he sat stroking my breasts, fingering my nipples. As we watched the woman dance, my body began to feel heavy. I imag-ined I was sinking into Sal, our bodies becoming one.

Time had become a complete blur. Before I knew it, Sal had finished his pipe. I didn't even remember the vendor bringing it to him. Sal settled our bill and led us back outside.

"Let's go to the beach," he said.

I was glad that Sal was more sober than me. Comino, while it had a winding path to the beach below, also had very tall cliffs. One misstep would lead you to a rocky death. What seemed like moments later, Sal and I were standing knee-deep in the Blue Lagoon.

I was feeling too high to fear the water. Besides, there were other couples in the water, other shadows pressed against one another in the darkness. I was completely naked. I splashed water at Sal; he picked me up and carried me to the beach. Soon we were making love in the moonlight, the waves lapping at our feet. Sitting on top of him, I could see Sal's eyes on me. My thighs, covered in sand, burned when our skin was pressed together. I leaned over and kissed him deeply.

"I love you, Sal," I whispered to him. "We should be together."

"Yes, we should. I love you too," he replied and kissed me tenderly, "so very much."

We lay on the beach until the buzz started to wear off. After, we got dressed and headed back to St. Mary's for a drink. On the rooftop, one could always find good liquor and good music. When we reached the roof, we headed for the bar where Sal ordered us absinthe.

"Chasing the green fairy again, eh Stargazer?" a voice called from behind me.

When I turned around, I found Edward Trelawny, a close associate of Byron and me, standing there.

"Well, Edward Trelawny. I thought you were in Greece," I said. Clearly, Trelawny was no more sober than me. His black curls were wildly out of place, and his clothing was a disheveled mess. He struggled to stand upright.

"I thought you were in Italy," he replied with a slur.

"Does the whole world know every move I make? I was in Italy. I'm headed back in the morning. I was craving Malta."

"There is much to crave in Malta," he said with a laugh.

"Why are you here?"

"I have, in fact, come to collect a little something for Byron. There," here said, pointing upward.

I looked up. "What the hell is that?" I asked. Above us, a floating warship boasting double propellers and double balloons was anchored in the southern tower. It quite nearly blocked out the light of the moon. It was the most enormous airship I'd ever seen.

"The *Hercules*. Commissioned by Byron for his expeditions. You do know you dear lord is about to go to war on behalf of the Greeks? I am headed to Athens to meet him with the ship. I bet he would be very happy if I arrived with you *and* the *Hercules*."

I looked at Sal. He was leaning against the bar and watching the exchange with a look of annoyance on his face.

"I'm very sorry," I told Sal. "Edward, do you know my associate, Salvatore Colonna? Sal, this is Edward Trelawny."

Sal raised his glass in toast, took a drink, then turned away. I had never seen Sal act in any degree less than cordial. I was confused.

"Pleasure," Trelawny replied absently, barely looking at Sal. "Come on now, Stargazer. Move that pretty little ass of yours onto the *Hercules*."

"I'm already about business that is of interest to Byron. Sorry, but no side trips until that matter is settled."

Trelawny sighed. "Well, no doubt you can elbow your way through a war zone if the mood strikes. George would love it. You know, Stargazer, of all the women he has, I think Byron might actually love you. Anyway, I'm off. Sure could use you on the *Hercules*. My air jockey is a lazy git. Safe travels," he called then headed back downstairs.

After he was gone, I turned back to Sal who was now working on his second glass. I ordered another and stood beside him in silence. My head was a fucked up euphoric mess, and the morphine had left my heart an open book. When I looked at Sal, I realized that the opium had the same effect on him. All this time, I thought Sal didn't care I had other lovers or about Byron in particular. In fact, I just assumed he had other lovers as well. Maybe that was not the case after all. Maybe I had misread Sal. The look on his face, one I *had* seen him hide before, told me the truth. He was jealous of Byron. This was a problem.

I took his hand. After a moment, he met my eyes.

"I've noticed something," I said.

Sal tossed back the last of his drink. "Yes?"

"You always call me *my* Lily."

"Do I?"

"Yes, you do."

"And what do you make of that, *my* Lily."

"I love it."

Sal smiled at me, kissed me on the forehead, and then pulled me close to his chest. "Let's go back to the ship, my Lily."

The first hint of light was beginning to show on the horizon by the time Sal and I made it back aboard the *Bacchus*. We crawled into our private sleeping area and slid into each other's arms. Sal held me tight, and I slept soundly, without dreams.

CHAPTER 20

I woke a couple of hours later to the sound of Celeste's gentle voice on the other side of the door. "Lily, sun is up," she called.

I groaned tiredly. This was not the way to start an all day cruise. I crawled out of the cot, shaking Sal who snored in reply. I decided to leave him where he was.

The sun was shining annoyingly bright. I pulled down my dark glasses and went to look for the crew. They were sitting on a small rug on deck eating freshly roasted goat meat and Maltese bread rubbed with tuna. The smell of the fish and the hot, fatty flesh assailed my nose and moments later I was leaning over the side of the *Bacchus* throwing up yellow bile. When I was done, I lay my head on the rail of the ship and hoped God would just kill me where I sat.

"Water?" Celeste said, pushing a cup toward me.

I took it and drank greedily. My hands were shaking, my head pounding.

"Here," she said, handing me a small vile of

laudanum. "At this point, it is the only thing that can help you, unless…"

I took a drop from her vile and passed it back. "Unless what?"

"Unless you quit."

"Quit?"

"Eating opium… and anything else."

I was not in the mood, and I didn't know why people always wanted to have this talk with me. What I did was none of their business. I took another drink of water and handed the cup back. "Do you have the journal? I want to verify the coordinates," I said brusquely.

Celeste frowned then went to look through her things.

I whistled to Roni's crew. They wrapped up what was left of their breakfast and got the ship ready to debark. I was at the wheel checking the instruments when Celeste returned.

"Any problems last night?" she asked as she handed me the journal.

I double checked the coordinates. The ship was ready to go. Unfortunately, it seemed like Roni's altimeter had stopped working, but I had no interest in going into high altitude. My head pounding, I was still high enough by myself. As for problems, as the memories of the night unfolded, I saw a number of issues now lying before me, none of which had anything to do with Celeste.

"Nothing to worry about," I told her.

Roni's gearman signaled that we were anchors away, and he was on his way below. The burners fired with a roar, and the balloon pulled us aloft and out of the docking bay. Once the balloon had lifted above the towers, I rang the galley. The propeller clicked on. I turned the wheel and set my compass east. After spending the whole night with her stalking me, I was on my way to hunt Aphrodite.

I was grateful for the silence of the skies. Shortly after takeoff, Celeste disappeared back into the crew quarters, and Roni's crew minded their own business. I was left alone to feel the wind on my skin and to look at the sky. It was a clear day. The clouds were high up in the atmosphere. The *Bacchus* chugged along, floating above the blue waters of the Mediterranean Sea. The wind was not overly brisk making the ride rather easy. For a moment, I even fantasized that the Goddess Aphrodite had conjured clear skies for us. That was good, because in my condition, I was not entirely sharp. I loved the feel of morphine, and I rarely came by it, but even I had to admit that the aftermath was horrible. Despite taking laudanum to keep the edge off, my head still ached terribly, my back and legs felt sore, and my nose kept running. I leaned against the wheel of the *Bacchus*. It was going to be a long day.

A few of hours later, Sal came out of the quarters

looking like I felt. He had let his hair hang loose. His long salt and pepper locks blew wildly around him. He looked tired. Perhaps, at his age, running around all night with a mess like me was bad for his health. He smiled as he approached me; he was carrying two cups of something hot. Steam rose from the drinks. Hiding behind my glasses, I was able to avoid meeting his eyes. I remembered very clearly what I had said to Sal and what he had said to me. I just wasn't sure that either of us meant it.

"The gods are at work this morning, my Lily. Tea," he told me and handed me a steaming cup.

"Thank you," I replied, smiling carefully at him.

Sal stretched, the muscles on his arms flexing, and grinned at me. "How are the skies?" he asked and went to the side of the ship.

"Calm thus far. We've had the wind on our back so we're making good time. I suspect we can put in by late afternoon." I looked at Sal as he watched the waves below. How handsome he was, his brilliant mind tucked inside his lean, athletic body. I tried to imagine us building a life together in London. The picture seemed to fall in place very easily. "Sal?" I called quietly, still unsure of what I was going to say next, but then Sal spoke over me. He had not heard me.

"Look, Lily. A whale," Sal said as he peered below.

I locked the wheel and joined him, clasping my fingers in his as I came up behind him. In the deep blue waters, a large dark shape was skimming below the surface. We watched as it moved quickly under the waves. The *Bacchus* cast her own shadow on the water. It seemed as if the whale was keeping pace with us. Perhaps our shadow had confused the creature. Then I noticed something odd shining amongst the waves. A flash of light, like a mirror's reflection, glimmered very briefly upward toward the *Bacchus*.

"Did you see that?" I asked.

"Yes, I did," Sal said and set his cup down. He grabbed a spyglass from one of the storage cases and peered below.

I watched the whale move. Something did not seem right. It lacked fluidity. "There it is again," I called as the reflective light flashed once more toward the airship.

A moment later, the *Bacchus'* balloonman yelled down to Sal. I looked up to see that he too was watching the shadow moving under the water. I didn't need to understand his words. His voice held the sound of warning.

"What is it?" I asked, pulling on my goggles and snapping down the telescopic lens.

The water at the surface began to froth as the creature rose up. The waves retreated violently as the beast emerged from the sea.

"Here she comes," Sal said with a mixture of terror and awe in his voice.

As if in slow motion, it emerged from below the waves. I had heard of experimental underwater vessels but had never seen one. Some said the French were developing a marine weapon. Indeed, more than once I'd heard sailors whisper of seeing a shadow pass underwater that looked like the sea monsters of lore, but I just assumed it to be fantasy. Yet, as the copper hulled behemoth rose up from under the water, I started to panic. It was every bit machine. From its copper skin to the strange shaped piping on its roof, one could see that it was manmade. And everything in the shape of its construction told me to fear it. Logic told me that it couldn't do anything to us because we were aloft, but my instincts defied that. I trusted my instincts.

"Altitude!" I yelled at the balloonman, pointing up. "Now!"

At once, he set the burners on high. The *Bacchus* started to lift. I rang the bell to the galley calling for speed and grabbed the wheel.

"What do you see?" I called to Sal as I began to turn the airship leeward. From the wheel, I could not see over the side of a ship.

"The crew has come out from below. They are launching a sail on the top of the ship. They've got some sort of hand crank. The sail is rising up from a storage locker in the hull. It's not large, but it seems to be fully functional. They are trying to catch the same wind you're riding. There is a propeller at the back of the vessel. I can see it churning the water. The craft must be twenty feet long. They are moving with some considerable knots, Lily. They are keeping pace with you."

The door to the crew quarters slapped open and Celeste rushed out. "What is it? Pirates?" she asked alarmed. She joined Sal at the side of the ship.

"You won't believe until you see," Sal replied then handed her the spyglass.

"What is that?" she asked, a tremor in her voice. "My god, it looks like a metal sea monster! Is that copper?"

"So it appears," Sal replied.

"There are windows all along its side under the water. And I think, as well, at the front. You can just barely make them out," Celeste said and handed the spyglass back to Sal.

"They are assembling some kind of apparatus on the top of the ship. Get higher, Lily!" Sal called and shouted in Italian at the balloonman who pushed the burner. It roared as the flame found its limit. The *Bacchus* groaned, and I started to worry about the old balloon catching fire with so much hot air circulating inside. The ropes on the balloon creaked as it began to pull quickly upward.

Celeste ran from the bulwark and opened the door to the gear galley. She yelled below. A moment later the propeller turned harder.

"Elven Rue... the name of the ship is pounded into the metal," Sal called again looking through the spyglass, "some call number after... S7081J. Elven Rue S7081J."

"Could be English or French. They post an ensign?" I asked.

"No, it appears they are too busy assembling some kind of weapon," Sal replied.

"Weapon!" Celeste shouted aghast and rushed again to the side of the airship.

"Let's hope your Aphrodite is truly on our side today," I called to Celeste. "I need your eyes, baby," I yelled to Sal.

"They are keeping pace with you. You're going to have to get above or dodge whatever is coming."

"Fuck!"

Sal shouted up to the balloonman who responded in such a way that I understood there was nothing more he could do. We were, however, still gaining altitude.

"Lily, remember what Roni said. This isn't the *Stargazer*," Celeste warned.

From the water below, I heard a strange popping sound. It sounded almost like a cannon.

"Turn! Turn!" Sal yelled.

I yanked the wheel hard and tried to find a wind draft to get some extra speed. I was lucky. The wind pushed us leeward and whatever had been shot toward us flew just behind the ship, missing us. I watched as something attached to a line shot about twenty feet above the stern of the *Bacchus*. Sal ran astern to get a look as the device fell back into the sea.

"Some kind of grappling hook," Sal called.

I heard the device splash into the water below with a crash.

"They are reeling it in fast," Celeste called. "They have some kind of crank pulling it in."

I scanned the horizon. On the port side, two sea hawks were spiraling upward in a thermal. A small, rocky archipelago was causing a heat draft the birds were riding. I turned the airship toward the birds.

"They are reloading," Sal called.

I was not going to make it in time.

Again I heard the popping sound. There was a whoosh as the hook flew up just behind the wheel-stand. It fell just short of snaring the balloon. Instead, it snagged one of the *Bacchus'* ropes tethering the balloon to the gondola.

The balloonman shouted in panic and threw a knife down to the deck. The blade stuck in the wood. Sal grabbed it and ran toward the rope. Just as the line on the grappling hook grew taut, Sal severed the balloon tether. Above, the *Bacchus'* balloon rocked as her grip on the gondola loosened. The grappling hook slid off the rope and fell onto the deck of the ship. It slid across the deck.

"No you don't," Sal said and kicked it hard. The hook pulled off a small piece of rail as it went over-board, falling back toward the sea.

Sal turned to me. "Whatever you're planning... be fast."

I rang the galley again and giving a final heave, the *Bacchus'* propellers pushed us forward. Moments later we floated over the small, stony island. Hoping the balloon, one tether short, would hold, I rode the *Bacchus* into the thermal. Up we went. I pulled the bell to the galley, and the propeller went still. One of the sea hawks cried to see us infringing in his air space. The *Bacchus* rode the heat upward, gaining altitude fast. The only downside was that we, like the birds, had begun to slowly pivot in the heat draft. The effect was dizzying.

"They are turning aside to miss the island," Sal called.

While Sal watched what has happening below, I watched the sky above. Not too far above us, a lateral wind was cutting off the thermal. Some smaller cumulus clouds were forming at the top, a foaming bubble on our thermal boil. This was a good thing in that the thermal was releasing. Not being able to keep an eye on altitude would lead us to the same worries we had when we outran the *Burning Rook* in the *Stargazer*. On the other hand, when we reached the top of the thermal, the wind shear could grab us, and it would be a hell of a ride backward or worse. If we were sideways, it could spell disaster. I was not sure that the *Bacchus* could handle it.

"Lily, we must be out of range. They are pulling

down the sail and packing in the grappling gun," Sal said then.

"Fantastic. Now, if the clouds don't kill us, we might just make it to Kos." I looked at the sky and calculated.

After a few moments, Sal reported that the metal sea monster was once again diving below the waves. "It's gone," he said. I couldn't help but notice the awe in his voice.

I asked Celeste to have the balloonman keep the burn pan on high. The galleyman had stuck his head out. I instructed him to keep the propeller off. An argument then ensued between the balloonman and the gear galleyman, and for a moment, I felt like Angus and Jessup were with me.

"They are debating, but they think you should turn the propeller on," Sal said as he listened to the exchange.

Celeste stood at the center of the ship. She had gone completely pale and was holding onto a rope for dear life.

I looked back up at the clouds and considered. "No," I said then.

Sal looked thoughtful. "No doubt you know best, my Lily." He then turned and instructed the men to keep as we were.

Silence filled the space as we waited. The cloud bank at the top of the thermal neared. We were still spinning. I held the wheel. The rush of the wind stroked my face, and I began to feel the cool air from the approaching clouds. I closed my eyes. I remembered then the story of Aphrodite, Adonis, and the anemone flower, the blossom that could bloom in and be destroyed by the same strong wind.

It happened so gently. The *Bacchus* popped out of the thermal. A wind caught the ship from behind and pushed it softly forward. Since I'd kept the balloon overfull on hot air, the change in temperature once we were inside the cool cloud never caused the ship to stir. The lift simply slowed, and the *Bacchus* settled into the lateral wind shear. We were inside the cloud. The air felt dewy. I opened my eyes to see the deck of the *Bacchus* draped in mist.

Celeste looked around in surprise. Sal and Roni's crew were smiling from ear to ear.

"Now, turn the propeller back on. Easy as she goes," I told the gearman; Sal translated.

The gearman said something in Italian, smiled at me, then went below.

Sal chuckled.

I raised an eyebrow.

"He said, 'That's why the Italians can never beat her. She carries the winds in her heart'," Sal translated.

I smiled. Maybe I did.

CHAPTER 21

After we were clear of the metallic sea beast, Sal immediately went about taking notes on and drawing everything he had seen. Celeste took a position on the prow of the ship like a masthead as we floated through the clouds toward Kos. I kept our altitude high and in the cloud-cover. The deck of the ship stayed draped in fog, just like it had the evening Mr. Oleander and I had returned to London without Nicolette.

Mr. Oleander had not spoken a single word to me the rest of the trip to Dublin. When we arrived, much to my great relief, Mr. Oleander had gone into the city and had returned with a common street whore. I had lived in terror that he would make me take Nicolette's usual role. Too frightened of what Mr. Oleander would do to me if I didn't comply, and grieving over the loss of Nicolette, I had guided the ship into the towers at Dublin with a sick stomach. I had even considered throwing myself overboard. For me, death would have been a better fate than being handed to lusty men. The wild blonde Mr. Oleander had picked up, however, spent the entire trip from Dublin to London naked and dancing on the deck of the *Iphigenia*. She was more than enough entertainment for the hungry-eyed men. They never even noticed me.

When we arrived in London, it took some time for the customers to depart. Mr. Oleander gave the Irish girl a small bag of coin, and she went happily away.

I busied myself taking care of the *Iphigenia*. It was late evening, and the Thames had created a thick bank of fog. The gaslights in the street below shone dimly, their hue dampened by the mist. Once I had gotten the ship tucked in, I sat along the bulwark near the wheel-stand and considered what to do. I could not go to the constables. Why would they believe a throwaway like me?

Mr. Oleander crossed the deck of the *Iphigenia* toward me. In this mist, I could not make out his features. He lumbered toward me like an evil spirit in the fog.

"Go down to the gear galley," he said, his voice rough and serious.

I didn't move.

"I ain't gonna hurt ya, girl. Just go," he told me.

I rose, my hands and knees shaking, and went below.

The gear galley is a cramped space suitable for two adults at maximum. The complex mechanical gears for the propeller lay just below the deck of the ship.

A small galley increased the aerodynamic features of a ship and weighed less: the smaller the galley the better. The *Iphigenia*'s galley was tightly built. Below, a small lantern burnt. The sharp smell of grease and metal filled the space. It was a smell I usually loved. In that moment, however, I feared it would perfume my dying breath.

Mr. Oleander crawled in behind me and pulled the galley door shut with a bang. Still drunk, he was barely able to keep himself upright in the narrow space.

"Take your clothes off," he told me.

I froze and tried to back away.

"Aye, pretty kitty, I know Fletcher is keen for you, but we need to come to an understanding. I'm going to teach you why you need to keep your mouth shut," he said as he began to unbuckle his pants.

"I won't tell. I promise. There is no need. Please, Sir. There is no need. I won't tell," I said. I was trapped.

Mr. Oleander reached forward and ripped my shirt open. I stood aghast. Just a girl, I had little to show for my womanliness. In fact, my courses had only come on me a few months preceding.

"Come on now, pretty kitty," he whispered dangerously, reaching toward me. He grabbed my shirt by the sleeve and tugged it off of me.

I turned and fled, slipping between the galley gears. The propeller off, I was able to slide deep into the back of the ship where Mr. Oleander was too large to follow. He reached out and tried to grab me, catching hold of my foot, but I pulled my leg free, leaving my boot in his hand. I scratched my skin on a piece of sharp metal in the effort, but moments later, I had escaped Mr. Oleander's grasp. Behind me, the old man cursed.

"Have it your way, pretty kitty. Let's see how you like spending the night in the dark. Come morning, perhaps you will be more receptive to our new arrangement," Mr. Oleander said with a laugh then crawled out of the galley. I heard the galley door slap shut. Mr. Oleander laughed as he slid the bolt through the lock.

"Try that for size," he yelled then strode off the ship.

Moments later I was alone in the dark. The *Iphigenia* rocked in the cool evening air. I put my head on my knees and cried. There was no way to get out of the galley. Nicolette was gone, and I was trapped. I sat in misery, half asleep and half hysterical, until I was awakened by the sound of steps on the deck of the ship. Thinking Mr. Oleander had returned, terror seized me. I listened and soon heard the familiar humming of Mr. Fletcher.

"Sir?" I called from below. "Mr. Fletcher? Is that you, Sir?"

The boot steps stopped. "Lily? Where are you?"

"In the galley," I moaned miserably and started climbing back through the gears toward the door.

"Why is the galley locked?" Mr. Fletcher puzzled

aloud as he slid the bolt. "Lily?" he called as he opened the door.

I shimmied through the gears.

Mr. Fletcher caught sight of my shirt and boot lying on the floor. He picked them up and looked at them. "Lily? What happened? Come out, girl."

He led me back onto the deck of the ship. It must have been very early morning. It was still very dark, and the mist was very thick. He removed his coat and dropped it over my shoulders.

"My girl," he said, taking me by the chin, "are you hurt?"

I shook my head but the tears had already started flowing.

"Where is Oleander?" he asked, bewildered.

I could not answer him. I burst into tears in reply.

Mr. Fletcher, who had previously looked perplexed, started to put the pieces of the puzzle together. His face went red and stiff with anger. "Where did Oleander go?" he asked me again.

"I don't know, Sir."

"Where is Nicolette?"

I moaned miserably. It was too terrible to speak.

Mr. Fletcher put his hands to his lips and considered. "Come," he said. Carrying his lantern in front of us, he led me to the Captain's Room. He sat me down on a chaise. "Lay down, Lily. Rest. Don't come out unless I call you. I'll be on the deck," he told me. Just before he blew out the lantern, I saw that the lines on his face look deeply grooved. His eyes looked wild with anger.

I pulled his coat up to my chin and breathed in the smell of him. My savior. As Mr. Fletcher opened the door to go back onto the deck of the ship, I finally found the courage to speak.

"He pushed Nicolette into the sea." The words heaved out of me in a giant exhale. I sucked air back into me after I spoke, just barely keeping myself from hyperventilating.

Mr. Fletcher had his back to me. I saw him stiffen at my words. He did not turn around. "I know," he said and closed the door behind him.

I did not move from the chaise, but I heard Mr. Fletcher moving around on the deck of the ship. About an hour after Mr. Fletcher rescued me from the galley, I heard Mr. Oleander mumbling to himself as he made his way down the loading platform toward the *Iphigenia*. His heavy footsteps hit the deck of the ship with a thud.

"Good morning, brother," I heard Mr. Fletcher say. His voice was low and dangerous.

"What, ho! Back so soon? By God, about time. The Dublin trip was a disaster, by God."

"By God, was it so?"

"Indeed, brother. You won't believe what ill fate has befallen us."

"Perhaps I won't. Do tell," Mr. Fletcher said, and I

heard the warning in his voice. Mr. Oleander, too lost in the bottom of a bottle of something, had missed it.

Now more curious than afraid, I quietly slid off the chaise and snuck to the door. The seal on the Captain's Room never closed properly and left a sizeable gap. If I knelt, I could see outside. Mr. Oleander was leaning against the side of the ship. Mr. Fletcher stood at the center of the ship holding onto the balloon ropes.

"Ehh, yeah. Nicolette has run off. Turns out she was pregnant by some lad. She musta stolen away to meet the boy."

"How do you know she was pregnant?"

"Oh, our Lily, solid little lass, told me."

"Where is Lily?"

"I left her sleepin' in the galley. She was tuckered out from the trip. Curled up down there amongst the gears. It's bad luck, brother. Bad luck, I say."

"Bad luck. Just like when Laura died. Bad luck then too."

"No, my brother, that was the worst of luck. Your sister was beautiful, but lord knows, she was none too graceful. I can't cross the Channel without seeing her ghost in the waves."

"How, exactly, was it that Laura came to fall? Can you tell me again?"

"You know, I've had a bit to drink, brother, and would rather not live over again something more than twenty years behind us," he slurred but continued. "My heart hurts for that little bird. She just toppled in, right over the rail and into the brink. Waves took her before I even got the ship low enough to look for her."

My hands flew to my mouth as I suppressed a gasp.

Mr. Fletcher was silent for a long time. In the mist, I could only see the shadow of his figure. Mr. Oleander started to fidget.

"Fog is thick tonight," Mr. Fletcher said then.

"Isn't it though? I half worried about falling from the tower on my way back. Can't see five feet in front of ya."

Mr. Fletcher laughed. "Come on now, brother. Can you give me a hand? I purchased a new chronometer. Come take a look."

"I can't see a damned thing. Where is your lantern?" Mr. Oleander asked.

"I left it at the back. Wick got too wet to light."

Their voices retreated toward the back of the ship. I stood to watch them from the window. Their figures became mere shadows in the fog. I gripped the handle on the door so hard my hand hurt. I knew it was coming. I knew. I just didn't do anything about it. It seemed like it took an eternity. But in reality, it was just moments later when I heard Mr. Oleander scream. His loud yell echoed through the foggy darkness as he fell to the ground. In the lingering silence of the early morning, I even heard his body hit cobblestones below.

I clambered back to the chaise and pulled Mr. Fletcher's coat over my head, feeling both relieved and sick. I heard him cross the deck of the ship and open the door of the Captain's Room.

"Mr. Oleander fell from the ship. Come with me. We need to call the constables," he said then opened a trunk and pulled out one of Nicolette's old lacey blouses. "Put this on. I need you dressed," he added and handed it to me.

I slid his coat off and pulled on my boot. He lit the lantern as I redressed. I could not help but feel his watchful eyes on me as I moved, topless, in the glaring light of the lantern. His dark eyes were glued to my small breasts. I turned from his gaze and slid the top on.

Mr. Fletcher pulled his coat on and took my hand. We crossed the deck of the *Iphigenia* hand in hand. I could hear footsteps pounding down the loading platform as someone ran toward our ship.

"He was drunk. He fell," Mr. Fletcher whispered, looking down at me.

"I know. I saw," I replied.

"Sweet Lily," he said, kissing me on my head, and we went together to tell a lie.

CHAPTER 22

We snuck past the southern tip of Greece toward the islands just off the shore of the Ottoman mainland in the Aegean Sea. After the excitement that morning, the last thing I wanted was to find myself in the middle of a military conflict. We were lucky. Wherever the Greeks and Ottomans were fighting, it was not over the isles of the ancient world.

It was early evening when we closed in on the location provided by the kaleidoscope. The late summer sun was still in the sky. We would have a few hours left to explore the small isle of Kos. The landscape below the western coast where we flew in was dotted with groves of olive and date trees. When we reached the coordinates indicted by the kaleidoscope, we found ourselves hovering above a cypress grove.

Celeste looked puzzled. "There should be a shrine here. The Kos Aphrodite was kept at the Asclepeion."

"What was the Asclepeion?" I asked.

"A medical center, like an ancient hospital, built in worship of the god Asclepius. Kos boasted the most famous Asclepeion in the ancient world. That is where Hippocrates learned his trade. People came from all around for healing. It was an enormous temple, probably as large as St. Mark's Square, with three levels. Thousands of people would come here to take restorative. Yet all I see is trees."

"Perhaps the passage of time has buried the world you seek," Sal suggested.

"Well, there is no way to know for sure until we go look."

I lowered the *Bacchus* to tree level and climbed down the rope ladder. It didn't take us long to figure out we were in the right place. You couldn't take two steps without stumbling over a piece of fallen stonework. The problem was that the ruins were a complete disaster. Columns jutted out of the ground, floor stones were half heaved up in the dirt, and chiseled rocks lay everywhere.

Celeste looked completely exasperated. "We'll need a team of people to dig," she said. "We'll need to excavate the site. She's here. I know it. We'll just need to unearth her."

Sal and I exchanged a glance.

"Celeste," I began, but I was not sure what to say. Even if she did excavate the site, by the time she found what she was looking for, the Dilettanti would be all over the dig.

Celeste looked at me with tears in her large, golden eyes. The early evening sun made her hair sparkle. She was a picture of sadness. "It has to be here," she whispered desperately.

I turned to Sal to discuss the matter when I noticed he was looking at something in the distance.

"What is it?" I asked him.

"A boy. Just there," he said.

A young boy, perhaps eight years of age, was looking from us to the ship and back again. He leaned against a wooden staff. His small herd of goats was stepping carefully between the fallen rocks, nibbling on the grass.

"Why don't we ask him?" I said, gazing at the boy.

Celeste looked puzzled. "Ask him what?"

"Where the statue is. After all, he must know this land," I replied.

Celeste looked uncertain, but with no better recourse, we decided to give it a try. Cautiously, Sal approached the small boy. The boy looked like his common sense was telling him to cut and run, but sheer nerve made him stay. I liked the lad. Sal knelt down to talk to the boy at eye level. The boy waved his hands toward the balloon then at the landscape around us. After a few moments, Sal stood up, ruffled the boy's hair, and waved for us to join them.

"I asked him where the Asclepeion was," Sal told us when we joined him, "and he told me, 'you're standing in it,'" he added with a laugh.

I smiled down at the lad. He wore rustic looking cotton trousers and a patched shirt. The child had dirt smeared on his face, and his pants were stained on the knees. His smile was wide and toothy, and his eyes showed innocence rarely seen in children roaming the streets of London. When he clicked at his goats, they obeyed his command. The boy led us uphill through the cypress grove. The goats followed obediently along.

Sal and the boy chatted along the way. "The temple is his family's grazing land. The boy's father told him much of the temple was destroyed in an earthquake many years ago, but he knows where we can see the best parts of the ruins," Sal said.

Celeste smiled, not a coquettish sidelong grin, but a smile of raw joy.

We entered a clearing. There we found what we had initially expected: the ruins of the temple. Their view had been hidden by a rise in the earth and a thicket of trees. What was left of the stone walls outlined the space. In one area, the walls of the temple were still erect. Temple buildings, constructed with small round stones, shimmered with a golden hue in the fading sunlight. Fallen marble columns lay amongst the wildflowers. Some of the ruins seemed to be in relatively good condition. The buildings were mainly roofless, but you could still see the arched hallways with ornately chiseled stonework.

The boy was talking quickly and pointing toward a rise before us.

Sal nodded.

"You can see, just there, how the earth does not rise in a natural way but looks more squared. Under the earth, the temple expands upward toward a shrine that would have crowned it at the top. You can just see the exposed stairs. Your temple is yet undiscovered, Celeste," Sal said then turned to the boy and asked the child a question.

The boy looked thoughtful then pointed toward an area in the ruins.

Sal smiled happily. His silver eyes crinkled in the corners. "I asked him if he knows of any statues within the ruins. He said the statues are 'in there,'" Sal said, following the boy's gaze.

"Oh, please, let's take a look," Celeste said excitedly to the boy who smiled up at her in return. The boy led us through the high grass toward the ruin. Along the way, he pointed to fallen stones which bore chiseled lion's heads, leaves, and flowers. I could not help but notice the snakes, many very large, lying on the stones soaking up the last of the sunlight.

"There are snakes everywhere," I commented to Sal, motioning toward the copper, almost yellow, colored snakes lying on the rocks.

The boy followed my glance and stopped. He motioned to the snakes and began explaining.

"These are temple snakes," Sal translated. "They used snakes during the healing rituals in worship of Asclepius. The temple is gone, but its snakes remain. They are not venomous. In fact, his grandmother still puts a snake in his bed when he is sick. He says it stays in the bed with him until he is well then crawls away."

The boy plucked one of the smaller snakes from a stone. Celeste took a step backward. He handed the creature, which wiggled to be free of his grasp, to me.

I extended my hand. The boy set the snake in my palm. The small creature curled into a ball and lifted its small head as if to look at me.

The boy smiled up at me and spoke.

Sal translated, "He says it wants to help you."

I looked at the little creature. "Sorry, but I think it will take longer than you have," I said, gently setting the creature back down on one of the warm stones.

The lad grinned and led onward. We moved into the temple and travelled the ruined hallways of the ancient hospital. Like any other English child, I had wandered around my share of ruined medieval haunts, but this was totally different. The structure was ancient. It both awed and unnerved me. I remembered feeling the same magical sensation the first time I'd flown over Stonehenge.

The boy chatted, Sal occasionally translating details of interest. I was mostly quiet as I absorbed the enormity of the experience. I understood then why Richard Payne Knight and the others wanted to haul the ancient world back to London. There was something magical about being able to touch the past. I reached out to feel the stone walls, my fingertips stroking the rough stones. How many people had come before me to this ancient place? What had they been searching for? I closed my eyes, just for a moment, and tried to envision the place as a bustling place of healing. The thought of it touched me deeply.

The boy led us to a part of the wall that was lined with deep niches. In one niche, a working fountain poured water from an image of Pan into a half-moon shaped basin. The lad scooped up a drink with his cupped hand, encouraged us all to do the same, and then waved us onward.

We all drank, Celeste muttering a little prayer to Pan, and then Sal and Celeste followed the boy toward the eastern side of the terrace, closer to the cypress grove over which the *Bacchus* hovered. I sat on the stone retaining wall around the spring.

I waved to Sal. "I'll catch up," I called.

He nodded.

It was terribly hot in the late afternoon sun. My stomach was feeling nauseous. I swore to myself I would never take an injection of morphine again. A breeze coming off the sea cut the heat, but I was sweating nonetheless. I took off my cap, dipped my hand in the water, and mopped down the back of my neck and splashed water on my face. The startlingly cool water had a minty taste, and I could smell fresh mint in the air. I looked around to see both mint and basil growing in large clumps near the fountain. I took another drink of water, wet my face, and put my cap back on.

I then followed the direction toward which I had seen the boy lead Sal and Celeste.

I worked my way back through the ruins, passing through the arched hallways of the ancient structure, listening for Sal's voice. I found myself in an area the boy had not yet shown to us. I was in the courtyard of a temple. At one end of the temple were the remains of a sculpture. Its body was charred, and its head and arms were missing. I got a sick feeling in my stomach. I approached the sculpture to see that is was, in fact, the sculpture of a woman. Was this all that was left of the Aphrodite? I looked upward and caught sight of the bow of the *Bacchus*. If the kaleidoscope's coordinates were exact, then this was not the statue we hunted. Our statue would be east of here. I looked around to see a set of crumbled stairs leading downward into a mostly collapsed hallway that led underground-and east. I went to the stairwell. Someone had cleared the fallen rock. If I kneeled down, I could enter the ruin. That is, if I wanted to enter. Then I noticed one of the smaller golden colored Aesculapian snakes working its way over the rocks into the underground passage. The space looked tight and dark. The snake turned and looked toward me, pausing for several moments before it slithered into the darkness.

"Fantastic," I muttered.

Someone had left a small white candle at the entrance. A fellow opium eater and chemist who lived on the Strand had given me a small box of his experimental sulphur timbers which I always carried. I struck up my nerve, lit the candle, and entered the underground passage.

My imagination had me going, and I expected the place to be squirming with snakes. To my luck, only the small, golden snake was moving on the ground before me. The place had suffered at the passage of the hands of time. Rubble was everywhere. The roots of trees overhead had grown down the hallway walls. Many of the walls had completely caved in. Yet I could still see some of the ancient beauty of the place. On one wall, I saw the faded colors of a still-striking painting of a goddess in an ocean setting. Where the soil had not encroached, small white tiles and mosaic patterns appeared on the floor. The passage was dark and winding. Small rooms, many entirely filled by earth, sat just off the hallway. One room, which had remained untouched by time, had a number of stone bathing tubs. I followed the hallway until it reached a "T". I flashed the candle around before me and worried about getting lost. The flame's light caught the glowing scales of the snake, which had turned left.

"I guess you're leading," I said, knowing just how crazy I sounded, and followed along.

Here the ruins were even more collapsed. In order to follow the serpent, I had to climb over a tall pile of rubble. I had just about made up my mind that I'd had enough risking my neck looking for an old piece of stone when I saw light ahead. Thinking the temple wall must be open to the outside, I went forward.

A golden hue illuminated the end of the hallway. The glow bobbed on the hallway wall, almost as if it were sunlight refracted by water. The temple snake kept a steady path toward the light.

I turned at the end of the hall and sucked in my breath in awe. The temple was not open to the outside light. Instead, a statue, shimmering brilliantly from the dusting of gold that covered it, filled the room with liquid light. The statue was celestial, but it was not the statue I sought. I immediately understood that I was in the temple room of the god Asclepius. The statue in gold was the god of healing.

Boasting a broad chest, curly hair, and draped robes, Asclepius was an imposing figure. He leaned against a staff around which two snakes had entwined. The golden dust on him gave the state a lifelike hue. At Asclepius' feet, water poured from the open mouth of a marble serpent into a basin. The snake climbed up the statue, twisting around the god's staff, until its head rested on the god's shoulder.

I took off my hat and knelt before the statue. Given my upbringing, I was not a religious girl. And I had never before sensed the divine except at the edge of an opium high. In those moments, where I sometimes lingered too long, the wind of the otherworld had blown ever so lightly upon me. Standing there, however, in that ancient place, I felt... something. The forgotten god's eyes, still outlined with faded paint, seemed to look down at me. And they seemed to pity.

I leaned my head against the basin and wept. At once, every terror I carried inside of me welled up and wanted to be let loose. I wanted to be rid of my mother. I wanted to be rid of Nicolette. I wanted to be rid of Mr. Fletcher and Mr. Oleander. I wanted to be rid of the drinking, and the opium, and the emptiness. I wanted a real life. I wanted to be something different. Couldn't I be Lily Stargazer, airship racer, but not have to be an opium eater? Couldn't I have just one man in my life who loved only me? And couldn't that person be Sal, who I knew in my heart, I loved? Why had I always let others' decisions unmake me? Why did I have to feel so broken?

I felt stupid sitting in that place weeping like a child. I tried to pull myself together, but I couldn't. I looked up at the old god, and in that moment, I had the strongest hallucination of my life. The god leaned down, cupped water from the fountain inside his hand, and put the drink to my lips. I sipped the water, startled by the warmth I felt from the statue, as if it were flesh. The water, ice cold, chilled my throat. I felt its coolness slide down my body to my stomach. I closed my eyes. The god then put his wet hand on my forehead, spoke a word I did not understand, and stood again.

In that moment, I knew I had to stop running from myself. It was time to accept the past for what it was and move on. I had to quit my habits. It was time to have a real life.

I took a deep breath and opened my eyes. I was startled to see that the room around me was dark save the small candle I had brought with me. The gold on Asclepius was gone. I stood and wiped the tears from my eyes. I lifted the candle and looked at the statue. Faded paint, now just a shadow, had once given color to his lips and shaded to his eyes. Otherwise, now, he was only marble. The room was dark as night, and the snake that had led me there was gone.

$$\bullet\!-\!\!\bullet$$

From the other end of the underground temple, I heard Sal's voice. I lifted the small candle and went back to the hallway. Before I left, I looked back once more at Asclepius. I was not certain what had happened, what I had seen, but I knew something within me felt different. I'd had my share of drug-induced hallucinations, but this was not the same thing. The tangy taste of the cold water still lingered in my mouth, yet the basin at Asclepius' feet was dry. I smiled at the marble statue, now seemingly cold and dead, and went after Sal-and Aphrodite.

Trying not to stumble over the shifted stones, I followed bits of light toward the other end of the temple. I could hear Sal's and Celeste's voices but could not make out their words. The hall turned toward the east. As I got closer, I noticed that the stones on the walls were carved with the anemone flower, apples, doves, and swans.

I then heard Celeste exclaim excitedly.

I entered the room behind them. Sal and the boy were holding up lanterns as they gazed at was, without a doubt, the Aphrodite of Kos. While time had worn away her paint, she was a statue with classic beauty. Celeste had said the Kos Aphrodite was draped, but it seemed that Praxiteles had done little to hide the erotic curves of the Goddess of Love. His carved draping of the goddess accented her round hips, full breasts, and long legs. Her lips were slightly parted as she gazed at a mirror she held in her left hand. In her other hand, which was carved to appear to hang loosely before her pubis, she held a marble replica of the kaleidoscope.

Sal turned. He gazed at me with a look of wonderment in his eyes.

"Chasing Aphrodite," Celeste whispered with both awe and frustration in her voice. "All my life I have been chasing Aphrodite."

"Well, in Kos, we have found her," I said, my eyes still locked on Sal's.

Celeste, just realizing I was there, looked at me. "This is the Kos Aphrodite. The Knidos is not here. What should we do now?"

I looked at Sal. "Indeed. Now what?"

CHAPTER 23

F our hours later we were sitting in the moonlight enjoying dinner with the young boy's family. The small boy, whose name was Selim, had insisted we come home with him. After some debate as to whether or not it was safe—for them or us—we agreed. It turned out that the family owned a vast olive and almond farm. Their rustic yet beautiful villa sat nestled into the hillside.

We had stayed in the temple with the Kos Aphrodite until dark. Sal, who had studied the sculpture with great scrutiny, had fallen into near complete silence as his brilliant mind went to work. In the temple, he had examined the carving of the kaleidoscope, the Aphrodite's mirror, her face, and even her bracelet. He took notes while Celeste sat in prayer at the base of the Aphrodite's feet. It was unlike Sal to be so silent. Sal loved to teach, to narrate as he worked, but he'd lost himself in the puzzle of the kaleidoscope. I sat on a small patch of an ancient mosaic and watched him. I, too, was distracted, but by my hallucination. I felt emotionally exhausted. I gazed up at the Aphrodite. The statue was beautiful, but in the end, it was just a statue. Her cold marble eyes gazed into the mirror she held. I wondered how she saw herself. I put my head on my knees and tried not to think about how I saw myself.

After it had grown dark, we left the temple and walked with the boy to his farm. The child led the way, clicking at his goats as he blazed a path. Sal took my hand and kissed it gently.

"My Lily," he whispered in the darkness.

The small act almost made me burst into tears.

At the boy's farm we were met with great curiosity. Once Sal explained that we'd come to look at the ruins, we were welcomed. The large family, from which the small boy was only one of many children, was a loud, happy, and excited crew. The father, Yunus, even knew a little English. The women of the group eyed me with stunned curiosity when Sal explained to them that I had piloted the airship to Kos.

"You are flying that ship?" Yunus asked. He gazed toward the horizon where the red lamps on the *Bacchus* were still visible.

I nodded. "I'm a pilot."

Yunus looked thoughtful but said nothing more.

The older boys, a good looking lot with dark hair, had clustered around Celeste and were eyeing the courtesan hungrily, inexplicably pulled toward her. Their mother shooed them away.

"Please," the boy's mother, Emine, had said, then led us to their el fresco dining terrace under the stars.

She seated us at the long dinner table. Soon Emine and five girls—no doubt Selim's sisters—had loaded down the table with wooden bowls filled with olives and platters of feta cheese, lamb roasted with rosemary, and a large round of bread with a yogurt and oil porridge baked into its center.

Yunus led the table in a toast. "To our guests," he called.

"To Aphrodite," Celeste added.

Yunus laughed. "Yes! To Afrodit!"

Everyone at the table cheered and soon we were delighted to a feast.

As we ate, the discussion turned to the ruins. As it turned out, the shrine of the Kos Aphrodite had recently been damaged. Originally, the shrine had boasted a domed roof with a skylight. A tremor a few years earlier had caused much of the roof to collapse.

"But we protected her. We laid planks over the roof. We keep her safe," Yunus explained. He was proud of the statue. It was part of Koan history. From how many villages just like this one had the Dilettanti simply come in and taken what they wanted? What right did they have?

"This opening in the roof, how large was it?" Sal asked.

The man stood. "Like this," he said, extending his arms to make a circle. "Like a barrel," he added.

"Was it directly above the statue?"

Yunus nodded. "When rain came, or sun, it fell only on her. It was beautiful."

I looked at Sal. His mind was busy, but he put his arm around me and pulled me close.

It was a beautiful night. The outside patio where the dinner table sat was partially enclosed by a wisteria arbor. The sweet purple blossoms perfumed the air. I was leaning my head on Sal's shoulder, fighting off a headache, and watching the couple's two smallest children playing with a nearly feral kitten when Emine asked a question.

"My wife... she is wondering if you have children," Yunus asked.

Sal looked down at me and stroked my cheek. "Not yet," he said then kissed me on the forehead.

Before his answer would have either amused or terrified me. I gazed deeply into his eyes. His gaze was loving and serious. Things between Sal and I had changed forever. Sal smiled then turned back to Yunus.

"Does your wife have a looking glass?" Sal asked him.

"Yes," he replied curiously.

"May I purchase it from you? I need something at least this big," Sal said then framed his hands to show he was after a mirror no smaller than the lid of a hat box.

The man exchanged a few words with his wife who looked perplexed. After a moment, she shrugged and went back into the villa. She returned with a wood framed oval mirror that looked like she'd taken it from the wall. She handed it to Sal.

Sal looked it over, nodded affirmatively, then set it aside. He dug into his pocket then slid a very generous amount of lira across the table to Yunus. The farmer began to protest, but Sal waved his hand gracefully to dismiss any argument and said nothing more.

It was not long after that we decided to head back to the ship. Yunus led us through the darkness to the ancient healing temple and our airship. When we arrived, he'd looked up at the *Bacchus* with wide-eyed fascination.

"Come have a look," I offered.

I could see from the starry look in his eyes that he truly wanted to see the ship, but he was cautious. And in the end, maybe a man with a home full of children was wise to be cautious. "No, but thank you. Please come see us again before you leave," Yunus said.

"Thank you for everything," Celeste said, kissing Yunus on both cheeks, causing him to blush. She climbed back into the airship.

Sal and I too parted ways with the kind man who stood in the dark holding a lantern aloft to illuminate our steps up the ladder. Sal, climbing up behind me, hauled the mirror on his back.

Once on board, I leaned over the rail and waved to Yunus. "Thank you," I called.

The man waved, and I watched his lantern bob through the night back toward his villa.

Roni's crew, who had been sleeping when we returned, looked relieved to see us alive. Sal let them know we would be anchored in this location for a while longer. They seemed satisfied with that and then went back to sleep.

Celeste went to the bow of the ship and leaned against the bulwark trying to catch a glimpse of the temple on the other side of the trees. Sal headed into our quarters with the mirror. I went to the wheelstand and checked all the instruments then climbed into the basket to check the burners. Everything seemed to be in working order. I busied myself to keep my mind off of what was really bothering me. It had been several hours since I'd last taken any laudanum. And I could feel it. I climbed back down to the gondola and sat down, my back against the wheelstand. I gazed up at the starry sky. My head was aching, and my hands had started shaking two hours before. I didn't want to take more laudanum. The craving was horrible. I knew that if I waited longer, I would start sweating and feeling nauseous. I also knew that if I ate opium I would feel better, and I would forget again. But for the first time, I did not want to just forget the past. I wanted to be finished with it. If I kept burying it under opium, it would never end. I gazed up at the stars. The sky above the ancient world looked different from the sky above the London. Somehow the sky above Kos seemed wiser.

I heard Sal return from our cabin with a jangle of instruments. He lit several lanterns, and I heard the clang of metal as he set equipment down on the deck of the ship. Curious, I rose slowly and went to see what he was doing.

Sal had laid Emine's mirror down on the deck of the ship and was looking over his notes.

"What is it?" I asked.

Sal took out a drawing compass, centered it on the mirror, and began to sketch out an oval.

"The Aphrodite's mirror," Sal said as he worked. He then opened his tinker's kit and removed a number of sharp looking precision instruments. "The mirror… the way she holds it in her hand… it was not angled to reflect her face. I didn't understand why until Yunus mentioned the opening above the statue."

Celeste had come up behind me and was watching Sal.

"What is she looking at?" I asked.

"Indeed, a good question, my Lily. At first I thought there used to be something on the ceiling. But now I don't think so. I think there is something else reflected in the mirror."

"The sky?" Celeste asked.

"The stars," I said.

Sal looked up. "The stars," he repeated and turned back to his instruments. With a fluid circular motion, Sal cut an oval out of the mirror. It was the same size and shape as the looking glass Aphrodite held. He stood, holding the mirror in his hand, and shined it at the night's sky. Celeste and I gathered behind him and looked up. It reflected the stars.

"We need to go back into the temple. Tonight. But we need that roof removed," Sal said.

Celeste smiled. "I'll wake up the crew."

CHAPTER 24

An hour later we were once again inside the temple of the Kos Aphrodite. Above ground, Roni's crew worked carefully in the darkness to remove the timbers over the statue's head.

"I feel guilty," I told Sal. "We need to put it back just the way Yunus made it."

"Don't worry. We'll make it right."

While the crew removed the planks, Sal carefully placed his cut looking glass onto Aphrodite's mirror. It was a perfect fit.

We waited breathlessly as the men removed the last of the timbers. Moonlight slanted into the temple. It showered the goddess with celestial light.

Celeste snubbed out her candle to take in the view. "Beautiful," she whispered.

She was right. The moonlight, cascading over the pure white marble, made the statue glow with other-worldly light.

Once the ceiling was open to the sky, the three of

us crowded around the Aphrodite like curious children. We all tried to see into the mirror.

Sal chuckled. "We must see what she would see," Sal said. "At this angle, I only see your face, my Lily."

"What better thing is there to see in Aphrodite's mirror than your true love?" Celeste asked.

Sal laughed. "Well put."

He then went behind the statue, gazed over her shoulder, and looked into the mirror. Tall as he was, once he balanced on the statue's pedestal, he was able to follow the sculpture's gaze.

"Lily, please find the star chart in my satchel," Sal instructed.

I dug through his bag. I pulled out maps, blueprints, and a variety of unusual instruments. I even found what felt like an enormous piece of rolled silk cloth.

"What's this?" I asked.

Sal glanced quickly toward the bundle. "Just something I'm working on."

I set the bundle aside and finally pulled out the chart. "Here it is," I said, and handed it to him, "but Sal, we don't even know what time of year or time of night we should be looking in the mirror. Won't that determine what is reflected?"

"Yes, but the mirror only catches a small band of stars no matter," Sal said then drew a set of parallel lines across the chart, boxing in the stars the mirror could possibly reflect. "Of course, we also have to calculate precession. The sky overhead looks different from when Eudoxus made the kaleidoscope."

Sal climbed down and set his star chart on the dusty floor. Celeste leaned over the chart while Sal began pulling instruments from his bag.

I gazed up at the Aphrodite. I wanted to look into the mirror as she saw it. As I searched for a foothold on the pedestal to push myself up, I glanced down the hallway toward the temple of Asclepius. Again I saw golden light emanating from the room. I stopped for a moment and looked. Then I got an idea. I climbed up and looked into the mirror. The star garden overhead twinkled brightly.

"I can make some adjustments to my instruments to get a rough estimate on precession. I believe the symbols carved around the frame of the mirror are intended to show us when, seasonally, we are supposed to look. Her bracelet seems to direct one to the signs of the zodiac. I believe it is key to knowing where in the night's sky-" Sal was saying when I cut him off.

"The god Asclepius... does he have his own constellation?" I gazed back down the hallway toward the golden light emanating from the other temple.

Sal stopped. "Yes... we call him Ophiuchus today. It can be seen in the summer sky."

Sal rose and looked up through the open slats in the roof. "It is there," Sal said. "Do you see Ophiuchus' bright star? That's Rasalhagues, the figurehead. Look," Sal said then drew a box in the sky with his finger.

I looked into the Aphrodite's mirror.

"Is it there? Can you see it in the mirror?" Celeste asked.

I stood up on my tiptoes and looked over the statue's shoulder. Trying to follow her gaze as best I could, I looked into the mirror. "It's there. It's a little out of alignment, but it's there."

"Celeste, give Lily the kaleidoscope," Sal said with urgency in his voice.

Celeste dug into her bag, pulled out the kaleidoscope, and handed it to me.

"Aim it right on Ophiuchus, Lily. Try angling your gaze the same way the Aphrodite is holding the mirror," Sal advised.

I put the kaleidoscope to my eye and leaned awkwardly against the statue trying to get a look. At first the kaleidoscope showed only faint hues of red and blue. After a moment, I began to see flecks of clear colors filtering through.

"Try to catch the Rasalhagues, the head of the constellation," Sal advised.

I pulled the kaleidoscope from my eye, took a look at the constellation with the naked eye again, then adjusted the kaleidoscope. Sal gripped my waist, supporting me so I could lean back safely and look up. Once the angle was just right, the colors rolled into place.

"A blue sea. Something that looks like two harbors, one large and one small. A temple near the larger harbor? A theater. And in the distance, in the water, a small island. The figurehead star is shining above the small island. It's a landscape."

"But where?" Celeste asked.

I crawled down and let Celeste take my place. Sal and I supported her so she could look.

"Oh my god," she said when she had finally gotten the colors aligned. "Oh my god. That's Knidos! That's the twin harbors of Knidos!"

"Are you sure?" Sal asked.

"I am, but I don't understand. My order... the Dilettanti... we've been all over Knidos. And Temenos reportedly moved her. She isn't there."

"Well, she is, after all, the Aphrodite *of Knidos*," Sal said as he helped Celeste down.

I gazed down the hallway toward Asclepius' shrine. The room had gone dark, and my head didn't ache anymore.

❧

Since Knidos was only a few miles from Kos, Sal and I convinced an exuberant Celeste to wait until morning to take off. Even after Sal and I had gone into our crew cabin, I still heard Celeste moving around on the deck of the *Bacchus*. She was singing a low chant that sounded like prayer. I envied her deep love of and attachment to the divine. Sadly, it was an attachment I'd never felt with anyone or anything.

But that night, as Sal and I got ready to sleep, I

could not take my eyes off him. I don't know if it was the influence of Aphrodite, but something between us had changed, permanently. When Sal moved to touch me, to stoke my hair, to gaze into my eyes, I could feel I was in love with him. And from the expression on his face, I could see he loved me too. I rose and gently lifted his shirt over his head, pressing my face against his chest. I heard his heart beating and could smell the sweet scent of sandalwood on his skin. When he wrapped his strong arms around me, I was overcome. I reached up to touch his face, to stroke his cheek, to pour myself into the depths of his eyes. Every fiber in my soul called out for him; it was a feeling I'd never had before. Sal and I had been lovers for two years. When we made love, I'd always sensed there was something special about him, something special between us. But in reality, maybe I'd never made love to Sal, or anyone else, before. Maybe really loving someone had always lain just beyond my reach.

Gently, Sal helped me remove my clothes, and he lay me down carefully, entwining his fingers with mine. He kissed me slowly, moving gently, moving like we were more than lovers. My hands stroked the muscles on his back, touching his skin, smelling the fragrance in his hair. We were patient. We kissed each other, feeling one another's body in a way we had never done before. My heart felt like it would burst. And when we finally made love, Sal's eyes locked on mine, and I was surprised to feel tears trailing down my cheeks.

"My Lily," he whispered in the dim candlelight. "My Lily."

I kissed his wrists, his fingers, and began to dream what life might be like from now on, now that I'd let Aphrodite have her way with me.

❦

CHAPTER 25

My head was ringing when I woke. Despite my earlier hopes that somehow I had been permanently cured of my opium cravings by the experience in the temple of Asclepius, that was not the case. I was overcome with nausea and was soon ungraciously vomiting into the bedpan. My head ached like someone had hit me with an anvil.

"Are you all right?" Sal asked quietly as he wet a cloth and handed it to me.

I dampened my face and tried to calm my stomach. My face flushed red with embarrassment. It was one thing to face your habits alone; it was another thing to have someone you admired see you at your lowest.

"I haven't had any opium in a while," I confessed.

Sal poured me a glass of water. I drank it greedily as I shifted my hand through my satchel. I'd almost finished the bottle of laudanum Byron had given me back in London. I held the bottle of amber colored liquid in my hand. If I quit in that moment, I would be unfit to fly the ship. I had tried to break the habit before. It would take a week, at least, to feel even a little human.

"I'm going to stop. Soon," I said and looked up at Sal.

He kissed me on the forehead and pulled me close to him.

I took two drops of laudanum and closed my eyes, waiting for the liquid to work its magic. I pressed my head against his chest and listened to his heartbeat. Within five minutes, my headache started to pass. Sighing heavily, I opened my eyes and gazed out at the sunrise. The sky was cherry red with streaks of gold and lavender.

"We all have difficulties we must pass," Sal said quietly as he stroked my hair. "For many years I could not understand why my father, my brother, did not accept me, what I lacked. But I learned it was not in my hand to change the past. Sometimes your world must get turned upside down for you to truly see yourself."

I looked up at him. "Never think of yourself as lacking. There is no one else like you in this world."

"And what about you, my Lily? What drives someone so loving, so gifted, to the bottom of this bottle?" he asked, taking the vial of laudanum from my hand.

"I guess I'm just... running... hiding."

"From what?"

"From," I said, and then I didn't know what to say. From myself? From the past? From that tender place inside me that thought I was so worthless I could just be trashed in a river. My eyes started to water. How could I explain it to him? Should I tell him what had happened?

"Ahh, Lily," he said, pulling me tight. "The past does not have to define you."

I sniffed and wiped my nose with my sleeve. "You should listen to your own advice."

Sal chuckled. "You're right."

"Well," I said, and taking a breath, I tried to pull myself together, "maybe the Goddess of Love will help us. I think Celeste has been pacing the deck since the sun rose. Shall we see Knidos?"

Sal nodded.

I dressed and got the crew up and going. We set sail. First we guided the *Bacchus* to Yunus' farm. We found him and his sons working in the olive grove. His boys clustered around him. They stood staring, eyes wide, up at the airship.

Sal and I went down to bid the farmer farewell.

Yunus removed his hat and shook Sal's hand. "Best of luck on your journey," he said smiling. He waved up to Celeste who leaned over the rail of the ship.

"Thank you for your hospitality. May your family be blessed," Sal said with a slight bow.

"Thank you for sharing your ruins with us," I added. "But please... I don't mean to alarm you... please consider hiding the Aphrodite... and the Asclepius. My countrymen—you may have heard what they are doing in Athens—they will take your statues if they find them."

The man looked at me as if he had not clearly understood every word I had spoken but got my warning nonetheless. He nodded stoically.

With that, we made our way back to the *Bacchus*, Sal pausing to ruffle little Selim's hair once more. Once we were aboard, I set the ship's coordinates to Knidos, and the propeller kicked hard as we made our way out to sea.

"What did you mean, the Asclepius?" Sal asked.

"There was another shrine near the Aphrodite. It was a temple of the healing god. Didn't you see it?"

Sal shook his head.

"I stumbled upon it. It was… remarkable."

As we made our way toward Knidos, Sal studied the notes he had taken. He set his star chart, astrolabe, and sextant out before him. He was swinging a pendulum over the chart.

"The carvings in the mirror indicated that we should look in the mirror during the summer months, so we are lucky there. The bracelet gives an orientation in the zodiac, but precession has shifted placement in the sky. Ophiuchus was just out of alignment. The zodiac would have made shifts from Eudoxus' time, but I cannot be certain how much. My talent with astronomy is rather limited," Sal said.

I grinned. What Sal thought of as limited likely

bested many of Oxford's brightest. "Once we get to Knidos, we'll know if we are in the right place or not."

"Have you ever met the Scotsman Alexander Jamison?" Sal asked. "He stops by Tinkers' Hall from time to time. He gifted me this copy of his *Celestial Atlas*. It is a remarkable piece of work."

"Isn't he the school master? The little mathematician married to that prudish travel writer?"

Sal laughed. "Yes, that's him. Here is his plate of your Ophiuchus," Sal said, showing me the engraved image of the god Asclepius. Jamison had drawn the god standing astride in the evening sky. Between his muscular legs, Asclepius gripped a massive serpent by the head and tail.

"That serpent... seems the Scotsman doth protest too much."

Sal laughed. "Most Scotsmen do."

"Don't let Angus hear you say that."

"I wouldn't dream of it. That lengthy constellation is Serpens."

"Serpens?"

"Asclepius clutches the serpent, conquering it. You see, my Lily, with determination, all monsters can be overcome. It is written in the stars."

"One can hope."

"I can see Knidos!" Celeste called to us from the prow of the ship where she had perched since we'd set sail.

Kos and Knidos were not far from one another,

and soon the twin harbors of the ancient city of Knidos came into view. Sal joined Celeste at the front of the ship. A strong wind blew across the Aegean. Celeste, her long hair flying in the wind, looked every bit the part of the goddess she sought. A sharp wind came in and snatched the white silk scarf she had tied around her neck. It floated in the air and fell toward the blue-green waters of the sea below.

The Knidian coast was rocky with high cliffs pocked by caves. Intermittently, we also saw sweet secret coves boasting sandy beaches and jewel colored waters. The landscape had waving golden grasses, dusty earth, tall Cypress trees, and thick green shrubbery. I sensed the ancient path of the sea captains who had come before me as I guided the *Bacchus* over the small, eastern Knidian harbor. Knidos was built in part on an island and in part on the mainland. A land bridge separated the two, making two harbors: one smaller and eastern, the other larger and more western. I envisioned the ancient warships docked in the lapis colored waters.

The island part of Knidos was rocky and shrub covered. Near the land bridge connecting it to the mainland, I could see the ancient stone walls of Praxiteles' city. The concave shape of an amphitheater was visible as were many other ruins. It looked just as I had seen in the kaleidoscope.

I yearned to look over and see more, but the

Bacchus, struggling in the harsh sea winds, demanded my attention.

"We need to bring the *Bacchus* down!" I yelled, gesturing to the balloonman. He nodded and began to release warm air from inside the balloon. We dropped altitude. I navigated the ship in, looking for a spot somewhere out of the harsh breeze. Once I had gotten the ship out of the wind shear, the jostling eased. I lowered the *Bacchus* below the mountain range and settled into a calm spot just east of the ancient theater. There, the *Bacchus* seemed to find a remarkably calm harbor from the wind.

"Let's hover here until we see what kind of company we are in for," I said. The crew and I anchored the ship while Sal and Celeste began packing their bags. To my surprise, Sal pulled out his sidearm.

"Bring yours as well," he told me.

He was right. If the Dilettanti thought we were after the Aphrodite, they may certainly be waiting for us in Knidos. Sal dropped the rope ladder. I grabbed an anchor line, and holding tight, leapt off the rail of the ship. I slid down the rope twenty feet to the ground.

My boots hit the dusty earth with a thud. Below my feet were marble floor stones. Green grass shot up from between the cracks. Behind us, the rocky remains of the ancient city wall were nestled against the mountainside. Directly ahead of us, a sandy bar jutted out between the mainland and the island.

"Cape Krio," Celeste said as she joined me,

motioning to the island. She rubbed her hands. Her palms were red from gripping the ladder.

"That's not the island we saw in the kaleidoscope," I said.

Celeste shook her head. "No, that was east of here."

Sal joined us. He had been talking to the crew of the *Bacchus* who now stood, rifles in hand, on the deck of the ship.

We scanned the horizon. We spotted two tan colored tents on the other side of the land bridge on Cape Krio. No one seemed to be moving around. This was either a very good thing or very a bad thing.

"Here we go," I muttered.

"Let's be friendly," Celeste suggested.

"Let's be cautious," Sal corrected.

We headed across the sandy land bridge. Around us, the landscape was dotted with low green scrub and creeping purple flowers. Although I expected I would be shot at any moment, I could not help but be taken with the landscape. I don't think I had ever seen a more beautiful sight in all my life. The ancient city, like the Asclepeion, was in complete disarray, but it seemed that more had survived in Knidos than had in Kos. In fact, the owner of the tents seemed to have set up camp near the ruins of an ancient watchtower at the entrance of the eastern harbor. We crossed onto Cape Krio and followed the old wall toward the tents. As we neared the camp, I began to smell roasting meat and could hear someone singing.

Sal pulled his weapon.

As we came upon the tents, we found two very sleepy looking Ottoman workers laboring over the campfire. Both men wore a red fez, a traditional Ottoman cap, and loose, ballooning pants. Their clothing looked rather disheveled. Apparently they had recently woken. Both men stood bolt upright.

"Professor," one of them called, and my stomach dropped to my boots. Sal gripped his gun harder.

"Ja, ja, was ist los?" we heard someone reply from inside one of the tents.

A moment later, a very old man with small, round glasses and a white moustache that curled at the corners emerged from the tent. He eyed us with great curiosity.

"Humm… Italiener?" he asked Sal.

"Ja, und Engländer," Sal replied.

The old man blew air through his lips. "Engländer," he said like curse. "Do you all speak English?" he asked.

"Yes," Sal replied. "We don't mean to bother you… Professor, no? We've come to see the ruins and wanted to ensure we were not imposing."

The man looked at Sal's gun, his eyes quickly darting to my own weapon. "Imposing. Expecting trouble, were you?"

Sal shrugged. "We did not know what to expect."

The old man laughed a long and hearty laugh and then looked Celeste and I over with great curiosity.

"Nice company you keep. Come. Have tea. These Ottoman's will drink tea when it's a hundred degrees, but it is morning and not yet hot, and this old man would like to sit and have a look at your beautiful comrades. I'm Professor Herzog," he introduced.

Sal smiled. "It is our pleasure, Professor. I am Salvatore, my wife Beatrice, and my sister Viola."

The professor smiled and holding open the tent door flap, gestured for us to go within. Sal holstered his gun, took my hand, and we entered. Inside, the old man had strung up maps and sketches of Knidos. He had collected a fabulous array of marble pieces. Picks, shovels, and an odd looking pole with a disc on one end leaned in the corner of the tent. Large boxes were stacked to the top of the tent. On one table, a marble hand sat under a magnifying glass. The hand clutched a fist full of arrows. On another table were about a dozen palm sized figurines.

"I've been hunting the sun god," the old man said. "In fact, I have finally revealed his temple."

"Apollo?" Celeste asked, raising her eyebrow. The Ottoman workers poured us tea into small, glass cups.

The professor smiled at her. "Ah, a woman educated in the classics. Yes, my dear, but how he has eluded me! I have been on this cove for the last ten years hunting him down, fending of the British who would have me kicked out of this dig. But I have convinced them I am simply an old man on a tired pursuit, and they leave me in peace. Besides, all they want is the Aphrodite. What do they care of my Apollo?"

The three of us exchanged glances.

"To be honest, I expected to find an Englishman in your tent, Professor," Sal said then, sipping the hot tea.

I pick up the cup, nearly burning my fingers. "Bloody hell," I grumbled under my breath.

"Like this, dear," the Professor told me, demonstrating the correct grip as he held his glass with his fingertips by the rim. "You've just missed them. They packed it in two days ago and headed back to Constantinople. Good riddance. No offense," he added, smiling at me.

"None taken."

"Would you mind, Professor, if we have a look around?" Celeste asked.

"My dear, with eyes like that, all you should do is look around," he said with a laugh. "Drink up. I'll give you a tour," Professor Herzog said and then hurried us along.

We polished off the hot tea, which made me sweat in the early morning heat, and headed outside.

"Come, I'll take you to the shrine of Apollo," the Professor said, taking a walking stick with one hand, and his strange disked device in the other. "Where is your ship—Gott, is that an airship?"

"We travel in style," Sal said jokingly.

The old man laughed a long, hard laugh. After a

moment, it became clear that it wasn't Sal's comment that had amused the professor.

"Professor?" Sal asked.

"Ah, my Italian friend, I laugh because you have docked your ship—isn't that the wine god on its balloon—directly above the ancient temple of Dionysus. I guess the old boy knows where he belongs," the old man said and led us back across the land bridge.

As we walked, I eyed the landscape. I was trying to find the image I had seen in the kaleidoscope. It seemed that the image I had picked up in the lens was oriented from the land side of Knidos. As we hiked up the hill along the seaside to the shrine of Apollo, I shaded my eyes with my hand and looked out at the water. The kaleidoscope had clearly indicated there should be a small island just off shore, but I saw almost nothing on the horizon. All around me, however, pieces of the ancient city were found in plenty.

"Here is one of the east-west roads through the city," the old man said as he pointed his walking stick toward a flat area carved into the mountainside. "And a row of houses. Some shops are still under the dirt along there. No doubt the Dilettanti will dig them out."

Sal and I exchanged a glance.

The old man, who was soon breathing hard and sweating profusely, led us to a section of wall quite near the sea cliff looking out over the ocean. Below us, on the city side, a pit had been dug into the earth. Marble stone floors and a pedestal had been unearthed.

"Here we are," the professor said, flourishing his hand toward the dig. "Besides me and my workers, you are the first eyes to see the temple of Apollo in more than a thousand years," the old man said then, his voice rich with satisfaction. "Are you pleased?" he called, facing upward toward the bright morning sun. He turned back to us again. "Granted, not much to see, but once we get the earth moved there will be more!"

"Congratulations on your achievement," Celeste said with a smile. "It is quite moving."

"Moving indeed! Ten years on this cape and more years than I can say buried in the archives of my university chasing Apollo," the Professor said then took Celeste's hand. "I must say, my dear, my heart nearly gave out when I saw that old stone floor. It was like passion."

"Passion is something I understand well," she said flirtatiously. She then turned back to the dig. "It is like a miracle," she whispered.

"Yes, yes indeed," the Professor agreed.

"What led you to this location?" Sal asked him.

"This," the man said, patting the strange instrument he carried.

"I did indeed notice this device, Professor. What is it?" Sal asked.

"Ah, you see, it is a device of my own creation! I began to wonder if there was some way to sense the presence of marble structures, walls, temples, under the earth without having to dig. I realized I could find them if I look by vibration! I have employed the use of crystals in what I call my clockwork dowsing rod. The vibrations given off by raw earth opposed to the linear lines of cut stone, manmade objects, are different. Using crystals, I catch the resonance. As such, I found the structure."

"Quite amazing," Sal said. I noticed that several times Sal's hand had moved toward the device as the professor waved it about.

The old man, lost in his thoughts, had not even noticed. "I tried to assist the Brits, but they think they know better, mucking around in the mud. They are not even looking in the right place for their Aphrodite."

"How do you know?" I asked.

The old man laughed. "It is written in the *Erōtes* exactly where she can be found."

"On a hill above the harbor. Aphrodite Euploia, the lady of safe voyages, blesses the ships as they pass, and she can be seen from the sea. She has a rotunda, an open air temple, where laurel trees grow and fruits and flowers. It is a place where lovers meet and practice her art under the eyes of Apollo," Celeste said dreamily.

"Indeed, by Apollo, she has it," the old man said, smiling at Celeste appreciatively. "One would almost think you are an Aphrodite scholar. Now, young lady, if that is an accurate description of the temple, where would you look?"

"Somewhere high. At the seaside. Somewhere

visible from all around. Somewhere where laurel trees still grow."

"The Dilettanti have been digging this site since 1812, yet you've put it together with more logic than all those so-called experts combined!" he said and pinched her cheek.

Celeste grinned. "Do you know where the Aphrodite temple is?"

He smiled. "Come with me."

He led us away from the Apollo temple and upward, following the sea cliff, toward an impressive rockslide that had shifted from a nearby crag. We crawled carefully around the rocks until we were standing at the cliff's edge. It was a steep drop to the water below. I noticed that mature laurel trees dotted the location. A soft, warm breeze floated in.

"What better place from which to see the Aphrodite?" the old man said. "I nearly broke my neck trying, but I explored that heap with my dowsing rod. Looking. Just looking. And do you know what is under all the scree?" With his walking staff, the Professor drew a large circle in the dirt. "Something large, round, and manmade."

"The temple of Aphrodite?" Celeste more breathed than asked.

The old man shrugged. "What do I know? I am just an old man chasing Apollo. Let the Dilettanti take the next hundred years figure it out!" he said with a laugh.

I had to join him. British prattishness, of which I

was sometimes prone when it came to talking about racing, was an unflattering quality. I stared out at the sea. The view struck me. I recognized it immediately as the view from the kaleidoscope.

I nudged Sal. "Nice view," I said, looking out at the blue-green water.

Both he and Celeste turned. Celeste had been staring intently at the pile of rubble; her eyes had a far-away look. I imagined she had been envisioning the ancient temple of the goddess lying underneath. In a world where Catholics and Protestants burned one another at the stake every other hundred years, it was a dangerous thing to have a faith so far beyond the pale. Her faith revealed, Celeste surely would have gone to the stocks, glossy hair and all. Her eyes widened as she looked out to sea and realized that we were seeing the image from the kaleidoscope.

"Looks pretty clear out there. Any islands off-shore?" I asked. On the far horizon, Kos rose from the sea like a gray-green shadow.

"Just rocks. Not much to see. Except, of course, Aphrodite's fingers," the Professor said.

"Aphrodite's fingers?" Celeste asked. I could not help but hear the excitement in her voice.

"Just a pile of rocks, really. Five rocky fingers sticking out of the sea, waving" he said and wiggled his fingers. He then pointed toward the horizon. "North of the harbor. You can see it from here. Look," he added. And where he pointed, I just made out a small island that looked to be exactly where the kaleidoscope had indicated.

Celeste released a small, excited "Ahh!" but held herself in check.

I noticed then that the old man looked rather gray around the lips.

"Can we help you back? The heat is rising," I said.

"Ah, yes. We've been in a duel, Apollo and me. Either I'll find him, or his sun will kill me. Seems I am triumphant," the Professor said with a laugh.

Sal gently took the old man by the arm, and we walked back to his tent. Along the way, I noticed that there was a small sailboat docked in the harbor.

"Is that ship yours, Professor?" I asked.

"Yes, but I haven't used it in ages. I used to like to sail around. Lots of lovely beaches along the shoreline. Fit for the foam-born daughter herself," he said, patting Celeste on the arm.

Celeste raised an eyebrow at him.

"I hate to impose, but would you mind if we borrowed your boat? We would love to take a look at the shoreline, but the weather is too rough for the airship," I said.

"Have you got any ale on your dirigible?" the old man asked with a twinkle in his eyes.

I turned to Celeste.

"Yes, there should be some there," she said.

"Then you have a deal! The boat is yours to use.

Just bring the ale with you when you come by tonight for dinner. We'll drink to Apollo!"

"Of course," Sal said.

When we reached the tent, Sal helped lower the old man into a chair, and the Ottoman assistants came at once to remove his boots and give him water.

"Thank you for the tour. It was an honor," Celeste said, kissing him on the cheek.

"Ahh, you smell better than the Goddess of Love herself," the old man said, whisking a handful of Celeste's long locks toward his nose.

Celeste smiled and kissed the old man playfully once again, allowing him to stroke her hair once more before he let her go.

"We'll be back at sunset… with ale!" I said.

The professor was fanning himself with his hat. "Now, that is something to look forward to!"

We left the Professor's tent. It had grown extremely hot in the midday sun. The sea breeze cooled us to some degree, but there was little by way of shade in the ancient city.

"The boat… what do you have in mind, Lily?" Celeste asked.

"Well, it seems the Aphrodite is literally waving us in, but it will be practically impossible to explore by air," I said, knowing it was the truth. I scanned the teal colored waters. While the vista was striking, a lump rose up in my throat. I knew I had to try to put my fears aside. We were too close to stop now. Besides, we had a boat. It would be fine. It would be safe. I turned to Sal: "Can you sail?"

He shook his head. I was surprised. I guess I'd come to think that Sal knew everything.

"I can," Celeste said. Again, I was surprised. She caught my expression. "I grew up on an island," she explained.

"Well then, shall we set sail?" Sal asked.

Celeste looked out at the sea. "That's why we are here. Let's pray Aphrodite gives us safe voyage."

CHAPTER 26

While I clung to the boat and pretended I was not frightened to death of the water, Celeste showed a side of herself I'd never expected. Her hands moving quickly, she readied the small boat and guided it out of the Knidian harbor with finesse. The small white sail, discolored with age and disuse, flapped in the breeze. Part of me thought that even if Celeste had not known how to sail, she still would have helmed the ship. She was a woman on a quest that was nearing its end. In those moments, a person will risk anything to win what they love.

Sal panned his spyglass across the water as we set out of the harbor. We had not gone far when he spotted Aphrodite's fingers. "There," he said pointing. "I can see the rocks jutting out of the water."

Celeste adjusted the sail, and the small ship pushed through the waves.

I gazed down into the turquoise colored waters. You could see the sea bottom. Below, I saw the dark shapes of rocks and the quick movements of silver fish. The water was beautiful albeit terrifying.

It was not long until the rocky island came into view of the naked eye. To say it was an island was a bit of an exaggeration. In reality, it was five tall rocks sticking out of the water. Like a hand waving at the shoreline, the rocks really did look like fingers. The back of the hand seemed to face the sea, its dark black stones looking like knuckles. The palm faced the coast. The rocks looked like slim fingers jutting out at different angles.

Celeste guided the boat toward the rocks, all of us looking intently for any sign of a cave or anything else.

"Let me drop anchor here," Celeste said as we came within several feet from the rocks. "I don't want to risk damaging the boat. We can swim over," she said. Sal nodded in agreement while I looked at both of them like they'd lost their minds. They didn't seem to notice.

Once she had the ship anchored, Celeste began pulling off her boots, and Sal tied his hair back and pulled off his shirt. I sat perfectly still, gripping the rail of the boat as sea spray splashed over its side.

"Lily?" Sal asked. His forehead furrowed with confusion.

"I'll stay and mind the boat," I said.

Celeste and Sal both looked questioningly at me.

"Are you all right?" he asked.

I nodded. "Fantastic. I'll just stay here and mind

the boat," I said again. I could feel that all the blood had drained from my face.

Sal peered deeply at me. "Very good. We'll take a look."

"Be careful swimming near the rocks. Don't get pulled under," I told them both.

Celeste nodded, and with a jump, she splashed into the water and started swimming toward the stones. Sal slipped off the side of the boat and followed her. A few moments later, they appeared on the rocks, helping one another get a handhold. The rocks were much larger up close, perhaps twice the size of a man. I looked at the rocks, taking in the surroundings, as I sat on the rocking boat. I pulled out Sal's spyglass and examined the shoreline. In general, the coast had high cliffs, but I did spy one small cove nestled into the curvature of the land. There was a small, private beach.

"I don't see anything," Celeste called.

"No, me either," Sal answered.

"It's all stone. Just wet, slippery stone. You see any carvings? Anything? They might be faded from erosion," Celeste called. She sounded exasperated.

"Not yet," Sal answered. "Maybe there is something under the water. Look for a chain or something leading below," Sal called to her.

I gazed up at the fingers. Professor Herzog was right. The Aphrodite's fingers did seem to waggle, almost like she was waving toward the shoreline. I then noticed that one of the fingers was bent lower than the others, more lateral to the ocean. Given all the fingers seemed to be pointing, just in different directions, I didn't think much of it at first. But then I realized that the lowest and most lateral finger was, in fact, the ring finger of a left hand. I lifted the spyglass and looked. Following the line of the finger, it seemed like it was pointing directly to the small, hidden cove.

"Sal?" I called.

"Nothing yet, Lily. Are you all right over there?"

I took a deep breath, reached down, and grabbed Celeste's satchel. From inside, I removed the kaleidoscope. Getting my balance as best I could, I stood, aligned myself with the finger, and aimed the kaleidoscope toward the shoreline.

"Sal?"

"Lily? Everything okay?" he called from the other side of the rocks.

"You and Celeste should come back to the boat."

"Why? What's wrong?" Celeste called.

I smiled. "Nothing. It's just… well… I know where to find the Aphrodite."

In the kaleidoscope's colored glass, clear as day, was the image of the Aphrodite of Knidos.

CHAPTER 27

The small boat made a soft scraping sound as it hit the sandy shoreline of the beach. We jumped into the startlingly warm, topaz blue water and pulled the boat onto the shore.

The cove turned out to be even more secluded than it had initially seemed. The rocky shoreline formed a crescent shape, secluding and protecting the view of the much of the beach from the sea. As we stood on the beach, it became clear that this was a perfect hiding spot. Where, exactly, the Aphrodite was hidden remained to be found. Sal, Celeste, and I scoured the small beach for any sign of the Aphrodite. I panned the kaleidoscope around but was treated only to colors.

We spread out to scan the cove. I must have been looking for at least fifteen minutes when Celeste finally called out: "Here! Here!"

She was standing in one of the most secluded spots on the cove near the cliff wall. There, the cliff was open, just a crack. If you knelt, you could just see the sky on the other side. Above the narrow slit, however, was a carving. It was not large and time had worn it down, but carved into the rocks above the crevice was a swan with an anemone flower in its beak.

"I'm confused," Celeste said. "Is she buried in the sand? Under the water?"

Sal waded in and examined the rocks. Waist deep in the water, he stood in the middle of the inverted v-shaped opening. He turned and smiled at Celeste. Grabbing hold of the rocks, he pulled himself up out of the water and disappeared into the sea wall. He looked back out with a grin. "A cave."

Without another word, Celeste went after him.

I looked at the water. It wasn't that deep, maybe only thigh high. I followed behind them.

The cave was very narrow but passable. We crawled through the cavern deeper into the cliff side. It seemed to me the cavern turned to the right with the shape of the crescent moon. Soon it grew very dark.

"Watch your step. I can see some light up ahead," Sal called from the front.

I reached out for handholds, afraid I would feel the squishy body of a bat or worse. The stones were wet and grimy. The sharp smell of seaweed and earth filled the place, and the cave floor was jagged and slick. More than once I scraped my leg on the rocks. Before me, I heard Celeste struggling, but she never complained. Perhaps she had not even noticed. The passage, while rough, was short. Light began to filter in from the other side.

"My Lily?" Sal called back to me. "Are you all right? Almost there."

Sal was the first to emerge. I saw Celeste struggle out of the cave before me. Finally dragging myself over the damp rocks and out of the cave, I emerged into what can only be described as a natural cathedral.

Inside the cliff was a massive cave that was maybe thirty feet in height. Small openings, from which sea-birds flew in and out, let light into the place. The cave floor, sandy on the bottom, was submerged in just a few inches of clear water. Vines with small purple flowers grew everywhere, their cheery faces turning toward the sun, their scent perfuming the place. In the middle of this natural house of worship, on a pedestal adorned with seashells, sat the Aphrodite of Knidos. Sunlight slanting in through cliff side crevices bathed the goddess in the golden light of Apollo. The sun's rays mixed with a thin coat of crystalline dust that had fallen on the statue. She glimmered gold. The sight was breathtaking.

Celeste took two steps toward the sculpture then fell on her knees and burst into tears.

I came up behind Sal and took his hand.

We all stood in awe, not of what Praxiteles had made—though the rarity and delicacy his sculpture was without equal,-but of what that moment meant to each of us. This was what the Dilettante did not understand. It wasn't what the sculpture showed us of herself, or of Praxiteles, that made her so important. It was what we saw through her that mattered. Through her, I saw hope. I squeezed Sal's hand.

After a few moments, we approached the sculpture. With a disconnected eye, you could see it was a divine work of art. Why Praxiteles had made the sculpture was unknown, but there was something special about it. Energy seemed to pulse from it. I'd felt the same thing in the shrine of Asclepius.

Celeste reached out and touched the naked toes of the goddess. I heard her murmur under her breath. When she removed her hand, I noticed that her fingers had lifted off the golden dust. White marble, almost translucent in color, was revealed.

"How did they get her in here?" I wondered aloud.

Sal, who had a strange, faraway look his eyes, seemed to pull himself back from beyond. "The cave entrance is wide enough for her but not practical," he said.

"How about from above? Maybe they widened one of the crevice openings and lowered her in," I suggested.

"That could very well be. And even if that is not how they brought her in, certainly that could be a way to get her out."

I frowned. "The *Bacchus* is not strong enough to lift marble. Even if we modify the gear shaft to pull her, it can't be done from aloft. It would destroy Roni's ship. Maybe Profess-"

"We can lift her. She's not heavy. The *Bacchus* will

be able to lift her out," Celeste said. Her voice sounded thin.

"Didn't you hear what I just said? A piece of marble that siz-"

"She's just a woman. She weighs no more than you or I," Celeste corrected, her eyes locked on the face of the Aphrodite.

I looked at Sal. This is exactly the kind of zealot-like behavior I feared I'd get from Celeste.

"Celeste, we don't have time for this. If you want to get her moved, we need to get help."

She shook her head and looked at Sal. "You understand? You feel it too, don't you? You feel it. Just try. Let's see if we can lift her. It will work."

Sal looked up at the Aphrodite. I suddenly started to feel like a person left out on a joke. I watched Sal's face as he considered. He had a strange look in his eyes.

I looked up at the statue. The face shined with great luminescence. For just a brief moment, my vision seemed to double. It was almost like the statue had vibrated. I closed my eyes, trying to clear the blurry vision, then opened them again.

"Stand back, my Lily," Sal said and walked behind the Aphrodite. "Come. You'll need to help," he called to Celeste.

Had the two of them lost their minds? I was about to tell them so when Sal wrapped arms around the waist of the sculpture, and with a slight heave, moved her from her pedestal. He stepped backward, slowly setting her onto the sandy floor of the cave. Celeste took the Goddess' arm and steadied her.

I realized then that they were not seeing what I was seeing. What I was seeing was impossible. Or, she was not made of marble. Or, something else was going on, and I had not been invited to the party.

"We'll need to go back and get the *Bacchus*," Celeste said then, dusting her hands off on her wet trousers.

I opened my mouth to speak then closed it again.

Sal nodded. "We will pull her out from above. I'll harness her in and get her lifted using the gear assembly. It will work. Does that sound all right to you, Lily?" Sal asked.

What could I say? "Of course, my love."

Sal smiled. "All right. Let's head back."

We turned back to the cave opening when suddenly we realized the water around the edges of the cave was significantly higher and that the entrance to the cave was almost entirely submerged.

"Tide must have come in," Celeste said.

"It's not a far swim. Looks like we'll have some air at the top of the cave for another minute or so," Sal added.

Celeste nodded and headed into the mouth of the cave. Moments later, without another thought, she disappeared under the water.

Sal turned and looked at me.

I had not moved an inch. I stared at the water.

"What's wrong?"

I stood frozen.

"It's not far. Use the cave walls to guide you. I'll be right in front of you. You just need a little nerve, something you always have in abundance," he said with a wink. He reached out for my hand. I stood still.

I couldn't do it.

"Lily?" Sal said, confused.

After a moment, I said, "Go ahead. I'm coming."

Sal looked worried. "The longer you wait, the higher the water will get. I promise you, I'll be right in front of you."

Sal took my hand and led me into the water. As we neared the cave, the water inched high and higher: first to my waist, then to my torso. When it reached up to my neck, we stopped.

"Remember, the cave bends a little to the left. Pull on your goggles," he said, pulling them from my pocket, shaking out the water, and handing them to me. "That will help you see. Use your legs to guide you and take a deep breath." With that, Sal dove under the water.

I uttered a faint "wait," but he was already gone. I pulled my goggles on. I was deep in the cave. The light from Aphrodite's chamber glimmered faintly behind me. My hands started to tingle as the water began to rise toward my earlobes. I felt the tears coming, and my chest started to hurt. The water seeped into my ears. I could do it. I didn't have to be broken. I could do it.

I took a deep breath and plunged under the water. The feeling of being completely submerged alarmed me so severely that I felt a sharp pain in my chest. I braced myself against it and pushed off into the darkness, feeling the cave walls with my fingers, pushing myself along with my feet.

Further and further I pushed. I opened my eyes. The water was pitch black. I pushed forward, my chest beginning to burn. I expected to see light at any moment. I started to panic. What if I didn't make it? What if the water finally got me? I pushed forward again, still not reaching the end of the cave. I needed air. I had to breathe. Then, in the water before me, I saw a face. At first I could only make out feminine features: it was a woman with alabaster skin. She was swimming toward me. I stopped. My chest screamed for air. Then, I thought I saw light. Golden light illuminated the dark waves. Sunlight slanted into the water, and I found myself face to face with Nicolette. Her hair moved wildly around her. She reached out, took my hand, and pulled me forward. She led me toward the sunlight. Smiling at me, she pulled me by both of my hands then pushed me toward the surface of the water.

I broke through the surface with a gasp. Celeste pulled me out of the water. I sputtered, half choking.

"Oh my god, Lily. Why didn't you tell us you can't swim," Celeste scolded, leading me to the sandy beach.

Sal pulled off my goggles, pushed my hair away from my face, and sat me down on the warm sand.

I coughed hard, getting the last of the water out of my lungs.

"I didn't understand. I'm sorry. I'm so sorry," Sal said, pressing me against his chest.

I nodded, waving my hand dismissively at them, and caught my breath. "It's okay. I'm okay now," I said, and I meant it.

◆—◆

In silence, the three of us sailed back to Knidos. Sal kept his arm protectively around me. Celeste looked radiant. I stuck my hand over the side of the boat and let my fingertips glide along the water's surface. Nicolette. I closed my eyes and felt the wind on me. Nicolette. What had I seen? In the end, it didn't matter. My aching heart felt like it had been soothed. My sister. Nicolette. I closed my eyes and relished the experience.

Before I knew it, we had returned to the harbor at Knidos. I think we were all relieved to find it just as empty as we had left it. I shook myself from my dreamy thoughts and tried to focus.

"We cannot delay," Celeste said when we had anchored the sailboat. "There is no telling when the Dilettante will return. Sal, do you think you can make the harness tonight?"

He nodded. "I must start now. I was working on a project for Lily that I can modify."

"What kind of project?" I asked.

"You saw the roll of silk?"

I nodded.

"Based on a model by Da Vinci, I have been working on a kind of parachute such as Lenormand and Blanchard have used, but this one will be harnessed around the chest like a vest. It is a prototype, but it seems quite effective. I have the harness completed. I can modify it just a bit and use it and a pulley system to lift her onto the ship."

As usual, I was amazed, but then I remembered something: "We did promise the Prof-" I began, but Celeste cut me off.

"We really must act quickly. I can't bear the thought of the statue alone in that cave," Celeste said.

"Well, she has been alone in there for hundreds of years. I think she can wait until we finish a pint."

Celeste frowned.

"My Lily, take the professor his ale and our thanks. Celeste and I will get the ship ready."

While I wasn't wild about the plan, I agreed. The *Bacchus* had several stoneware jars of ale in stock. They weren't exactly cold, but I suspected the Professor would not mind either way.

I wound my way back to the Professor's tents where I found the Ottoman workers packing a mule cart with the Professor's boxes.

"Are you leaving?" I asked them, confused.

It was clear something was afoot. After discussing the matter for a few minutes, they led me inside Professor Herzog's tent. Inside, Professor Herzog was laid out on his cot. His skin had already started to turn ashy. I sat on his bedside. His eyes had been closed. I opened one of the jars, toasted the man, and took a drink. Setting the jar down, I sighed and took his cold hand. There was a shadow of a smile on his lips, and the aura of a fulfilled life emanated from him. I closed my eyes and prayed his Apollo would bless his path. I hoped that I would be lucky enough to die so satisfied.

CHAPTER 28

We sailed from Knidos and travelled the coast until we reached the cove where the Aphrodite lay hidden.

"Are you sure it's strong enough to hold you?" I asked as Sal pulled on the harness. We had reconfigured the *Bacchus'* gears to be used as a makeshift pulley.

"It can hold two grown men," Sal said, pulling on the straps. "It is woven metal and leather. Don't worry." He then tied a rope to a hook on the front of the harness, working it until it was tight. He had extra straps, hooks, and clasps in a bag belted around his waist. Nervous, I bent and looked the rope over. I didn't know where Celeste had found it, but it was very high quality, strong enough to carry marble.

Sal motioned to the galleyman. The man removed the pins that held a hatch door under the gondola closed. The door swung open. A breeze from the sea blew in, making the ship rock.

The galleyman swore.

I agreed. The hatch door was only opened to make repairs or to change parts, not to lower people into caves.

"Sal, this is dangerous."

Sal grabbed a miner's pick and motioned to the galleyman who began cranking gears.

"It's a leap of faith," Sal said with a grin then dropped out of the bottom of the ship.

I held onto a rod and looked down, afraid I would see Sal smashed to pieces below. Instead, he wagged in the breeze about six feet below the ship.

Sal yelled up to the galleyman who lowered him toward the cliff. Once he reached the rocks, he called "Stop." I watched from above as Sal peered through the opening into the cave below.

"I can see the statue. Celeste is there too," Sal called. Celeste had gotten off the *Bacchus* at the beach and had gone back inside through the beachside cave. "The rocks are loose here. I can open a space," Sal said. Getting into position, he began to pick away at the rocks and sediment. He opened up a gap large enough for him and the sculpture to fit through.

My teeth clenched tightly, I watched as he worked. It seemed to take an eternity, but soon he called: "Good! I'm ready."

I motioned to the crewman to begin again. Sal crawled into the crevice, disappearing into the cave.

"Sal? Salvatore?" I called.

"I'm okay," his voice echoed from within the cave. A few minutes later, he called "Stop. I'm down." I motioned to the crewman to halt. I shook my head. This felt like lunacy.

I went back on deck to see if I could get a better look. I stared down at the crevice into which Sal had been lowered. I felt like I was frozen in place. After what seemed like an eternity, Sal called up to me. His voice echoed from the expanse of the cave.

"We have her. Up and slow," he called.

I went back down to the galley and nodded to the crewman, motioning for him to go slowly. As the line on the harness grew taught, the *Bacchus* put up a little resistance. The gears groaned a bit. For a moment, I feared we really were trying to lift marble. The crewman applied a little more torque and soon it began to lift.

I leaned back over the open hatch door and waited.

"Stop," Sal called. His voice sounded like he was just near the opening. I saw the harness shake.

"Sal?"

"I'm all right. Just adjusting," he called. A moment later he yelled, "Begin again. Easy."

I nodded and signaled once more.

A moment later, Sal and Aphrodite emerged into the sunlight. The statue glimmered blindingly bright.

"Ave Maria!" the galleyman exclaimed in surprise.

It was an amazing sight. Sal had lashed her tightly

against him, gripping the statue under the arms and around the waist. He guided her carefully out of the crevice, protecting her head as best he could as she neared the sides of the opening. The two of them slipped through.

I breathed a sigh of relief. I headed to the deck and leaned over the rail so I could see when Sal made landfall. He used his legs to guide them around the rocks, clutching the statue as he moved toward the flat, grassy landing above the cliff.

Once his feet were flat on the ground, I called stop. The gears on the *Bacchus* ground to a halt. Sal unharnessed himself and the statue.

"Lily, bring the *Bacchus* down as low as you can. Let's crate the statue and get her stowed in the galley," Sal called.

Airships do not like to be low. It risks damage to the rudder and propeller. I frowned and signaled to the balloonman. He frowned in agreement but opened the balloon value a crack. The ship began to lower.

"Watch the rudder, Sal," I called.

When we came within ten feet of land, Sal called "Stop!"

I dropped the ladder overboard and went down. We had traded Professor Herzog's workers a spyglass and a case of Italian wine for a long, wooden crate in which we could transport the statue. There was just enough room in the galley to stow her there, out of sight.

"Let me talk to the crew. I'll need more muscle to get her loaded without damage," Sal said as he positioned the statue on the grassy cliff-top.

In the bright light of day, the statue was truly stunning. It was not made of marble, at least not any kind of marble I had ever seen. I didn't know what it was made of, but it was beautiful. I reached out and touched her cheek. I could see why she had scandalized the ancient world. It was not so much that she was nude that was so shocking, it was the way she stood that made her so provocative. While they might have called the statue "Modest Venus," her pose was anything but modest. The Aphrodite was not shyly covering her feminine parts with her hand. Instead, her hand was tipped forward; she was offering her body to the viewer.

Sal and the galleyman returned with the crate. Carefully, we lowered the Aphrodite of Knidos into the box. She lay in a bed of golden straw. Her eyes were blank, but the playful smile on her lips made me think that she was enjoying all this intrigue.

Once she was secure in the crate, the box was lashed with rope, and the pulley system lifted the statue into a small space in the gear galley. The galleyman and I reboarded the ship and guided the crate to rest between the rods. She barely fit, but we had her.

I could not help but smile. "Let's pick up Celeste then head out," I said.

"To where?" Sal asked.

Indeed, where could you hide the Goddess of Love?

CHAPTER 29

"Lesvos," Celeste said.

We were standing on the deck of the *Bacchus* debating—more disagreeing-our next move.

"Celeste, the isle of Lesvos is situated right in the middle of the Ottoman-Greek conflict," Sal said.

"Perhaps we should take her back to Venice," I suggested.

Celeste shook her head. "We have a sanctuary on Lesvos that is secret. She will be safe there. In Venice, our moves are watched."

Sal looked at me. "Lesvos is not a hotly contested piece of land. It's what may lie between us and Lesvos that is a problem."

"We've come all this way, Lily. We must take her somewhere safe. Cyprus is compromised. In Venice we are watched. Athens is a disaster. I must move her, at least for now, somewhere secret. She must be taken somewhere secluded until our order decides what is best. Please!"

"And if the *Bacchus* is blasted out of the sky?"

"Fly an Italian ensign. With Bacchus on the balloon, people will know we are not about war," Celeste said.

This was exactly the kind of mess Jessup and Angus had worried about. "I don't know."

"Please, Lily. Please!" she said, taking my hand. Her eyes brimmed with tears. "Please help us."

I sighed. "Let me see a map."

I looked over Celeste's proposed flight path. She was asking us to fly into a war zone.

"Is there no other option? I could fly the *Bacchus* to London or Paris. You could transport her elsewhere by land or sea."

Celeste shook her head. "We can move in and out quickly. No one will ever know. I just need to get her to Lesvos."

"You could have mentioned your plan to fly into the middle of a war before we left Venice," I chided.

"I was afraid you wouldn't come."

"You were right."

I handed Celeste the map. "In and out. After the drop, no more side trips. I have a race to worry about."

"Yes, I understand. Oh Lily, thank you so much!"

"Yeah, okay," I said with a sigh and then turned to Sal. "You all right with that?"

He shrugged nonchalantly. "It is for you to decide."

"Then let's get the crew ready," I said.

Sal nodded and went to exchange words with the crew.

I was feeling irritable, and it was not just because Celeste had me potentially dodging canon fire. I had already started to stretch out my laudanum intake. As delighted as I was that we had found the sculpture, I was already headed back to London in my mind and was in no mood for a detour. That, and I wanted to smoke opium. I really wanted to smoke opium.

Fly fast. Move quick. Get it over with. That was my mantra as I took the wheelstand and guided the ship northbound into the belly of the Aegean. If we caught a good wind, and the *Bacchus* showed me what it was made of, I could have us in port by midnight.

It was late afternoon when we flew between Kos and Knidos. I took the *Bacchus* up. I wanted to get well out of eyeshot from anything on land or in the water. The cloud bank promised some cover. When it got dark, I would keep the lanterns off. The stars had guided me this far, maybe they could shed a little light on the rest of the journey.

I asked Sal to have the galleyman run the *Bacchus* at full speed. Something inside me made me feel like I was on the run.

Gliding along the coast of the Ottoman Empire, I kept my eyes peeled for any sign of trouble. Sal and Celeste watched over the side of the ship looking for action in the water below. Thankfully, the waters were clear. There was no Greek incursion on Trojan shores that night.

A couple of hours into the trip, I found myself rooting through my satchel for my laudanum. I was feeling frustrated with the world for no good reason other than I had not indulged my habit for hours. It was a horrible feeling. I tried to keep my cravings at bay, tried to focus on Sal, on the Aphrodite, on the race, on getting to Lesvos, but nothing was working. The longer I waited, the more agitated I became. Once I finally dug out my bottle, I took three healthy drops of the opiate. It would be enough to make the trip tolerable. I closed my eyes and drifted. The feel of the drug made my body tingle, and suddenly I felt lighter. I felt less irritable. My head was swimming in a foggy haze. I rocked with the ship, feeling the *Bacchus* shift in the wind. It was so peaceful.

It was not until Sal was standing before me in a fit of panic that I realized I had missed something, something important. Sal moved my hands from the wheel and cranked it hard.

"Starboard! Starboard!" Celeste was shouting.

I tried to focus. On our starboard side, a small ship was flying in very fast. Someone aboard the deck of the opposing ship was loading a harpoon. It was aimed at the *Bacchus*.

"Oh my god!" I exclaimed and reached for the

wheel. "I've got it!" I told Sal. "We need to drop elevation!"

Sal yelled up to the balloonman then pulled out his sidearm.

If we got the ship low, they would not be able to harpoon the gondola. If they wanted us alive, they would not take out the balloon. The *Bacchus* did its best, but in the end, the ship was bulky and slow.

The harpoon hit the prow of the *Bacchus* with a jolt. I gasped to see the metal claw puncture through the prow. Wood shrapnel sprayed everywhere. By luck, they had missed the propeller assembly. Since we'd already begun dropping altitude, when the harpoon caught the ship by the nose, it heaved us up. I clutched the wheelstand as the ship began to tip from the prow. The small ship that attacked us used counter maneuvers to avoid being dragged down. They increased their altitude. Soon, they were pulling us upward.

With no better recourse, Roni's balloonman heated the *Bacchus*'s balloon to keep pace before we all got dumped into the ocean or the balloon buckled into the burners.

I looked at the opposing ship. This was no pirate vessel. Nor was it a Greek or Ottoman warship. The ship was a sleek, expensive, and well-equipped private ship. It was the kind of ship an aged antiquity dealer could afford. On the ship's side, I noted the vessels' name: *Hephaestus*. No, this was no coincidence; on the deck of the ship was the man I had outrun in Venice. The Dilettanti had us.

Celeste headed below.

Sal, weapon drawn, came to my side.

I let go of the wheel. There was nothing more I could do.

CHAPTER 30

"Well, Miss Stargazer, what are you doing so far from home?" an Englishman in a dark suit asked me from the deck of the *Hephaestus* as they moored to the side of the *Bacchus*. Inconspicuously, I pulled my gun from my satchel and stuck it into the back of Sal's pants. Anger made my hands shake. While I felt rage toward the Dilettanti, I was angrier with myself. This was my fault.

"I suggest you don't come closer," Sal said, aiming his handgun toward the Englishman.

"Signor Colonna, we are after your sculpture, not your woman. Miss Stargazer just needs to tell us the location of the sculpture, and we'll let you limp to port," the man said.

They did not know we had the Aphrodite.

"What sculpture?" I asked. While my head was still a mess, I forced myself to focus.

"Come now, Miss Stargazer. We know what you are up to," he replied.

"Perhaps she needs more motivation," one of the

henchmen said, and before we could react, he pulled his sidearm and fired, shooting Roni's balloonman in the shoulder with startling accuracy. The man screamed and clenched his wound.

"Do watch the burners. I'd hate for the ship to explode before Miss Stargazer gives us the information we need… oh yes and the kaleidoscope," the man said. "Now, where is the courtesan?"

We did not reply.

The ringleader sighed. "We'll be boarding your ship now, Lily. Do mind your manners. Signor Colonna, I suggest you lower your weapon. The five of us," he said, motioning to his crew, "are all armed, and we'd hate to see you meet with an accident."

The five men boarded the *Bacchus*.

"I'll take that," one of the men said, wrenching the gun from Sal's hand.

"Go below. Bring the galleyman up and find the courtesan," their leader said. "Someone get the wounded bird out of the nest and tie him up," he added, looking up at the burner basket.

"Stay close," Sal whispered to me.

"Now, Lily, why don't you be a good girl and pass me the kaleidoscope," the ringleader said.

I scanned the deck of the *Bacchus*. Celeste's satchel had slid toward a storage hold.

"All right. Let me get it for you."

"No games," the man holding a weapon on Sal said, pushing his revolver into Sal's ribs.

"I wouldn't dream of it," I replied.

I grabbed Celeste's satchel and pulled out the kaleidoscope. I handed it to their leader. "I guess we'll be parting ways now," I said.

"Ahh, but something tells me you might have information to share. Do you know where the sculpture is, Lily?"

I heard Celeste grunting as the henchman yanked her and the galleyman, both with hands bound behind their backs, onto the deck. Celeste's lip was bleeding. The galleyman came along quietly. I saw him scan the deck. He saw his crewmate, bleeding from the shoulder, sitting bound against the bulwark. He lowered his eyes and cooperated.

"Ah, the lovely Celeste. How are you, dear?"

"Go to hell," she replied.

"Mr. Holloway," one of the henchmen said. "You should come below deck, Sir. There is something down there."

"Something? Be more specific."

"A crate, Sir."

"A crate?"

"Large enough to hold a statue."

Holloway smiled at me. "Well done, Miss Stargazer. You've made it easy for me." He and two of the Dilettanti henchman headed toward the galley. One guard kept a gun on Sal and me, another man guarded Celeste and Roni's crewmen.

"I've had enough of this," Sal whispered.

"I agree."

"Now."

Moving fast, Sal grabbed the gunman closest to us and knocked the weapon from his hand. I grabbed a wrench lying on the deck, and moving quickly, came up behind the henchman holding the gun on Celeste and slammed him in the back the head with the wrench. He went down with a screech. The others turned back and soon we were in a fray.

Sal pulled the gun from the back of his pants, but before he could get off a shot, two men jumped him. They pushed him down on the deck. I reached out to help him but instead took a blow to the right cheek; my mouth filled with blood. I spat out a tooth. Celeste came up from behind. She tried to use her shoulders to push the man they called Holloway off the ship. He tossed her onto the deck like a ragdoll. I heard her head hit the deck of the *Bacchus* hard. I kicked one of the men pummeling Sal in the ribs, and he toppled over, clutching his side.

"Someone knock that bitch out," Holloway yelled.

I turned in time to get clocked in the face. I heard my nose bone snap. I staggered backward. Blood sprayed from my nose.

"Throw the Italian overboard," Holloway commanded.

"No!" I screamed and ran toward Sal. One of the henchmen grabbed me.

"Sir? Sir! What is that!" one of the henchmen shouted urgently.

"What are you talking about? Get some rope and tie Stargazer up."

One of them grabbed my arms, and I felt the burn of rope around my wrists.

"That! Sir! Port!"

"Sal!" I wailed as they began hauling Sal toward the side of the ship. I struggled against the man who held me, and then, in a desperate move, I shot my leg backward, kicking the henchman between the legs. He groaned and went down.

I ran toward one of the men dragging Sal toward the rail. I slammed into the henchman, knocking him onto the deck.

"Sir! Sir! Port!" the henchman screamed again.

This time we all looked. An enormous dark shape dropped from the clouds. It was like the hand of a god was descending upon us.

"Oh my god," one of the henchmen whispered.

Everyone stared in wonderment as an enormous warship came out of the clouds and headed directly toward us. Its cannons gleamed in the dimming twilight. At once, I recognized the double-propelled war machine dubbed *Hercules*. And at its prow, I saw a poet.

CHAPTER 31

"George! George!" I screamed, fearful Byron would not recognize me or the ship.

Hoping to silence me, Holloway hit me hard. I fell onto the deck of the ship.

"Lily!" Sal called, reaching for me.

A split second later, I heard a gunshot. Holloway fell onto the deck beside me; blood poured from a bullet hole between his eyes. His men scattered.

I closed my eyes and sent out a silent prayer of thanks.

"Lily! Lily? Are you all right?" I heard Byron call from the *Hercules*.

I was now.

"Here, let me help you up," Sal whispered. His face was a bloody mess. He lifted me and helped me to the rail.

"I'm okay," I called to Byron.

"Stay there. We're coming. My crew has your new friends in their optics. I suggest no one moves."

The four remaining henchmen stood frozen as the *Hercules* came up alongside us.

Byron signaled to his crewmates. They extended a plank between us and the *Hercules*. Byron was the first to cross over. Four young men, by their appearance I guessed them to be Greek, followed him. Byron took in the scene and directed his crew to watch the remaining henchmen.

Byron took me by the chin, smoothing the hair away from my face, and looked me over. "My Lily," he whispered.

Beside me, Sal stiffened and took a step away from Byron and me.

Reaching into his pocket, Byron pulled out a hand-kerchief and wiped the blood from my face. I caught his intoxicating orange blossom and patchouli scent in the soft material. "What have they done to you?" he asked and pulled me close to him. Part of me wanted to fall into the crush of his chest, but then I opened my eyes and saw Sal. I pulled back.

"Can you cut me loose?" I asked.

He let me go. I turned my back to Byron so he could snip the ropes. I looked at Sal who looked straight ahead and not at me.

"Who are they?" Byron asked.

"The Dilettanti. They have been tracking Lily since she left London. They were after the kaleidoscope," Sal answered.

"Colonna, isn't it?" Byron asked.

"Yes, my Lord."

Byron laughed. "No need for formality. I am a fan of your inventions, tinker" he said, clapping Sal on the shoulder. "But your face is a mess."

"That is their handiwork," I said, motioning toward the henchmen who stood silently on the other side of the ship. I rubbed my wrists where the rope had burned them.

"Who do you work for?" Byron asked them. His voice was dark and serious.

They all looked at the ground.

I saw a sparkle in Byron's eyes, the glimmer of madness which I had seen before on only a few occasions. I knew it to be dangerous.

"Let me ask you again," he said, and I noticed his cheeks had begun to flush red as he crossed the deck toward the men. As if the look in his eyes was not telling enough, Byron's limp became pronounced. Always self-conscious about his condition, Byron usually took great care to hide the birth defect. When he was distracted, however, that was another matter. "No one wants to talk?" he asked them.

None of the men spoke.

"You work for Knight, don't you?" I said.

One of the men looked up.

"Richard Payne Knight?" Byron asked me.

I nodded. "He paid me a little visit in Venice. He was looking for the kaleidoscope."

Byron turned back to the men. "The lady asked you a question," he told them.

No one spoke.

"Well, this is boring," he said then turned to his crew and gave orders.

In a heartbeat, the soldiers turned and shot three of the henchmen. They then unmoored the *Hephaestus* and tossed lit lanterns onto its deck. Oil spilled across the gondola. With a great boom, the ship caught fire. As the vessel floated from us back into the clouds, it became engulfed in flame, and soon the burning wreck fell toward the sea.

The remaining Dilettanti henchman watched the ship burn. "She's right. We work for Knight," the man said.

"Thank you for confirming," Byron replied and motioned for his crew to throw the man overboard. The henchmen fell screaming from the *Bacchus*.

Lady Caroline Lamb was the one who had called Byron "mad, bad, and dangerous to know." And in that moment, I suspected this was the side of him to which she was referring. But this was the Byron who had saved us.

Byron looked around the ship. Spotting Celeste, he knelt down and helped her up.

"Celeste? Whatever are you doing here?" he asked.

I felt my eyebrows furrow but tried to hide my reaction. Apparently the instinct I'd had in Venice was right.

"Lord Byron," she whispered.

"Looks like you've had quite the adventure, Lily," he said with a smile. His blue eyes twinkled.

"That is an understatement. But we do have an injured man here," I said, motioning to the balloon-man who was nursing his shoulder. "Is Dr. Thomas traveling with you?" I asked.

"He is. Let's get you and your crew aboard the *Hercules*. I'll tow your ship to Athens."

◆—◆

I half expected Celeste to protest against leaving the Aphrodite aboard the Bacchus, but she made her way onto the *Hercules* without complaint. Perhaps she was feeling just as I did: safe.

Roni's crewmen went with Byron's physician while Byron led Sal, Celeste, and me to his Captain's quarters. The space was small but voluptuously decorated. Windows looked out onto the deck on three sides, and the wood paneling gleamed. He had a small meeting space outfitted with expensive chairs that had blue velvet upholstery. Behind them was a large captain's desk upon which he'd spread several maps. In the back of the quarters was a curtained space where, no doubt, one could find his sleeping area.

Byron's servants cleaned us up. My nose throbbed. And it never felt good to lose a tooth. I eyed Sal over. He had a black eye and a bruised cheek. He flinched as he settled into his seat.

"Is your rib broken?" I asked him.

Sal's eyes met mine. There was a strange expression on his face. Was he angry? Had I done something wrong? "I'll be all right," he said and sat back.

Byron also looked a little rougher than I was used to seeing him. His hair did not curl as primly as usual, and his clothing looked less than freshly pressed.

"You were lucky. I just broke the ship in. We are returning from a campaign," Bryon explained as he poured us all a drink.

I polished mine off and held the glass out for a refill. Byron smiled at me and filled the glass to the rim.

"There are no words to express our gratitude," Celeste said.

"Well, words were never your strong suit, my dear," he told her then turned to me. "Now… someone tell me… what exactly is going on? Lily?"

I looked from Sal, who would not meet my gaze, to Celeste, who begged me with her eyes to keep quiet. Again, Byron's reputation had preceded him. In that moment, I realized that I was the only one in the room who really understood Byron. And that realization struck me with a terrible sense of confusion. I was in love with Sal. Of that there was no longer any doubt. And Sal was in love with me. But somewhere along the way, I had forgotten to really process what I had with Byron. We were lovers, that much was true, but Byron trusted me the way he trusted few others, and I would not betray his faith for the world. After all, I trusted

Byron the way I trusted few others. In that moment, I realized I would never break his faith, but I might have to break his heart. Then, I worried that they might be the same thing.

I looked at Sal again. His long hair hung all around his face. He had closed his eyes and pressed his glass against his forehead. I understood what plagued his mind: me.

"The kaleidoscope led to the lost sculpture Aphrodite of Knidos. We recovered the sculpture, and it is stowed in the galley of the *Bacchus*. Celeste needs to take the sculpture to Lesvos where it can be safely hidden by the secret sect of Aphrodite to which she belongs."

Celeste's mouth hung open.

Sal opened his eyes and looked at me.

Byron lifted his drink to his lips, took a long sip, and smiled at me with his eyes.

"All right, Lily. Let's get the ships back to Athens, and I'll have a private vessel, someone I trust, take Celeste and the statue to Lesvos. Where are you and Mr. Colonna headed?"

"Back to Venice," I answered for both of us. I looked at Sal. He seemed perplexed.

Byron sighed and slumped down into his chair. He tossed back his drink and set the glass down on the table. He smiled at me. "Care for an aperitif?" he asked, motioning toward his opium pipe sitting on the table beside him. I had noticed it as soon as I'd entered the room. The sweet scent of opium still perfumed the air. Apparently he'd just used it himself.

"I'll pass tonight. I've had enough stimulation for one day."

Byron laughed. "Is there such a thing? I've never known you to find its limits before."

I turned and looked at Sal. It was clear from his expression that this entire situation was making him uncomfortable.

"Things change," I said with a smile.

"Too much change is unhealthy. You know, I was thinking it was rather lucky that the four of us are together," Byron said slyly. "Mr. Colonna, I have to tell you how much I admired the bodice you made for Lily. That was your work, wasn't it? Your hands are rather genius. I can only imagine what they must be able to do. It was a rather tedious campaign. I'd like to suggest we all have another drink and move our conversation to my sleeping quarters."

"All of us?" Celeste asked. I could tell from the expression on her face that she had not really meant to say it aloud.

Byron shrugged and poured himself another drink. "I didn't think it was outside your repertoire."

I wanted to bury my face in my hands.

"I'm afraid that is not my style, Lord Byron. But I do appreciate the compliment," Sal said and then rose, again nursing his broken rib. "If you will excuse me, I'll be on deck."

I feared then how Byron would respond. To my great relief, Byron laughed out loud. "How disappointing! But, it's no wonder Lily likes you. As you wish," Byron said then tipped his glass at Sal.

Sal nodded to him, gave me a long look, then left the Captain's quarters. My fingers itched to follow him, to nurse his wounds, to whisper in his ear and do away with any worries that plagued his mind. He knew how much I loved him, didn't he?

"Celeste?" Byron asked, turning to her.

"I, too, must pass, Lord Byron. I hit my head rather hard and need rest."

"As you like it. I'm beginning to think I'm losing my charm, Lily," Byron said and rose. He went to the door of the Captain's quarters and called to a crewman. He motioned to Celeste. "He will take you to a private room," Byron told her. After she left, he came and sat very close to me. He took my hand. "Are you all right?"

I nodded.

"It seems like your adventure was rather... revealing," he said carefully.

"Revealing?"

"How many years have we been together?" he asked me, stroking the nape of my neck.

"More than four," I said thoughtfully.

Byron nodded. "More than four years. Do you know what I've always liked about you?"

I smiled slyly at him. "I think there are many things."

He laughed. "That is true... no one understands me as you do. But what I love most about you is that you are honest, in your words and in your heart. I know you love me. And, in truth, I love you. But I can never love you the way that man who just left loves you."

I looked at Byron. "What should I do?"

"It depends. What do you want? You can come to my bed, or you can go after him. The choice is yours."

I looked at Byron. "I want you to see the Aphrodite."

He raised an eyebrow at me. "Now?"

I nodded.

He took another drink and considered. "Lead the way."

CHAPTER 32

It was already dark when Byron and I made our way back onto the *Bacchus*. I gazed up at the stars. Ophiuchus was visible in the night sky. We held our lanterns aloft as we crossed the deck of the ship. I stepped carefully around the puddles of blood. Roni was not going to be happy.

"It's in a crate in the galley," I told Byron.

"How did you get it in there?"

"Sal reconfigured the gears to be used as a pulley."

"Genius. I like your tinker, Lily."

I laughed. "So I noticed."

"You'll need to loosen him up."

"I like him as he is."

"Be careful. He may domesticate you."

"Is that a bad thing?"

"For you? Yes."

When we got below, I hung up the lantern and crawled over the gears to the crate. "Hand me the prise bar."

Byron passed it to me. I loosened the nails, pried

open the lid, and slid it off. Part of me half expected, well, something, but this was not my moment. The Aphrodite lay where we had left her amongst the golden straw. Wind blew in from the opening in the prow and ruffled the padding around her. It gave the effect that she was moving. I smiled at her. In the light of the lantern, she glimmered magnificently.

"Let me crawl out so you can see her. There isn't room for both of us," I said and slid back toward the galley opening where Byron waited.

We exchanged places. Byron slipped between the gears and worked his way toward the crate. I handed his lantern to him then crawled out of the galley to the deck of the ship.

Once on deck, I dug into my satchel and pulled out the tin of Cutter's tobacco and a pipe. I lit up. I gazed up at the stars. The tobacco didn't make my headache go away, but it comforted me. I blew smoke rings into the air and watched them twist away in the wind. Below deck, Byron was silent.

I finished the first pipe then smoked a second. Venus was no longer visible in the evening sky. On the deck of the *Bacchus* behind me, I heard something rolling. I looked back to see the kaleidoscope lying forgotten on the deck. It glimmered in the moonlight. I got up and retrieved it. I lifted it toward the night's sky. I was startled and saddened to find that the glass within was cracked.

I tried to center the kaleidoscope on Ophiuchus.

Not only did the image of Knidos fail to appear, but for a brief moment, I thought I saw Mr. Fletcher's face. I sat back down, leaned my head against the rail, and looked up at the stars.

The first two years after Mr. Oleander and Nicolette had died, my relationship with Mr. Fletcher was made up of a strange mixture of awkwardness and affection. The lie we shared seemed to cement us together. With Mr. Oleander out of our home, something changed between my foster father and me. We grew very close and were very sweet with one another. I began to feel certain that my foster father really loved me.

Mr. Fletcher had sold the flat on Neal's Yard and had rented a small loft in the building next to Rheneas' tavern. The flat only had one room. The space was fine for a father and daughter. I clung desperately to Mr. Fletcher who seemed to enjoy our closeness. I loved being loved. All my life I had wanted someone to really love me, to see me as someone worth keeping, worth loving. Through Mr. Fletcher, my father, I finally found what I was looking for: unconditional love.

In the meantime, we were still flying. Mr. Fletcher had sold the ill-fated *Iphigenia* to a Dutch crew and had picked up a new vessel, the Irish-built *Deirdre*. The *Deirdre* was fast and sleek. On her, I began to learn how to pilot like a champion.

In the year after Mr. Oleander's death, Mr. Fletcher had hired Angus to apprentice in the galley of the

Deirdre. From the start, Angus and I got along very well, but Angus never liked Mr. Fletcher.

"His eyes are too hungry," Angus would say.

It was the first time I'd ever heard the phrase and wasn't quite sure what he'd meant. One spring morning, however, I found out.

Mr. Fletcher woke me earlier than usual. "Get up, Lily. We've got some business to attend to today," he said, shaking my shoulder gently.

Since we lacked space, Mr. Fletcher and I had taken to sharing the same bed. He almost never got up before I did.

"But it's Monday," I complained. We never ran fares on Mondays. On the weekends we worked around the clock. I was exhausted.

"Not that kind of business. We've got legal business to get on with," he explained. "Get dressed. I laid out some new clothes out for you."

I woke tiredly and stumbled to the table where I discovered that Mr. Fletcher had purchased me not just new clothes, but a dress. I lifted the gown. The style was modern and very similar to the attire I'd seen the female air jockeys wearing. The bodice was constructed with black leather and purple velvet. The skirt, which was very short, had high splits up both legs. I set the clothes back down on the table and burst into tears.

"Lily?"

"How could you!"

"How could I what?" Mr. Fletcher looked confused.

"I can't. I can't be like Nicolette!"

"Oh, dear Lily, never! My sweet girl, you are grown now. You should dress like a woman. Today is an important day. You should dress the part!"

"The part?"

"You'll see. Put it on, and let me see you," he said, sitting down to watch me change. I slipped my house clothes off and pulled the dress on.

Between Mr. Fletcher watching my clumsy movements and the dress squeezing me, I felt awkward. "How is it?" I asked.

"Very nice!" Mr. Fletcher said and then rose to stand behind me. "I'll lace it for you. Push your bosom up a bit, Lily. Here, let me help," he said, his hand scooping under the fabric, adjusting my breasts. I could not help but notice the caress with which he touched me. It made me uncomfortable.

After I got the bodice on, he tightened the laces and unbraided my hair. He pulled a comb through my long locks.

"You're so beautiful," he whispered. Mr. Fletcher then spun me in a circle. "Perfect. Lily Fletcher, air jockey!" he said with a laugh. "Now, come," he said, and we headed out.

Mr. Fletcher had arranged for a carriage to take us across town. We road to a section of London with which I was unfamiliar. From the attire of the men moving busily about, I gathered we were near the Inns of Court. Mr. Fletcher led me into an office building. We entered a small, quiet office where two old men sat laboring over massive piles of paper. We sat waiting for a long time before we were called.

"John and Lily Fletcher?"

Mr. Fletcher took me by the hand, and we went to the back. Mr. Fletcher pulled my chair out, and I sat, struggling to find a way to sit in the short dress without showing the whole word what I was made of.

"Papers?" the clerk said, never looking up.

Mr. Fletcher handed a number of papers to him.

"And Mrs. Fletcher will be sole beneficiary of your estate?"

"That is correct," Mr. Fletcher said.

Confused, I looked at Mr. Fletcher.

"Sign here," the clerk said.

Mr. Fletcher signed his name.

The clerk stamped the paper. "Can your wife write?"

"Indeed."

"Sign here, Mrs. Fletcher," the man said then slid the papers toward me.

I looked aghast at my father.

"Go ahead, Lily," Mr. Fletcher said.

I signed my name on the paper and leaned back into my seat. I could feel the blood draining from my face.

"Your nuptials and estate are now confirmed, Mr. and Mrs. Fletcher. The fee, please," the clerk said.

Mr. Fletcher slid a small stack of coins to the clerk who counted them carefully, twice.

"Thank you. And congratulations," the man said absently.

Mr. Fletcher rose and took my hand, pulling me behind him. I followed him to the street. I felt like I was going to faint.

"Lily? What's wrong? You're absolutely pale!"

"Are we... are we married?" I stammered.

"Here," he said, pressing a vial of laudanum in my hand. "Take just one drop. It will calm you. Of course we are married. How else do you think I can ensure you'll inherit my estate if, god forbid, I die? Now, bottom's up."

I did as he instructed. The laudanum hit me hard. Moments later, I was lost in a fog. I vaguely remember being loaded back into the carriage. The ride home over the bumpy cobblestone jostled me.

Mr. Fletcher, my father, kept his hand on my inner thigh the entire ride. "You see," he said, "I promised you I would take care of you. I taught you everything I know! What a pair we will make! Maybe we'll even have a child, Lily! What-ho! Can you imagine what fun that will be?"

The carriage stopped outside our flat. I stumbled when I got out, scrapping my knees on the cobblestones.

"My goodness, Lily. You can't even hold a drop. Strong stuff though. I try not to use it much, but once it gets you by the nose, it doesn't let you go. Let's go upstairs and celebrate. Here, my girl, I'll carry you," he said and hoisted me up.

My head was a confused mess. I thought maybe I was dreaming… or maybe I was dead. In what seemed like moments later, I was standing before the fireplace in our flat. Mr. Fletcher, my father, was lying in the bed. He was calling my name. When I did not respond, he rose. He wrapped his arms around my waist.

"Come now, Lily. I'll be easy," he whispered.

"No."

"Ah, my girl, there is no need to fear. I'll be gentle. Come now."

"No."

"Don't make it come to this," he whispered in my ear. "We love one another."

"You're my father!" I wailed.

"Actually, Oleander was the one who officially adopted you. Come on now, Lily. Be smart," he said, his hands roving between my legs. "You stand to gain everything. Who could ever love you as much as I do?"

"Please don't," I whispered.

Before I could stop him, he turned me and slammed me, face down, on the table, my cheek pressed against the tabletop. I wailed miserably. "Please! No!"

In that same moment, the door to the loft opened. Mr. Fletcher had given Angus the key so he could drop off the fares.

"I'm sorry, Sir. It was dark. I thought you were

out—for Christ's sake, what's happening here!" Angus exclaimed.

I slipped from Mr. Fletcher and ran to Angus, clinging desperately to him.

"Get the fuck out of here," Mr. Fletcher yelled and grabbed me, pulling me away from Angus.

"No! Please don't go! Don't leave me here," I pleaded, reaching out to Angus.

"This isn't proper! That's your daughter there!" Angus exclaimed.

"It's not a bit of your business! Get out or find a new situation!"

"Come on, Lily. Come with me, lassie," Angus called and reached for me.

I pulled out of Mr. Fletcher's grasp. He came rushing after me. Trying to get away from him, I moved aside. Mr. Fletcher lost his balance and fell out of the open door and down the stairs. He landed on the street below, his body twisting awkwardly.

I ran to the bottom of the steps. Several people had already gathered around him.

"Call the surgeon! Call the surgeon!" someone screamed.

"What happened, Lily?" someone asked. I looked up. It was Rheneas.

"He fell!" I exclaimed. Tears ran down my cheeks.

I knelt beside Mr. Fletcher. He was still alive. His hand, jutting sideways, twitched oddly.

A constable came running up. "What happened?"

"She said he fell," someone repeated.

"What's his name?" the constable asked.

"That's Mr. Fletcher, the air jockey."

"Mr. Fletcher? What happened?" the constable asked.

Mr. Fletcher's eyes were already growing dim. A shadow seemed to hover around him. Blood trickled from his ears and mouth. It took him considerable effort, but he made eye contact with me. After a moment, he breathed, "I'm an old man, and I'll die like an old man. Slipped and fell," he whispered then he died.

I looked up at Angus. His dark blue eyes met mine. He set his hand on my shoulder.

My whole body shook. My father had tried to make me his wife, body and soul. Now he lay dead at my feet.

In the end, Mr. Fletcher, just like my mother, had seen me as someone to do with as he pleased. My entire life, I was always someone to be used or not, kept or left, at another person's will.

A shuffle from below deck startled me from my memories. Byron reappeared from the galley looking paler than usual.

"Are you all right?" I asked him.

He turned and looked at me as if he were surprised to see me there. "Lily," he said, his voice sounding hollow.

I didn't need to ask Byron what he had seen or

what had happened. By instinct, I had known, through and through, that Byron needed to see the Aphrodite. And from the look on his face, I was right. He'd seen what he needed to see.

"Let's go back to your ship," I said, taking his hand.

Once we'd boarded the *Hercules*, we stopped and looked up at the starry sky. We stood, hand in hand, in quiet contemplation.

"Athens!" a crewman called from overhead.

On the horizon, the airship towers of Athens were coming into view. The *Hercules* began to drop altitude. In a matter of moments, we would be docked.

Byron looked down at me, kissed me on my forehead, and stroked my cheek. "Don't forget me," he whispered.

"Never."

He pulled me into a tight hug, and I soaked up his warmth, knowing it would be the last time I would ever feel him like that. From now on, my heart belonged to Sal. It was time to leave the past behind.

CHAPTER 33

There was complete mayhem on the airship towers in Athens when the *Hercules* arrived at port, the *Bacchus* in tow. I couldn't find Sal anywhere. The platform was flooded with Greek soldiers, English ex-pats, and travelers trying to dodge trouble. In the midst of all that confusion, Celeste found me.

"We need to get the Aphrodite off the ship!" she said, wringing her hands.

"Have you seen Sal?"

She shook her head. "Oh my god, Lily. It's like we are in the lion's den! How are we going to smuggle her out of here?"

I smiled at Celeste. The *Bacchus* had already been pulled into a docking bay, and a repair platform had been cranked out underneath. Byron was shouting instructions to his crew.

"Stay with Byron. He will see her safely transported."

It was not until that moment that Celeste realized

my role in her quest was done. "Lily! I... I don't know what to say."

I shrugged. "It was fun."

"Your broken nose doesn't look like much fun," she said then smiled.

"I like you like this," I said, grinning at her. "Natural joy suits you. You should try it more often."

She laughed and pulled me into a hug. "I am happy, but Roni won't be. Her ship! Can you send word when you reach Venice? Let her know we'll be making a few minor repairs? I spoke to her crew. They want to stay in Athens until the ship is fixed."

"Of course."

"I'm afraid the Dilettanti may still follow you," she said as she released me.

"I sense that Byron might be able to handle that as well. After all, what can I tell them? I don't have the kaleidoscope," I said, and then pulling the kaleidoscope from my bag, I handed it to her. "And I don't know the whereabouts of any ancient sculptures."

"Just... please... be safe."

Celeste pulled me into a hug again.

"Celeste?" I heard Byron call.

We turned then to see him waving her to the *Bacchus*.

"May the Goddess of Love bless you," she whispered in my ear then disappeared into the crowd.

I waved to Byron.

He lifted his hand, smiled at me, held my gaze for several moments, then turned back to the ship.

My transport to Venice had already been arranged. Now I just needed to find Sal. I worked my way through the platform traffic to the tower where the European ships were debarking. From a distance, I saw Sal talking to the pilot of a Swiss ship. I was puzzled.

I walked down the platform toward him. "Sal?" I called.

He turned, spotted me, then spoke a word to the pilot who nodded. Sal walked across the platform toward me. As he neared, he kept his gaze on the landing. My stomach began to knot.

It was not until he was standing in front of me that Sal looked me in the eyes. The expression on his face was one I had never seen before. He looked anguished.

"Sal? What's wro-"

"I'm taking a transport to Zurich," he told me.

"What?" I searched his face. While he tried to pull on his mask, he could not. He looked like a man destroyed. "I don't understand, Sal. I thought we... Look, Byron and I-"

"My Lily," he started. He reached out to take my hand but pulled his hand back. "Lily, I can never be a Byron. I will never drop out of the clouds and save you. I'm just a tinker and that is... not enough," he said then turned to go.

"Sal? Wait! Please!" I said and walked after him. I grabbed his arm, but he did not turn toward me.

"I understand your choice," he said, his voice cracking. He shook my hand off and strode down the platform. Nodding to the Swiss pilot, he boarded the transport. The ship pulled up her anchors and lifted out of the dock. Moments later, Sal was flying away from me. I stood on the platform all alone. Only Asclepius, astride across the night's sky, was there to see me weep. I had gone on a quest to find the Goddess of Love only to return home empty-handed. And I had been discarded-again.

❧

CHAPTER 34

Two months later, I stood on the pilot's platform looking out across the green grounds of the Champs de Mars below the Paris airship towers. Thunder rolled in the clouds overhead. Cloud-to-cloud lightning cracked ominously. A cool fall wind blew across the field. Behind me, Angus swore under his breath.

I looked up at Etienne. He had sucked in his lips and was tapping his finger on his chin.

The crowd below was waving the Union Jack and chanting "Star-gaze-r-Star-gaze-r-Star-gaze-r."

"No pressure," Jessup joked sarcastically.

On my other side, Alejandro Fernando was arguing vehemently with his team.

"Attention!" a voice crackled from a huge brass horn at the Marshalls' platform behind us. We all turned. "L'équipe Américaine s'est retirée!" Cutter's team had withdrawn.

The mainly European crowd cheered jubilantly.

"Well, that's a great fucking vote of confidence!" Angus swore.

Angus was right. While Cutter had taken first in New York and London, I had deftly trounced him, and everyone else, in Valencia. I'd come in a full mile before him. Apparently racing sober, something I'd never done before, significantly improved my piloting skills. Cutter's team was banking on me to fail.

I saw Cutter and his crew following behind his well-shod sponsors who had, no doubt, made the final decision not to risk the *Double Eagle*. They headed toward the observation platform. To describe his expression as angry would have been an understatement. He gazed over at the pilot's platform and flashed me a thumbs up.

Despite their certainty that I would botch it, I knew better. What Cutter didn't know was that my team had been in almost continual training since Venice. Well, that and the fact that I was, in fact, sober. I spent the first month home killing my habit. It hadn't been pretty. Every ounce of me wanted to bury my broken heart under a bottle of absinthe and in an opium fog, but I didn't. I wouldn't. Not then and never again.

As if constant sweating, vomiting, headaches, body pain, and irritability were not enough, Angus had hauled me to his little cottage in Scotland where there was nothing to stimulate me except the trees. I suspect I sobered up quickly just to get back to London before I died from boredom.

Sal had not come back. When I returned to London after the stint in Scotland, I went to Tinkers' Hall. His stall was still closed. In that moment in Athens, I didn't fully understand why Sal had left me. As I reflected later, I realized that what had really happened was that the deep wounds inside both of us had rubbed against one another. Sal, who had been schooled his whole life that he wasn't good enough, had felt eclipsed by the blinding sun that is Byron. When I had not followed Sal to the deck of the *Hercules* that night, he must have assumed the worst. I wish he had trusted me to do right by him, but after a lifetime of being dismissed as worthless, what else would he expect?

I went to Zurich to set things straight. I'd hoped to find him at the workshop of Master Vogt. Sal had been there, but by the time I'd arrived, he'd left for Rome. Something told me Sal was sorting things out. I went back to London. I would wait. If he came back, he came back. If he didn't, my heart would heal in time.

To my great relief, Byron had understood my decision. His letters still came as regularly as ever. We were still the greatest of confidants even though we were no longer lovers. And through Byron, I learned that the Aphrodite had been safely stowed. In that, I felt a sense of peace.

I looked again at Etienne. "Well?" I asked him.

He blew air through his lips. "It's Paris."

Lightening cracked on the horizon before us.

Etienne sighed. "Mon dieu... we'll probably die,

but let's race," he said, raising the French flag, wagging it in the air.

The French crowd below burst into a loud cheer.

Etienne kissed me on both cheeks. "Be careful," he told me then headed to the *Étoile*.

A light rain began to fall. Lightning cracked again.

I turned to Alejandro and stuck out my hand. He was the only one close enough to me on the points' board, besides Cutter, to be a threat. "Vaya con Dios," I said with a half-smile.

Alejandro sighed, kissed my hand, and turned to his team.

Angus raised the Union Jack.

Alejandro's crewmate waved the Spanish flag.

The crowd below screamed.

"Fly low," Angus said as we made our way to the *Stargazer*. "We'll need to win on speed alone."

The announcer started listing the teams still in the lineup: France, Spain, England, Italy, Austria, and Germany. All good crews, but no one was better than us.

I looked up at the sky. There was a strange yellow hue on the horizon. My scalp tingled with the feel of electricity. Maybe Etienne was right. Maybe we would all die. Lightning cracked nearby; thunder rolled toward us in waves.

Angus and Jessup strategized as we walked down the platform.

"The new configuration has us running faster

than anyone else," Jessup said. "Low and tight. It's a straight shot to Le Mans."

"Lily! Lily!" I heard someone call from the notables' platform. Had Byron come?

I scanned the platform. To my shock, Sal was trying to push his way to the front of the crowd.

"Sal?" I whispered.

Out of the corner of my eye, I saw Angus and Jessup exchange a glance.

"Sal!" I yelled. I rushed across the platform. "Let him through!" I called to the guards.

They released him.

"Lily," he more breathed than said as he grabbed me by both arms. "Lily... I am so sorry. I crossed paths with Byron in Rome. He told me... Lily..."

I'd waited months to hear those words.

"Mademoiselle Stargazer, we need you on your ship," a Marshall said from behind me.

"Please, come later," I told Sal, taking his face into my hands.

Lightning crashed nearby. It made the ground shake.

"Here," Sal said, pushing a bundle toward me. I recognized the harness and roll of silk. "Let me put it on you," he said and quickly dropped the harness around my shoulders and under my arms, belting it around my waist. He pulled the belts tight. I relished the feel of his hands on my body. "The chute at the back will open if you pull here," Sal said, guiding my hand to a pin on the vest. "It should lower you safely down. God forbid, Lily. But this weather... please be careful. Lily..."

"It's okay. I love you, Salvatore," I whispered.

"My Lily." He pressed me against his chest. Sandalwood.

"Mademoiselle Stargazer?"

"I'm coming!"

"Good luck. Be careful," Sal called.

I walked to the deck of the *Stargazer* with tears in my eyes.

CHAPTER 35

The ring of the cannon signaled start. The *Stargazer*'s propellers kicked over hard, and she leapt out of her tower. I watched from the wheelstand as the other ships lifted toward the sky. Everyone went up except us. Low and fast. Low and fast.

Lightning rocked the horizon. We had barely moved from the green of the Champs de Mars, the official race gateway, when the sky flashed white. I winced. My ears rung as the lightning rocked my body. My god, had we been struck?

The *Stargazer*'s propellers stopped. I heard the door to the gear galley clap open. "Are we hit?" Angus called.

"Fuck! It was close! No, we're okay! Lily?" Jessup called down.

I opened my eyes and scanned the horizon. In the sky above us, the other ships were turning, moving back toward the airship towers. All of the ships were turning, that is, except the *Étoile*. In the sky above me, Etienne's airship was on fire.

"Oh my god... oh my god! Jessup! Take us up!" I screamed.

Jessup cranked the heat in the *Stargazer*'s balloon.

Angus ran across the deck of the ship and started pulling out the airship-to-airship highwire.

"Fuck! Jessup, hurry!" I screamed. Already the *Étoile's* deck and ropes were on fire.

"Where the fuck are the Marshall ships?" Angus screamed.

I scanned around. The Marshall ships that were supposed to fly with us were still docked.

The *Stargazer* blasted upward like a cork being shot out of a bottle. I turned the wheel to bring us alongside the *Étoile* as we lifted. We reached the burning ship just as the first of her ropes snapped.

"Lily!" Etienne screamed from the deck of the ship.

The *Étoile* started to tilt starboard.

"Now, Angus, now!" I yelled.

He cranked the high-wire launcher and shot the line to Etienne's ship.

Etienne was screaming at his crew to lash onto the hoops of two-way drag line.

"Come on! I'll pull you in! Hurry!" Angus yelled.

Grabbing safety belts, the crewmen started to hook on.

"The balloon isn't going to make it!" Jessup yelled. "Etienne! Come on!"

Another rope snapped. The ship shook as the gondola began to hang sideways.

"Burner is gonna catch! We've got to cut her loose or she'll pull us down too!" Jessup yelled down to me.

I locked the wheel and went to the side of the ship. "Etienne!"

The Frenchman held on tightly to the remaining ropes and tried to make his way to the back of the ship. Angus towed the crewmen toward the *Stargazer*. The high-wire machine cranked quickly and soon Angus was pulling both men aboard. On the *Étoile*, Etienne was hanging on for dear life as the gondola looked like it was going to capsize.

"He's not going to make it, Lily! He's not going to make it! Where the fuck are the Marshall ships?" Angus cursed again.

There was a boom as the burners set the soft fabric of the balloon on fire.

Etienne hung onto a rope, but as the balloon burned, the ship started to plummet toward the ground.

Angus disconnected the high-wire between us as the *Étoile*.

Etienne's crew stood speechless as they watched in horror.

"Take the wheel!" I called to Angus.

"Lily?"

Etienne screamed as he let go of the rope and began to free fall toward the ground.

"Angus, come take the fucking wheel and get the

Stargazer out of here!" I yelled and with a running jump, leapt off the side of the *Stargazer*.

"Lily!" Jessup and Angus screamed in unison.

The earth rises quickly toward you when you are falling from the heavens. I set my eyes on Etienne, narrowed my body as I'd seen every bird do, and aimed toward him. I gained speed, and a fraction of a second later, I came face to face with Etienne. The look of shock on his face was priceless.

"Let's try not to die," I said, and wrapping my arms around him, I held Etienne with all of my strength. I turned, and with my teeth, pulled the pin from Sal's harness.

A leap of faith. The silk unfurled with a swish like a woman's gown. The fabric yanked the halter when it filled with air. I nearly lost my grip on Etienne, but he was holding onto me so tightly I could barely breathe.

The parachute held. Our descent slowed. I saw a mob of people rushing across the Champs de Mars toward us.

"Lily," Etienne whispered aghast. Tears were streaming from his eyes.

"I owed you one," I said.

We still had some speed as we neared the ground. I pulled my legs up and tried to shelter my head against Etienne's chest. We hit the ground hard and were separated by the jolt. I rolled across the grass. The landing had knocked the wind out of me, but otherwise I felt all right. The parachute fell on top of me, and I lay under the blanket of white material. It was like lying in a cloud.

Moments later, I heard the *Étoile* crash to the ground somewhere not far from me. The burners exploded with a boom.

Voices drew close.

"Mademoiselle Stargazer? Are you all right? Are you alive?"

"Etienne est vivant!" I heard someone call. He was alive.

I breathed a sigh of relief.

They pulled the parachute off me.

Overhead, the clouds broke for just a moment to reveal the early evening sky. From the star garden above, a single bright star shone down on me.

ACKNOWLEDGEMENTS

A debt of gratitude to:

This book would not have possible without Cat Carlson Amick to whom the novel is dedicated. Thank you, Cat, for being my psychotherapist, astrologer, and cheerleader. And thank you for being Lily's greatest champion.

Muhterem Boz Karsak for creating the time and space for me to complete this novel. Without you, Lily would still be sitting in my laptop.

Naomi Clewett, José Otero, Toni Lestaz, Mark Fisher, Margo Bond Collins, Kamille Stone Stanton, Susan Houts, Carrie Wells, Andrew Forbes, Michael Hall Jr., and Christopher Adams for your contributions, big and small, to the creation of this novel.

I also want to thank my husband for his tireless support. Thank you for being the star in my kaleidoscope.

ABOUT THE AUTHOR

Melanie Karsak grew up in rural northwestern Pennsylvania where there wasn't much to do but read books and go for hikes. She wrote her first novel, a gripping piece about a 1920s stage actress, when she was 12. Today, Melanie, a steampunk connoisseur, white elephant collector, and caffeine junkie, lives in Florida with her husband and two children. She is an Instructor of English at Eastern Florida State College.

Keep in touch with the author online. She's really nice!

Blog: melaniekarsak.blogspot.com

Twitter: twitter.com/MelanieKarsak

Email: melanie@clockpunkpress.com

Facebook: www.facebook.com/AuthorMelanieKarsak

Pinterest: www.pinterest.com/melaniekarsak/

Authorgraph:
www.authorgraph.com/authors/MelanieKarsak

A Goodreads author